By Gabby Hutchinson Crouch
Darkwood
Such Big Teeth

GLASS COFFIN

THE DARKWOOD SERIES

GABBY HUTCHINSON CROUCH

BOOK THREE

Farrago

This edition published in 2021 by Farrago,
an imprint of Duckworth Books Ltd,
1 Golden Court, Richmond TW9 1EU, United Kingdom

www.farragobooks.com

ISBN: 978-1-78842-147-8

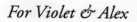

For Violet & Alex

Contents

Characters

Darkwood – a forest spanning the east of Myrsina and the West of Ashtrie, and the home to many magical beings.

Residents of Darkwood:
Gretel Mudd – who is not a witch after all, just a girl who can make inventions and do equations.
Hansel Mudd – the Mudd Witch. Can control the ground, draw vast pools of the sun's energy, turn shadows solid and lash out with tentacles of magical power.
Princess Snow – the White Knight of the Darkwood. A witch of small birds and animals. Usually followed around by seven hairy, stinky Dwarves.
Buttercup Brick – the Cake Witch. Accidentally turned most of her cottage into Gingerbread.
Jack Trott – a Flora Witch and petty thief. Accidentally got a Giant killed when he was seven.
Patience Fieldmouse – a Ghost. Was a huntsman before she was killed in a beanstalk incident but has since become deeply anti-huntsman.
Trevor – a spider. Has a collection of very small hats.
The Mirror – a magic, all-seeing mirror inhabited by the soul of the former King, Snow's father. Can show you anything in Myrsina as long as you ask in rhyme.
Charles the Magnificent – a Unicorn.

Gilde Locke – the Bear Witch. Has been living far away from humans for around 60 years and uses very old-fashioned turns of phrase as a result.

Scarlett Little – a Werewolf. Lycanthropy is hereditary, can't turn anyone. Uses her Granny's cloak to control her transformations (except at full moon).

Hex – a cursed Ashtrian man. Was turned into a raven by the Glass Witch. A magical shirt of nettles can turn him human again, except for one wing.

Nearby Village (pronounced 'NEAR-bee') – a rural village on the eastern edge of Myrsina, bordering the Darkwood.

Residents of Nearby Village:

Daisy Wicker – Gretel's best friend, and another inventor. Weaves a mean basket.

Mr and Mrs Mudd – Hansel and Gretel's Stepfather and Stepmother (don't ask how that works). Farmers.

Homily Goggins – an old lady.

Gregor Smithy – Nearby's elderly nightwatchman. And daywatchman.

Ethel Wicker – a basket-weaver and Daisy's mother.

Lisbet Grief – don't ask why she has a long running feud with Homily Goggins – she just does.

Carpenter Fred – a carpenter with some uncharitable views about magicals.

Coriander – a midwife.

The Citadel – the capital of Myrsina, a day's walk west of Nearby.

Residents of The Citadel:

Morning Quarry – the Head Huntsman and therefore ruler of Myrsina. Has a winning smile, a dog called Sausages and a thirst for genocide.

Fennel, Richard and Grey – high-ranking huntsmen and close allies of Morning Quarry.

Peter and Rose Piper – pickle-makers.

Salad and Rumpel – proprietors of a mysterious cobbler's shop.

Odette – another cursed Ashtrian. Often a swan.

Bellina – a Thumbling.

Old Nikolas – the Midwinter Witch.

Lucy Toads – a Lace Merchant's wife whom Hansel and Daisy met in Book 2.

Ashtrie – the country to the east of Myrsina. Something terrible happened there.

Residents of Ashtrie:

Ella – the Glass Witch. Formerly Queen of all Ashtrie.

Mopsa and Dorcas – Ella's stepsisters.

Several frogs – they are not supposed to be frogs.

1

A New Woman

To the south west of a great continent, hugging the Golden Sea, lie two small countries. This in itself is not unusual; most countries in this continent at this current, pre-industrial moment in history, are small. They're about the size of Wales, because most small countries are. The country in the far south-westerly corner is called Myrsina, and its neighbour to the east is named Ashtrie. Their climates are mostly temperate, their soil mostly fertile, and their people mostly healthy. There used to be a major trade route through here, stopping off at port towns on Myrsina's coastline and travelling by road across the land, through Ashtrie and on to the rest of the continent beyond. In those days, both Myrsina and Ashtrie were rich with trade. Those days are gone. Now, merchants will stop only briefly at Goldenharbour or Tide on Myrsina's western coast before continuing by sea, or else cut straight north through a narrow mountain pass, minimising the trip through Myrsina and bypassing Ashtrie altogether. There would be no land route east for them to take even if they wanted to. The road through the Darkwood that stands between Myrsina and Ashtrie has been reclaimed by the trees… and other things, besides. Bad things. Dark things.

Long story short, a bunch of dirty rotten witches ruined everything, as any of Myrsina's friendly ruling huntsmen would attest. For their part, the huntsmen are doing their very best to put a stop to the witch menace, once and for all. Why, they've only just installed a brand new Head Huntsman: a practical and forward-thinking woman, who has bold new plans to completely wipe the Darkwood and all of its wretched inhabitants off this plane of existence entirely. Yes, you read that right – a woman! They're *very* progressive, these days; they've got rid of the old 'abominations' list that used to limit what women in the country were allowed to do. They don't even fetch the pitchforks when they see a girl wielding an abacus any more. Turns out, powerful women in Myrsina are just as good at killing witches as men are. You go, sisters!

As for what the people of Ashtrie have been doing about the witch problem… well, nobody in Myrsina rightly knows, since to get into Ashtrie, one must pass through the Darkwood, and nobody goes into the accursed Darkwood. Because it's cursed. Nobody.

Nobody besides all of the residents of Nearby Village, that is. The hundred or so villagers pass quite cheerfully over the log bridge into the bordering cursed forest and back again on a regular basis, with the exception of Monday nights, when everybody hides because that's Bin Night, and if the Bin Men catch you in the Darkwood on a Monday night, they absolutely will kill you. According to the huntsmen, the small farming village of Nearby is essentially an annexe of the Darkwood and should be treated as such, since all of its inhabitants declared themselves to be witches and traitors in an ill-conceived display of solidarity with the forest's magical beings. That was a week ago, and everybody's still getting used to the new arrangement.

Mudd Farm, for example, isn't entirely functioning as a farm at present. It's currently more of a field hospital with some crops and animals attached. With both Mr and Mrs Mudd occupied practising their veterinary skills on magical creatures injured during the last battle against the huntsman army, running the farm itself has fallen to volunteers, from both the village and the Darkwood. Currently, the pigs are being attended to by a pair of Centaurs, which confuses the pigs no end.

The situation with the makeshift hospital in Mudd Farm's bedrooms also means that Gretel Mudd hasn't been able to return home from the witch cottage where she's been sheltering ever since she was wrongfully accused of witchcraft a few months ago. Instead, she's had to make room in the witch cottage's bedroom for her twin brother Hansel. Hansel has also recently been accused of witchcraft, although in this case, the huntsmen were absolutely bang on; he is a massive witch.

Currently, Gretel is just outside the witch's cottage in the accursed wood, in the small communal privy where her friend Jack was once attacked by Swamp Mermaids who wanted to drown him in slurry. She is also crying her eyes out, and it isn't about Mermaids or witches or her old bedroom at the farm or anything like that.

Gretel's friend Trevor has been alerted to the crying while going about his customary fly-hunt, and has decided to do what he always does when somebody is crying – namely, call for his housemate Buttercup to come and sort it out. Having slid back along his tether line to the house, Trevor is now running at top speed along the cottage's wall towards a crack above the kitchen door.

Oh, by the way, Trevor is a talking spider. Magic forest – these things happen.

'Buttercup! Buttercup!' Trevor locates Buttercup, and drops on a thread from the ceiling to her shoulder.

'What is it?' asks Buttercup. 'What happened?'

'I don't know, but Gretel's locked herself in the privy and she's crying and her brother's trying to talk to her but she says she can't tell him what's wrong.'

Buttercup's brow creases. 'Usually that means a heartbreak, but I didn't even think she was sweet on anyone.'

'When would she even have found time?' asks another housemate, Patience Fieldmouse. Patience is floating on the ceiling. She can do this because she died last month and is now a Ghost. Again – magic forest; Ghosts are fairly standard.

'I haven't seen her appearing smitten around anybody,' adds the magic Mirror on the wall, who would know this sort of thing because it's a magic Mirror inhabited by the soul of the dead King of Myrsina, and can see the whole kingdom at all times. Nobody bats an eyelid because, at the risk of becoming repetitive, magic forest.

'You can't always tell with teenaged girls,' frets Buttercup. She wraps a bit of cloth around her hand, which turns into puff pastry. This is because Buttercup is a witch, and her only magical power, as far as she's aware, is that she can turn anything that isn't alive into baked goods with the touch of her hand. The vast majority of the times this happens, it's an accident due to her being startled or stressed or unhappy. This explains why the cottage they are standing in is mostly gingerbread and cake. Buttercup sighs. 'Could somebody get the door for me? Cake hands again.'

'Um,' says Trevor, the house spider.

'Um,' add Patience and the Mirror, with their lack of corporeal bodies.

'Oh,' says Buttercup. She goes over to the hearth and apologetically nudges the Werewolf napping there with the side of her foot. 'Scarlett? So sorry to wake you, but it's a bit of an...'

Scarlett Little the Werewolf wakes up, sniffing the air. Her teeth and ears elongate slightly.

'I smell blood.'

'Oh no!' Buttercup cries, and then blinks. 'Oh, wait. I think I know what this is about.'

When Buttercup gets to the privy a few minutes later, she's calm. Scarlett trots beside her, carrying everything that Gretel's going to need.

Hansel looks up at them, clearly frightened by his sister's sobs. The shadows around him look unnaturally thick and dark, and move in entirely the wrong way – an indication that the powerful young witch is distressed.

'I don't know what it is,' he manages. 'She won't talk about it, won't even let me into her thoughts to see.'

'It's all right.' Buttercup gently shifts Hansel out of the way and takes his place at the door. 'This isn't a brother thing. Usually, it's a parent thing, but yours are off saving lives right now, so I'll just have to make do.' She taps on the door. 'Gretel, dear?'

'Mmmf?' comes a scared sob from behind the privy door.

'Your stepmother did tell you about the monthlies, didn't she, my lovely?'

'Mm-hmm,' manages the voice from behind the door, shakily. 'I just didn't know… I don't have time for this right now!'

'Nobody ever does,' Buttercup tells her. 'But unfortunately all women have to.'

'Not me,' Patience announces, with rather more pride than is necessary. 'No body, no trouble.'

'Nor me,' admits Scarlett shyly. 'Although I still go weird once a month, just in a different way.'

'Most women have to,' continues Buttercup. 'And that's what's happened today. You're a woman now.'

'Don't want to,' sniffles Gretel. 'If this is "being a woman", it's messy and it hurts and it makes me want to cry.'

'Yep,' replies Buttercup sympathetically, 'that sounds about right. Scarlett's just going to pass you some of the things we use, me and Snow. For under your underthings. Then we can see about a dram of medicine for the pains.'

Scarlett passes a couple of the clean rag wads over the privy door, along with a special looped belt. There is a pause.

'You use *these*?'

'They're fairly standard. I'm sure a clever girl like you can work out the loops and the…'

'They're so *bulky*! And fiddly!' There's another pause.

'You don't need to invent anyth—' begins Buttercup.

'I'm going to invent an alternative,' announces Gretel.

'I'm not sure we really have time right now, dear...'

Gretel comes out of the privy, her face tear-streaked and determined. 'Well, I'll put it on my to-do list, then. One, save the Darkwood; two, invent a new bandage for monthlies.'

Gretel is thirteen years old. She just became a woman, and it aches. She doesn't know it, right now, but she has four days to save Myrsina. Twice.

2
Love Hurts

There is a familiar cacophony coming from the rough track that leads towards Nearby Village. It sounds like a large woman in full, skull-adorned body armour, clanking uphill, while speaking imperiously to anybody who might listen. Sure enough, when Gretel looks over to the crest of the hollow in which the cottage nestles, that is just what she sees. The White Knight approaches, unkempt and dark and superficially foreboding as the forest itself.

Hardly anybody calls her the White Knight any more. There's little point in her trying to maintain a hidden identity; everybody knows who she is, these days. Most people call her Snow, because that's her name. Some people call her Princess Snow, because she used to be the princess. She hates being called Princess Snow. *Some* people call her Majesty, on account of her now technically being the deposed Queen of Myrsina. Snow hates that even more.

Snow has a tendency to be followed around by a train of people. She's just one of those folks that others can't help but gravitate towards, like a dense star. Currently in her wake are Daisy Wicker from the village, and six hairy Dwarves. Gretel is at least pleased to see her friend Daisy, but is concerned by the glumness on all of the faces. They are, as they have been all week, one Dwarf short. One of Snow's family of Dwarves was shot by a huntsman in a skirmish last week. The wound was not instantly fatal, but not all deadly or life-altering injuries do all their damage straightaway. The Dwarf is still in the makeshift infirmary at Mudd Farm, and despite the best care from the medically skilled villagers, has been feverish with infection for days.

Buttercup steps towards Snow as she approaches.

'How's Oi doing?'

The injured Dwarf is named Oi. If there's a story behind this, it's one that we're unlikely to hear any time soon.

'Same,' grunts Snow.

'She's in the best hands,' Daisy assures her. From the tone of Daisy's voice, it's not the first time she's told Snow this today.

Snow grunts again. 'How's everything else going?' She nods at Gretel. 'What have you been blubbing for?'

'Nothing!' Gretel scrubs at her reddened eyes self-consciously. 'Everything's fine here, got some new blueprints, and I think Jack's nearly finished with the nettle charm.'

Snow arches an eyebrow and peers over at the nettle patch where Jack is busily sewing. 'Already? He can certainly work hard on a project when he's properly motivated, can't he?' She nods again at Gretel. 'You *have* been crying, though.'

'It was over something called a monthly,' says Trevor loudly, from the top of Buttercup's head. 'To be honest, I didn't understand what it was. I think it might be a mammal thing.'

'Oh, is that all?' replies Snow, just as loudly. 'You'll get used to them, New Girl.'

Daisy leans into her. 'D'you want some fennel and pine tea? It tastes like feet but it helps with the ache.'

'Stop!' Hansel runs up to the group, waving his arms. 'Can everybody please stop talking about Gretel's... um...' He stumbles over the words, flustered. 'Her special lady... becoming a woman, and... what I mean to say is, she was really crying about it in the privy just now, so I think you should probably all just drop it.'

Gretel sighs, her embarrassment complete. 'Thank you, Hansel.' She meets eyes with Daisy, and whispers, 'But yes please on the feet tea.'

Jack Trott has indeed been working hard, and is indeed motivated. Jack, you see, is in love. Full-on, bolt-from-the-blue love at first sight stuff, with an Ashtrian he met in the northern woods, named Hex. There are, unfortunately, a few obstacles to their potential romance. Hex is a good decade Jack's senior, and although Jack doesn't mind this at all, he isn't sure what Hex's feelings would be about dating a man barely in his twenties. Another, more pressing issue is that Jack doesn't know any of Hex's thoughts about Jack's amorous intentions. Jack doesn't even know if his feelings are reciprocated. This is due to the most urgent problem of all: Hex has been cursed and turned into a raven. Jack's only chance to reverse the curse is to attempt to recreate the nettle shirt charm originally created by Hex's sister, to save Hex and his brothers many years ago. This is not an easy task. The original charms had taken Hex's sister a year per shirt, and with the threat of another huntsman assault looming over them all, Jack knows that he doesn't have this long. There's also the detail that, for the charm to have even a chance of working, from the moment the first stitch is made to the moment of completion, the witch who creates the shirt must do so without speaking a word. It's been a week. Jack *really* misses talking. It used to be one of his favourite things to do.

There are a few factors working in his favour, however. In the safety of the Darkwood's community, he doesn't have to hide his witchcraft the way Hex's sister would have done. He can work around the clock. He also has the benefit of the magical ability to grow any plant at will, and so is able to constantly surround himself with a patch of nettles to pick and stitch, instead of having to go off and find them. And then, there's Gilde.

Gilde, the old Bear Witch of the north, the one who told him how to make a nettle shirt in the first place, and spent the first couple of days watching him sleepily from the fur of a dozing bear while making sarcastic comments. Gilde, who surprised everybody by not following the bears into a nearby cave to hibernate, but instead carried on sitting outside, keeping Jack and Hex company. Gilde, who started bringing Jack water and food so that he didn't have to stop for sustenance; who started actually lifting cups and spoons to his mouth so that he didn't even need to stop while he ate and drank. Gilde, who after the third night of his sewing, ordered him to rest for a few hours, and when he awoke, he discovered that she'd picked hundreds of leaves for him, and brought him a new needle and two new reels of thread. Gilde, who now sits beside him, as tired-looking and as silent as he, passing him leaves, to make the process as quick as possible, her hands as reddened and sore from the nettles' stings as his. Gilde, who is doing everything that she can, short of stitching the shirt herself, which they both know would stop it from working. Gilde, who had lived with Hex in her mountain cottage for years before Jack met either of them. Gilde, who, in her own grumpy, sardonic way, also clearly loves Hex very much.

And now, the shirt is all but done. Jack is down to the cuffs of the second sleeve – the sleeve that Hex's sister never managed to finish, leaving Hex with one detested wing while in human form. Jack supposes he could have dispensed with making that sleeve, for time's sake. He could have found out a day and a night earlier if the charm had worked; and if it had, he could have found out a day and a night earlier if Hex loves him back. He could have got back to speaking and sleeping and living normally and allowing his hands to heal a day and a night earlier. But Jack, as was mentioned before, is in love. And when you're in love enough with somebody to spend a silent week sewing nettles, then you're in love enough to put in an extra day and night of pain in order to try to give them their left arm back.

Snow and Gretel watch Jack and Gilde quietly for a while. The others have all drifted off to their various jobs around the cottage and the small surrounding camp, for the magical creatures left homeless by the huntsmen's recent fiery assault on the Darkwood.

'Love,' sighs Snow, after a while. 'It's a mug's game. I hate feeling this bad about Oi, all the time.'

Gretel nods sympathetically. 'I used to feel like that about Hansel. You know. When the huntsmen had him.' She nods over to her brother, walking hand in hand with Daisy to fetch water. 'But that turned out all right, in the end. And we got the Mirror back safely, and Trevor, after we lost him, so...'

'So, we've been pushing our luck, so far,' replies Snow.

Gretel looks back at Snow. 'You're worried about going east.'

'I'm not worried about *me* going east, I'm concerned about what will happen when you lot inevitably follow me.'

Gretel snorts a laugh. 'Yeah, we're totally planning on tagging along.'

Snow scowls. 'I knew it. I should have snuck out in the dead of night already, before Jack had finished with the shirt, before you were done with your inventions for the village...'

'You wouldn't go without knowing Oi's on the mend,' Gretel replies. 'And even you have to admit we work best as a team. It's how we liberated Nearby; talked round the northern witches; how we survived Big Cave...' She counts off their sort-of victories on her fingers.

'The battle for Big Cave is the whole reason Oi is currently lying in your old bedroom, half-dead from infection,' growls Snow. 'I can't abide for that to happen again. My lads are tough, but they're small. They make themselves easy targets.' She looks down at the ground, a glimmer of shamefacedness passing over her usually haughty expression. 'When we go, I need to make sure they stay behind. I'm sure you can think up some plans, invent some busywork, ensure they're needed at home.'

'All right,' Gretel tells her gently. 'There's so much to do, here and in the village, everyone will be grateful for six more pairs of hands.'

Still, Snow doesn't look up. 'Buttercup, too.'

This startles Gretel. 'But Buttercup's one of the gang, she's…'

'Soft,' Snow says quietly. 'Soft, is what she is. Soft and precious and defenceless and hopeless and lovely and… and if anything were ever to happen to her… Not her.' She clears her throat, and her voice hardens again. 'Like I say, it's a mug's game.'

'She won't be happy,' says Gretel.

Snow manages a fond smile. 'I know she won't. I can live with that.'

'And Trevor will probably want to stay with her.'

'I can live with that, too. Spiders are fragile little things.'

'And if Hex ever gets his old form back, you know what he's going to say about going east…'

'Neat-oh finito like sweet poteeto,' cries a thin, elderly voice in triumph. Gretel jumps, having all but forgotten about Jack and Gilde silently working on the shirt across the way.

Gilde is measuring the shirt's sleeves. 'That's that, loverboy,' she tells the mute Jack. 'Yer done.'

Snow tuts, ambling over. 'Does that mean Trott's going to be able to talk again, then? I was really enjoying the peace.'

'Not till the shirt's in place,' Gilde replies. She beckons the watching raven over. 'You did the best you could, Jack the Lad, but there's only one way to prove the puddin'.'

The raven walks in its ungainly birdish way, to stop in front of Jack. Bird and man lock gazes for a moment, as if both have something they desperately want to say to the other, but can't. After a couple of seconds, the raven bows its head down, to indicate that Jack should place the shirt over it.

Jack does so, carefully, making sure that it's smoothed out and the right way round.

Gretel holds her breath, watching. She notices that, beside her, Snow has done the same. There's a distant cry of 'Wait, has Jack finished?' and the others come running over to watch.

To watch, as it turns out, a full minute of absolutely nothing happening.

'Oh Hex,' sighs Buttercup sadly, after enough time has passed to gauge that the spell hasn't worked, and then rather more time has passed for it to be polite to admit as such. 'I'm so sorry. You tried so hard, Jack.'

Gilde pats Jack on the shoulder. 'I did say it mightn't work. There were nothing else you could've done, lad.'

Jack kneels, crumpled, exhausted, broken, needle and thread still in his hand. He opens his mouth to finally say something, hurl an obscenity out into the unfair world… then, he stops. He squints at the shirt's collar. His eyes widen. He reaches out the needle and makes three quick stitches in a seam that has been left with a tiny gap. He bites the remaining thread off and sits back on his heels, watching the shirt…

Which suddenly has an otherwise naked man in it.

3
Love Heals

Both men speak at once.

'Jack,' stammers the newly human Hex, 'I never thought… that is, I never imagined… that is, I never expected…'

'I wanted to tell you but I couldn't,' says Jack, over him, 'the shirt is unconditional, I don't need anything in return, you don't even have to accept it if you don't want…'

'Of course I want to,' Hex blurts. He holds his arms out towards Jack.

Gretel and the rest of the watching crowd notice at that moment that the left sleeve of the shirt has already torn from the strain of holding one giant black wing. Even the complete shirt Jack made for him has not returned Hex's missing arm to human form.

'Oh,' sighs Jack, disappointed, noticing the wing.

'Yeah,' replies Hex with an apologetic tone. 'I think my body has just got too used to that limb always being a wing, now. Sorry you wasted your time on it.'

Jack puts on his cockiest, flirtiest smile. 'Wasn't a waste. When that shirt gets ruined and I have to make you another one, I'll make the left sleeve twice as big.'

'Mm,' mutters Hex, looking down at the shirt. It's about as well made as you would expect a shirt made out of nettles by a sleep-deprived needlework novice to be. 'When do you think you can start work on that replacement?'

Jack grins. 'I can make one a week for the next fifty years, if that's what you need. The feelings will still be there to sew into nettles again.'

'Aww,' sighs Buttercup softly, even as Gretel and Snow both roll their eyes at Jack going straight back into cheesy charm mode.

Still sitting next to Jack, Gilde looks similarly unimpressed. 'Anyone else already miss this 'un having ter keep schtum?'

'Gilde,' says Hex gently, 'I saw all the help you gave. Thank you so much.'

'Yeah.' Jack beams. 'Cheers, darlin'.' He gives the old woman a light kiss on the forehead.

Gilde stares at him for a moment, then casts her eyes down. 'Well, shucks. Weren't nothing.'

'And,' continues Hex timidly, 'if there's *anything* I can do to thank you, Jack…'

Jack turns the dazzle of his rakishness up to eleven, or possibly even twelve. 'Oh, I can think of a few things… which, as I mentioned before, you are not obliged to do if you don't want to…'

'Maybe I *do* want to.'

'Aww,' coos Buttercup again, her voice going impossibly high.

'No snogging in front of the rest of us, thank you,' snaps Snow.

'Nobody forced you to all gather round and watch this tender, private moment,' Jack replies.

The watching group exchange glances, silently sharing the sentiment that what Jack said was fair, and they should probably leave the imminent couple to a bit of privacy. They start trudging towards the cottage, but are startled by a cry coming from the path towards the village.

'Princess Snow,' comes the voice. Gretel recognises it as that of Coriander, the village midwife. Her heart leaps. Coriander is one of the villagers who's been caring for the injured in her stepparents' makeshift hospital.

15

'Princess Snow!' Coriander sprints into view, sweat-slicked and panting, muddy skirts hitched to the knees, still wearing, to Gretel's disquiet, a bloodied apron. 'Highness!'

'Less of that, kindly, midwife,' snaps Snow. 'Just spit it out.'

'Pardon... ooh...' Coriander slows to a trot as she approaches, bending at the middle with a stitch. 'The... Dwarf... I'm... ooh.'

Snow gives Coriander her usual supercilious glare down the nose, but the clanking of her gauntlets over one another betrays her nervousness. 'Just tell me what's happened with Oi.'

'The Dwarf...' pants Coriander. 'Passed... Fever...'

Snow's eyes widen. Her shoulders slump. 'She's... passed? The fever took her?'

'Oh, Snow.' Buttercup's hands are to her mouth. The Dwarves cling to one another in silent misery. Trevor sniffs, which is weird because spiders can't cry. Gretel, who is very used to Coriander's occasionally unfortunate turns of phrase, reserves any despair for now and keeps watching the midwife.

'No, sorry,' manages Coriander, getting her breath back. 'The fever's passed. It broke not long after you left. Should have been clearer, but I was all out of puff from running.'

Yep, thinks Gretel, standard Coriander. Mixed messaging in moments of crisis doesn't make for the most ideal quality in a midwife, it's a good job she's so proficient at the practical side of things.

'So...' Snow manages, 'Oi's going to be OK now?'

'Oh, she'll be bedridden,' Coriander tells her solemnly.

'What?'

'...for a few more days,' continues Coriander, 'but yes, we think she should make a full recovery in time.'

'She's going to be OK,' repeats Snow, for her own benefit as well as the Dwarves', who still cling to one another, now with a sense of quiet, shaken relief. Snow pats two of them on their scruffy heads. 'Let's go and see if she's awake,' she tells them. She casts Gretel a meaningful gaze. 'I'll be back by dawn. I'd like those plans by then, New Girl.'

'What plans?' asks Buttercup.

'The plans,' Snow tells her vaguely. 'New Girl can fill us all in tomorrow. Right, I'm off again. Don't wait up. Somebody make sure Jack gets some rest; I don't think he's slept properly in a week, we don't want him to start seeing things.' She starts leading the Dwarves and the midwife back towards the village again. 'You hear that, Trott?' she shouts. 'No time for snogging!'

'I wasn't,' calls Jack from beyond the nettle patch.

'He *was*,' murmurs Trevor conspiratorially. 'I saw him.'

4
Through the Looking Glass

'Ashtrie?' whispers Hansel. 'Really?

Gretel waves a finger at him and Daisy. 'But you see, that's exactly how we used to talk about the Darkwood, only a few months ago. And yet, here we are, safe and sound.'

'I suppose,' says Daisy, with a frown.

'Yeah, might I remind you that I was literally killed by creatures of the Darkwood,' says Patience, who was not technically invited to join the hushed conversation in the kitchen, but will do what she likes, because she's dead.

'True,' Gretel admits, 'but that's because you went in alone and unprepared, and refused to listen to our advice. That's the whole reason why I'll be going with Snow. She'll probably need *some* back-up. Or, at least, somebody to tell her to stop and think before running in, swinging axes at everything.'

'Then, we should come too,' Daisy tells her.

Gretel shakes her head. 'Hansel's still learning to control his magic. I'm not sure how the witch in Ashtrie is going to react to that sort of thing encroaching on her territory. Besides, the village needs you two to defend it.'

'Snow's scared of more of the gang getting hurt,' says Hansel softly, 'isn't she?'

'No,' lies Gretel, impulsively and unconvincingly.

'I didn't mean it as a bad thing, Gretel. *I'm* scared all the time. It's a normal response to being in a cursed forest that people keep trying to set on fire, and to planning a fight against genocidal zealots, *and* to going into a different country that nobody will ever tell us about.'

'I've been trying to ask the older ones what happened in Ashtrie for years,' admits Daisy, 'and they never say.'

'The huntsmen's rumours were just that,' Patience adds. 'Insubstantial rumours and rhetoric. All the years I was a huntsman, nobody ever actually went to Ashtrie, or came out of there.'

'Besides that Hex fellow, of course,' says Daisy. 'We can ask him all about it, now he's human again, if he ever stops snogging Jack…'

'They still at it?' asks Patience quietly.

Daisy nods, and Patience rolls her eyes.

'He won't talk about it,' says Gretel. 'All he'll say is that he was cursed, it ruined his life and broke his sister, and that we mustn't go out there. Whatever happened to him must have been decades ago, back before the huntsmen, back when Myrsina still had…' She trails off thoughtfully. '…the king…'

'Are we going to discuss that, at all?' Hansel says. 'We know someone who actually grew up in Ashtrie, and he's so traumatised by what happened out there that he won't even talk about it. Tad worrying.'

Gretel decides to set her brother's argument to one side. She goes over to the magic Mirror on the kitchen wall.

'Mirror, do you know anything about Ashtrie?'

'I can only see my own kingdom,' the Mirror tells her, in a weary voice that suggests he's had to answer this question many times before.

'Yes, but you'd have known what was going on in the neighbouring land, back when you were king,' Gretel reasons. 'Surely you can remember?'

'Surely…' echoes the Mirror, in unsure tones.

Gretel tries asking the Mirror properly, in rhyme. 'Mirror, Mirror, answer me; show what you know about Ashtrie.'

The Mirror's surface goes to the magical static that usually indicates that a magical vision is imminent, and then, it stops. The Mirror just shows the interior of the cottage's kitchen again.

'I'm sure I used to remember,' says the Mirror apologetically.

'That's all right,' Hansel tells it gently, patting its gilt frame. 'You're doing your best.'

'Wait,' says Gretel suddenly. She stares at the Mirror's image. 'Wait, this is wrong.'

She yanks her brother's hand away from the Mirror. Its surface is showing the interior of the kitchen, but it is not a reflection. The Mirror is showing them the kitchen, as viewed from behind their backs.

They turn, as one, to look at the spot in the corner from which the Mirror's image seems to be watching them. There's nothing there. Just an empty window. Gretel turns back, but when she does, her mirror image, still shown from behind, is still looking over its shoulder, into her eyes. There is static again, and the reflection goes back to normal.

'Sorry about that,' says the Mirror. 'That doesn't usually happen.'

'You don't think,' says Daisy, 'maybe this witch of Ashtrie can affect the Mirror, somehow?'

'It's possible,' the Mirror replies. 'Snow was able to affect what I could see, for years. And this Ashtrie witch… they *do* call her the Glass Witch, and I am mostly glass, nowadays.'

'That's not right,' says Patience, perturbed. 'Playing with mirrors, that's spooky stuff, that is. And I should know spooky. That's the sort of thing I'd do, if I were…'

'If you were trying to scare people into leaving you alone,' says Gretel. 'Like us, at the liberation of Nearby. Like the northern witches when we met them. Like Gilde at Big Cave. Making ourselves look fierce.'

'You do know that when somebody's trying to scare you into leaving them alone, it doesn't always mean you should go and bother them straightaway worries Hansel.

'True,' Gretel replies, 'but there's one surefire way to know whether this Glass Witch is actually as dangerous as she's rumoured to be.'

'What?'

'You! You're a walking magical early warning system. Have any ominous visions gone off over all this Ashtrie talk?'

'It doesn't work like that, Gretel.'

Gretel cocks her head at him, with an expression that clearly says, 'I have a feeling that it *does* work exactly like that, Hansel Mudd'.

Hansel sighs. 'No. There's been nothing. Not a whisper, not a dream. Not so much as a sense of foreboding.'

Gretel smiles brightly. 'Well, then!'

Hansel frowns. 'Nothing, at all,' he mutters. 'It's like it's… a blank. A void.'

A blank. A void. An empty, clear glass. A mirror, reflecting back on another mirror. The Mudd Witch cannot see her, with his magic thick and solid and earthy, but she can see them through their mirror and their windows. It has worked. She's piqued their interest. Her little raven boy can squawk and squawk about the danger as much as he likes; they won't take his warnings seriously. It's all woven into the curse she put on him. Even Trott won't listen. That's going to hurt her poor raven boy, but then after all, love is pain. Love is dancing on glass. They will all learn this, and soon. And then, the Glass Witch will have some new toys to play with, to smash into pieces and re-mould into shapes that please her more. Including the brat Queen of Myrsina – what a catch! What a coup! She might unite all of the woods, both nations under her control. Rule it all from her grand, sparkling palace. Keep Myrsina's pathetic, animalistic, unwashed, uncultured shadow of a Queen locked up in a glass box, so that all can see her fade away.

Yet, even the Queen of Myrsina pales into insignificance against the prize dangled in front of her now. The Mudd Witch. Earth to her ether. Warmth to her coldness. And such power! And so young! So mouldable.

She watches the Citadel and the huntsmen, as she always has, as insects scuttling around in a nest, outside her home. Not enough of an inconvenience to her personally to go to the bother of eliminating... yet. Humans will always be petty and jealous and mean. They will always attempt to unseat the Glass Witch. When this latest lot try, they will regret it, as humans do. She will dance on them, in a dress woven from their screams, and shoes of broken glass. She will have a ball on their re-moulded bodies, and she will dance all night with this new, powerful witch boy. Her brand new Prince Charming.

5
Homewrecker

'Leave the forest?' Buttercup's eyes are wide. 'Now? But we're not ready!'

'We are,' Gretel tells her. '*You* are.'

'But Oi is still sick,' Buttercup frets. 'We don't even have the bears; they've gone to hibernate...'

'We don't need them for this, it isn't an assault,' Gretel explains. 'In fact, if this mission goes really well, we may never need the bears at all.'

'Are you kidding me right now?' blurts Gilde. 'After all that fuss, after breaking my little cottage, you don't even think you're going to need my bears after all?'

'Your bears already saved us at Big Cave,' says Gretel diplomatically, 'and if this *doesn't* work, we're going to need them come the spring, but it would be after a long hard winter of holding the defensive line.'

'So, what is the mission?' Scarlett asks.

'Is it an espionage mission?' asks Trevor excitedly. 'Oh, *please* say it's an espionage mission.'

'Ain't gonna be an espionage mission,' mutters Gilde.

'It's a bit of an espionage mission...'

'YESSSSSSS,' crows Trevor, punching the air with six tiny feet.

'I got the idea from how Daisy and Hansel sort of accidentally got that horrible woman elected to Head Huntsman,' Gretel tells them all.

Daisy sighs at her knees, embarrassed. 'Still haven't stopped reminding everybody about that yet, then?'

'Hansel, you said you felt witches in the Citadel.'

Hansel nods. 'I think there might be more witches in Myrsina than we ever imagined. They're just hiding it.'

'Understandable,' sighs Buttercup.

'Yellerbellies,' declares Gilde, over her.

'What if Myrsina's ripe for change?' Gretel asks. 'I'm not just talking about recruiting the secret witches and their families, either, although they'd be a good start. The outskirting towns and villages have started turning huntsmen out; the civilians of the Citadel just voted to get rid of all the old abominations. What other cruel practices would they do away with, if only they felt they had the chance? The whole country might be willing to help us overturn the system; they just need a bit of a nudge.'

'You want us to infiltrate the Citadel?' asks Trevor excitedly. 'I could wear a fancy coat. Do they wear fancy coats, there?'

'I think,' replies Gretel carefully, 'maybe start with towns closer to Nearby, so you can have a safe base. Ham, Goosemarket, Miggleham, places like that. Sound people out, see what sympathies there are for magicals. There might be underground movements we don't even know about, or the situation could be ripe for you to start one yourselves.'

'Um...?' says Buttercup.

'Yes?' asks Gretel brightly, dreading the question that she knows is about to come.

'You said "you",' says Trevor. 'Which sounds like you're not coming, Gretel. You're not planning to just hang around your old farm, are you? We've got a system to overturn!'

'And surely people would recognise Snow,' Buttercup adds. 'Would she be in disguise, or... or is she not coming either...?'

Gretel draws breath to answer, and tries not to look Buttercup in the eyes.

'We,' interrupts Patience, 'are going to Ashtrie.'

'Oh…' manages Gretel.

'You're going to Ashtrie?' Scarlett asks, aghast.

'Mustn't go to Ashtrie,' mutters Gilde.

'You're going to Ashtrie, without us?' Buttercup adds, hurt.

'Mustn't *nobody* go to Ashtrie,' continues Gilde, aware that no one's really listening.

'I'm sorry,' Gretel manages. 'Patience, we'd rather you *didn't* go to Ashtrie…'

The end of Gretel's sentence turns to vapour in the air as the temperature in the kitchen tangibly drops. All of the forks fly violently from their various surfaces and cling to the suddenly frosty ceiling.

'Good start,' says Gilde through the freezing mist settling temporarily in the kitchen. 'Now, the *rest* of yers, don't go to Ashtrie neither.'

'You're sending me off on the babysitting busywork mission?' Patience seethes.

'Babysitting?' With every utterance, Buttercup sounds more and more aghast.

'Ain't you confident,' trills Gilde, 'for a Ghostie I managed to catch in a jar easy as a dead pie.'

'Is that why you're cutting me out?' Patience floats right up in Gretel's personal space. It's a terrible habit; Gretel wishes she wouldn't. 'I swear I won't get captured again, that was just a bad day, I'm usually really stealthy – I was once awarded Promising Young Huntsman of the Week! There was a certificate!'

Gretel sighs. 'It's exactly for reasons like that that I'll need you to look after the others… I mean, go with the others. Nobody's looking after anyone or babysitting, here.' She clears her throat. 'Patience, you know the huntsmen better than anyone; you'll be more useful there in their territory.'

'But…'

There is a bang at the kitchen door, and Snow enters, foot first as usual. There's something different about her, but it takes Gretel a moment to work out what that is.

'Good-oh,' barks Snow, clattering in, 'you've got everybody up to speed.'

'Where's your pack?' asks Scarlett.

That's what it is, Gretel realises. Snow doesn't have her usual train of Dwarves.

'Left 'em with Oi,' Snow announces. 'It was a touching scene; she started waking up and they all jumped on her to groom out her parasites. Who was I to break up something that adorable?'

'Yes,' says Buttercup pointedly. 'It's best for families to stay together.'

Snow's only reply to Buttercup is a weird, worried smile. 'Well, since everything's in order for now, I might pop out to have a little chat with this Glass Witch I've been hearing so much about.'

'Oh,' says Gretel breezily, 'I might tag along, I can add to the map of the forest. Daisy can take the new defence blueprints over to the village without my help.'

Snow shrugs, and looks around the rest of the cottage, not managing to meet Buttercup's gaze. 'Looks like everybody else has something to keep busy with in our absence.'

'Guys?' Jack and Hex's sleep-tousled heads appear, upside-down, from the trapdoor in the ceiling to the bedroom above. 'What in Myrsina's going on down there?'

It was never going to be easy for Gretel to say goodbye again to her brother and her best friend, especially so soon after having been reunited with them. It turns out to be even harder to do so than she imagined, although this is largely because she has to do so in the middle of two different arguments.

'Were you *ever* going to tell me yourself?' Buttercup asks Snow. 'Or were you just going to palm me off as somebody else's problem to look after, and march off into danger without me? Again?'

'No,' Hex tells Jack at the same time. 'Absolutely not. Not you. Not now.'

'Hex, the huntsmen could attack again any minute; I need to help where I can.'

'That doesn't have to mean you going east,' Hex frets. '*None* of you should be going east! I *said*! You *promised*!'

'We promised you would get a say,' replies Jack.

'But you won't *listen*!' Hex tries to get Gretel's attention, or anybody's, for support. 'Somebody tell him, please!'

Gretel just hugs Hansel and Daisy quietly, trying to ignore both rows. 'And you'll keep an eye on Buttercup via the Mirror?'

'If she or the others look like they're in trouble, we'll help them get out of there,' Daisy assures her. 'I wish I could say the same of you.'

'I'll keep my mind open to Hansel,' Gretel says. 'He should be able to feel it if I need help.'

'You're always doing this,' Buttercup continues to rail at Snow, 'you're always pushing me away, it's horrid. You're worried I'm going to be a liability, aren't you?'

'Of course not!'

'Then why are you taking Gretel and Jack, but not me?'

Snow gazes at Buttercup. She sighs. 'Fine. Trott, New Girl, you aren't coming with me either.'

'What?' chorus Gretel and Jack, dismayed.

'*Thank* you,' breathes Hex.

'So what am I supposed to do now?' asks Jack. 'Try to go undercover with the others? Everyone recognises Jack Trott the thief – I've been on wanted posters for thirteen years; everyone still connects me with the start of the huntsmen's purge against magicals.' He points at himself. 'This is the face that killed a thousand Giants.'

'I thought you said that wasn't even you.'

'Yeah, but people don't know that.'

'Jack really is too recognisable to go undercover,' says Daisy. 'But so are you, Hex. You know, with your Ashtrian accent. And your wing.'

Hex looks ruefully at his wing.

'Come back to the village with us,' Daisy continues. 'We can keep you both safe there.'

'More hiding?' Jack asks wearily. 'I've been hiding since I was seven.'

Hex takes his hand desperately. 'Can't you hide a little longer? With me?'

Jack splits a Jackish grin. 'I mean, I can't say it's not tempting.'

Buttercup points at Jack and Hex, glaring ruefully at Snow. 'You see? You see what happens when people *listen* to one another, and compromise?'

'Yes, nothing gets done.'

'We can still do stuff as a team,' Buttercup cries. 'We're *better* as a team, not with you just... just ordering us around like you're already queen.'

Snow manages a small smile. 'I thought you wanted me to be queen.'

'And I thought you didn't.' Buttercup frowns down at the ground. 'Maybe that's what all of this is about.'

She sniffs, and Snow softens like icing on a hot cake.

'Buttercup...'

'So,' Gretel manages, her hiking bag still slung over her shoulder, 'are... are we still going east, or...?'

Snow sighs. She takes Buttercup's hand.

Ah. Looks like nobody's going to Ashtrie after all.

'Your idea of starting an underground movement, New Girl,' says Snow.

It wasn't much of an idea; Gretel had been told to come up with some busywork for Buttercup and that was the best she'd managed, on the fly. She doesn't tell anyone this. She just smiles and says, 'Yes?'

'If we all chipped in, with those of us who are too recognisable coordinating from the cottage, how far do you think we'd be able to take it? Could we go as far as infiltrating the Citadel itself?'

'I don't know,' Gretel admits. 'We'd still have to work on defences as well…'

Snow indicates to Hansel. 'Early warning system, though.'

'It really doesn't work like that,' repeats Hansel wearily.

'Oh, Snow!' Buttercup throws her arms around Snow. 'You'll stay? For me?'

Snow gives her a wordless smile, and Buttercup squeaks with joy.

'Um, as I was saying,' attempts Hansel, 'I really wouldn't call my visions a reliable warning s—'

'I'm going to go in and make you a lovely scone out of something,' Buttercup tells Snow over him, flapping her fingers over her moist eyelids.

'That really isn't necessary,' calls Snow after her, but Buttercup is already trotting back towards the cottage. 'Should probably talk to her at some point about her compulsion to make people happy by giving them food. But her scones really are delicious.'

Hansel tries again. 'Sometimes it can take me ages to work out what a warning vision means,' he tells Snow, 'or sometimes, they just come too late, or…' He trails off, troubled.

'Or what? Daisy asks, frowning.

Gretel shares a glance with her friend. She recognises that expression on Hansel, and it does not inspire confidence in their prospects for the near future.

'Something's…' Hansel begins. He shakes his head. 'I don't know.'

Patience manifests next to Hex, making him jump. The Ghost looks worried. 'Something's freaking out your Werewolf.'

Indeed, Scarlett is already running up to them from the cottage. She barges with an uncommon roughness past Gretel, her nose and teeth elongated, pointed ears pricked with tension.

'Something's wrong,' she manages through a not-quite-human mouth.

Hansel looks confused. 'I felt something for a second too, but then I didn't any more, and I've never…'

There is a noise from above. It isn't anything like the ominous rumble of the huntsmen's flying machine from the battle at Big Cave. It's more of a whine – the sound of a much smaller contraption. Smaller, quieter and harder to detect.

'That one of your prototypes already, New Girl?' Snow asks.

Gretel shakes her head. 'Doesn't sound right.'

'Well, if it isn't us, and your big, powerful brother's magical warning system isn't going off...'

Something cracks, in the air, in the very fabric of the forest. It's brittle, like crystal, and spreads wide like a grin. It disappears as quickly as it spread, and leaves behind a subtly different forest.

Hansel gasps, as Scarlett suddenly turns full wolf in panic.

'Something's been blocking my visions,' Hansel manages. 'I couldn't even tell!'

'What could be powerful enough to block you?' asks Patience.

'Don't know. No time!' He points up to the sky. 'It's on us!'

A very small flying machine buzzes into view above the trees. It's huntsman made, likely only capable of carrying two or three, and it is indeed right on top of them.

The occupants of the nearby refugee camp immediately start to scatter off into the trees in fear of a fresh huntsman assault. Hex is out of the nettle shirt in seconds. He lets the rest of his clothes rip under the strain of his morphing body as he transforms into a giant raven. He takes off in the direction of the machine, Jack holding his nettle shirt and calling uselessly up to him to be careful. Hansel pulls great mounds of earth up from the ground with his magic. They hang in mid-air at his command, as he waits for a clear shot of the tiny machine.

It's just too late. There is a flash, and something is sent hurtling down towards them. Hex dodges it deftly, and carries on soaring up to meet the machine. Hansel hurls the lumps of earth at the missile to knock it off its course. This works, up to a point. The missile is no longer heading directly for them. It's heading directly for the house.

'Buttercup!' Snow is sprinting towards the house. Gretel, Scarlett and Daisy too. Patience vanishes, and can be heard an instant later, screaming inside the kitchen to get out, using a horrifying ghostly voice that she is not usually permitted to use indoors. One of Jack's trees springs up in the path of the projectile, but not fast enough – the missile will barely clip the top of the branches at the rate it's moving. Gretel knows none of them will make it in time – even Scarlett will barely make it to the cottage door before the projectile hits.

There can only be around three seconds left.

Hansel focuses on the cottage, grunting with effort. The whole cottage tilts violently towards the front. A very surprised-looking Gilde comes tumbling out of the front door, followed by the Mirror, with Patience controlling its fall telekinetically so that it doesn't smash. The stale sponge of the wall next to the door bursts outwards and Buttercup falls through it in a foetal, crumby daze. From his horrified shrieks, Trevor is with her.

The house smacks back down, shedding biscuits and cakey lumps from the sudden strain of being considerably more mobile than any house is supposed to be, let alone one mostly made of baked goods.

Whatever the house was about to do next will remain a secret that it takes to its cakey grave, because at that moment the huntsmen's missile hits. It ploughs straight through the gingerbread wall, into the kitchen, and explodes in a deafening, terrifying and surprisingly wet ball of gunpowder, splintered wood and rancid fruitcake crumbs.

6

Split

'My house!' Buttercup screams. 'My *house!*'

'Not very nice,' manages Gilde, brushing herself off, 'is it? Having your little cottage destroyed.'

'Not now, mate,' says Trevor. 'Let's get cover before that flying machine fires again, eh? Um… could somebody carry that Mirror, please?'

'Snow?' calls Buttercup through the smoke, and the hail of currants. 'Where's Snow? Where are the others?'

'Finding shelter, if they know what's good for 'em.' Gilde takes Buttercup's elbow. 'Come on, sugarwitch. Yer spider's right, as usual.'

'Thank you,' says Trevor, quietly.

'Wolfie,' Gilde tells the cowering Werewolf, still in full wolf form, 'grow yerself a pair of hands, fetch the Mirror and follow me.' She pauses, meeting Trevor's gaze and remembering their recent chat about Gilde's interpersonal skills. 'Please.'

The others aren't finding shelter at all. Jack has managed to create a rudimentary barrier of thick trees in the flying machine's path. Hansel and Snow are wielding rocks and axes respectively, and Gretel is rooting through her hiking bag for a handheld propulsion device she's sure she packed, but at present, nobody dares throw anything, for fear of hitting Hex. The magical giant raven is a swirl of furious feathers, railing against the tiny flying machine with his sharp beak and claws.

Gretel gives up on trying to find the propulsion device amongst the clutter of her bag. She peers up at the battle between flying machine and bird. 'Snow?' she calls. 'Can you get a message up to Hex? If he pecks out one of the middle struts on that thing's wings, I think he'd be able to bring the whole machine down.'

Snow whistles. A jackdaw flutters up towards the embattled Hex, croaking. Hex goes straight for the wing strut. It comes away easily.

'They used the wrong kind of wood, there,' murmurs Daisy. 'They want to use white pine or something.'

One of the machine's wings collapses, and the machine begins a descent. It's a considerably swifter descent than that of the bigger flying machine they downed during the Battle for Big Cave, since the broken wing is one of only two, rather than four.

Yes. It's coming down much, *much* faster than the last one.

Much faster, and straight for them. Oh, and it's gone on fire; that's helpful.

Jack flings up a tall, thin pine to knock it off course. It hits the machine's remaining wing. Gretel sees two black-clad figures leap from the open roof of the machine just before it goes into a spin.

'Ooh,' says Daisy, paying attention to the large fabric sheets that open up on ropes above the huntsman aviators' heads, safely slowing their descent, 'those look handy'.

'Not now, Daisy,' shout both Gretel and Hansel in unison, although Gretel has to admit, they *do* look handy.

The flying machine is now spinning, on fire, towards the makeshift refugee camp. Most of the Darkwood creatures have already managed to flee, but some are struggling. Gretel recognises one small Unicorn with an injured leg, frozen with fear staring at the burning, crashing machine that's now heading right for him.

'Move, Charles,' Gretel screams at the Unicorn, but Charles the Magnificent is rooted to the spot, shrieking.

Hansel pushes magical tendrils into the ground directly beneath himself and, accidentally, beneath Daisy at his side as well, and shoves their circle of earth towards the straggling refugees at speed. Hansel's magic causes the ground to knock the few injured Unicorns, Centaurs and Ogres off their feet and scoop them away from the path of the machine. It also has the unintended effect of leaving in its wake a deep trench, as the forest floor is pulled along with Hansel. Unintended as it is, it actually turns out to be pretty handy, since it is into this trench that the machine crashes and burns, out of the way of anyone it could harm.

It's almost the perfect outcome to this terrible situation.

Almost.

It is, of course, *not* perfect, because the cottage has been blown up, nobody can see Gilde, Buttercup, Scarlett, Patience or Trevor any more, and Hansel and Daisy are on the other side of a deep trench, which is now on fire.

Hex lands next to Jack, accepts the nettle shirt and transforms back into a very shaky man.

'What *was* that?' Jack asks. 'Why didn't we know it was coming?'

'It's her,' Hex breathes. 'That cracking feeling? That's her magic. She makes people see things… she's already able to stretch her magic all the way out here… I'm not safe from her even here…'

'She even overrode your brother's visions,' murmurs Snow.

'But why would she do that?' asks Gretel. 'Why would she put us in danger of the huntsmen? She's a witch; she's supposed to be on our side, not theirs…'

'She's on nobody's side,' Hex tells them. 'She plays people against each other, and picks off what's left. You see what I mean about how dangerous she is? She plays with minds as well, makes people forget…'

Snow glares off, towards the east. 'We can't fight the huntsmen with another witch trying to sabotage us.'

'I should have warned you about how she makes people forget stuff,' wails Hex, 'but I forgot.'

Jack pats him on the shoulder tenderly. 'It'll be OK.'

'No, it won't,' Snow replies.

'No,' agrees Hex, 'it won't.' He tries to gather his still incredibly shaky nerve. 'Snow's right. We have to stop her before we can stop the huntsmen.'

'Finally,' grunts Snow, and without any word to anyone else, starts striding east.

Gretel turns to her brother. He and Daisy are safe on the other side of the burning trench, checking the muddy and shocked refugees for any further injuries.

'Find the others,' she shouts. 'Go back to the village.'

'I'm so sorry,' Hansel shouts back. 'Something was blocking my magic.'

'I know,' yells Gretel. 'We're off to sort it now. Find the Mirror. And make sure Buttercup's OK, yeah? You know how she gets!'

'I only met her last week,' shouts back Hansel, 'so, no, I don't really know how she gets, but fine.'

'I'll see you both soon,' Gretel calls. 'Love you!'

'Love you too,' shouts Daisy back to her.

There's so much more that Gretel wants to say, but Snow is a very fast walker; Gretel's already going to have to run to catch up with her, and she definitely doesn't want to lose the trail. She turns, and hurries after Snow. Jack and Hex are already following, hand in hand.

'Um,' mutters Hex as she catches up, pointing down at what's left of his normal clothes, now shredded to scraps after his speedy metamorphosis, 'does anyone have any spare breeches? Because this ripped-up arrangement here is quite cold. And rude.'

'It's *very* rude.' Jack grins. Gretel speeds up her run, now as keen to get away from Jack in full flirt mode as she is to catch up with Snow.

7
Scattered

'Snow?'

With the smoke now clearing from the crashed flying machine, Buttercup stumbles out from the rocks she, Trevor, Gilde and Scarlett took shelter behind. The house is gone. Just gone. Her home, for all those years. Just a mess of masonry and broken biscuit, now. Mocking her silly, useless magic. Everything she touches falls apart under the slightest pressure.

'Snow!'

There is a large trench of furrowed earth, running right through what used to be Jack's vegetable garden. It's still smoking a little. The stench is acrid. The privy has been knocked down. And, oh! The little camp for the homeless creatures. All the tents have been either flattened or overturned. Buttercup hurries towards it, still calling for Snow.

She knows she's not alone. Not really. Gilde and Patience are calling for the others, too, Scarlett's still clutching the Mirror and she can feel the reassuring tickle of Trevor's feet on her shoulder. But with the house gone, with no sign of Snow or Gretel or Jack or even Hex, she feels as desolate as she did that terrible day, all those years ago, when she discovered the hard way just how little she and her magical accidents were wanted in her childhood town.

'It'll be all right, mate,' Trevor tells her gently.

'Snow!'

'You'll bounce back from this, you'll see. We all will.'

'*Snow!*'

'Tough as boots, you are. And Snow's got to be round here still, somewhere…'

Patience manifests. 'Snow isn't here.'

'Oh…' Buttercup frets.

'But Gretel's brother and that Daisy girl from the village are over there.' Patience points to two teenagers stumbling towards them over upturned earth, alongside a small and rather upset-looking Unicorn.

'Daisy! Hansel!' Trevor scuttles to the top of Buttercup's head and bellows at the villagers, waving several legs. 'Hiya!'

'…I mean, look at the *state* of it,' Charles the Magnificent mutters as Hansel and Daisy jog up to join Buttercup. 'Where am I supposed to sleep now?'

'They went east,' Daisy pants. 'They were determined.'

Buttercup's heart plummets, and not for the first time, no, not for the first time at all. 'Without even saying goodbye.'

'They were the other side of this great big fiery ravine that *used* to be my bed,' Charles the Magnificent tells her pointedly. 'They didn't exactly have the chance.'

'Besides,' says Trevor gently. 'If Snow had tried saying goodbye to you, chances are, you'd end up persuading her not to go, again.'

The fact that this is probably true only hurts Buttercup's heart all the more.

'I'll tell them to come back,' says Patience. 'They can't have gone far. I'll latch on to Jack.' Ever since her untimely death, Patience has been able to psychically locate and draw herself to Jack. It's a bond that neither of them particularly enjoys, especially since it's due to the fact that he was accidentally partially responsible for her getting killed on a Bin Night, but it can come in handy from time to time.

'He'll be with the others,' the Ghost continues.

'Unless he went off snogging again,' interjects Trevor.

Patience pulls a face. 'Not in the middle of a mission, surely?'

Buttercup considers this, in light of everything she knows about Jack. 'I mean, maybe? But it's still worth a try, thank you, dear.'

'Um,' Hansel attempts to interject.

'Any messages?' Patience asks. 'For any moody princesses, in particular?'

'Tell her if she just goes off and does this, I'll be very upset with her,' Buttercup says hotly. She softens. 'But also tell her to take care.' She feels herself getting angry again. 'But also tell her that if she gets herself killed not to come running crying to me.' She softens again. 'But also tell her that I love her.' She gazes at the Ghost, feeling pathetic.

Patience vanishes in a mist of freezing air.

'Um,' attempts Hansel again, 'I don't think they really have a choice, about this.'

He explains to them the situation he was able to glean, from the sense that something had been watching them, had been blocking his magical sense for danger, leaving them vulnerable to the huntsman attack. Buttercup is only just managing to digest all of this when Gilde and Scarlett join them, carrying the Mirror, and Hansel has to tell them about it all over again.

'The sensation of everything cracking,' says the Mirror. 'There was something about that, I'm sure. In the old days. Travellers from Ashtrie, speaking of seeing things that were all wrong, and sometimes it was like looking through shattered glass. But then...' It sighs. 'No, gone again.'

Buttercup's neck hairs stand on end and her breath becomes icy. She turns to face the pocket of chilled air expectantly, just as Patience manifests back. The Ghost looks perturbed, and drained.

'I couldn't get to any of them,' she explains. 'Not even Jack.'

'*Was* he snogging again?'

'I don't know! What's your fascination with snogging, Trevor?'

'It's just such a weird thing for you people to keep doing with your faces,' replies the spider. 'What if you accidentally get the other one with your venom?'

'We don't have any venom.'

'What?' asks Trevor, incredulous.

Scarlett sniffs the air. 'Hmm. They can't have got far, but… there's something weird about their scents, like someone's put them behind…'

'Glass?' Patience asks. 'Because that's the sensation I got whenever I tried to reach them. Smacking headlong into glass.'

'But you usually just drift straight through glass,' says Buttercup, with a faint frown, 'as long as it's not salted.'

'I know!' Patience snaps. 'That's part of what made it so frustrating!'

'So, we can't foller 'em and we can't send no word to 'em,' Gilde concludes. 'Such teamwork.'

'There's a plan in place, though,' says Daisy. 'We should all just carry on with what we agreed.'

Gilde throws her hands up. 'So Majesty's still bossing us about even after she's took off? Typical princess.'

Hansel puts one of his big, gentle, farm-worn hands on Buttercup's arm. 'Come on. Let's find you lot somewhere to stay. There's nothing here for any of us any more.'

Buttercup looks around at the sad, soggy ruins of her home again, and is hit with fresh despair.

'I've got a cousin in Goosemarket,' Daisy volunteers. 'It's nice there, like Nearby but a bit bigger. Maybe that's where you could start building this movement against the huntsmen.'

'No,' says Patience, in a tone that Buttercup would normally describe as 'heated', but which actually chills the air more than usual, due to the effect the Ghost's frustration can have on the microclimate around her. 'The huntsmen were able to send another aerial attack after us only a week after the last one. We don't have time to muck about in the smaller towns; I say we take this straight to the Citadel.'

The others look troubled.

'I *know* the Citadel,' Patience argues. 'And Hansel said there's witches hiding there. Lots. If we lead from the Citadel, it'll spread to the other towns quick enough.'

'But Snow said…' begins Buttercup.

'Snow said she wouldn't go east,' Gilde reminds her. 'You don't have to spend yer life doing what she says, whether yer soft on her or not. Yer your own sugarwitch, sugarwitch.'

Buttercup doesn't know what to say. She feels close to tears. Everything's gone, everything's smashed and scattered, everything that she's spent the past thirteen years working so hard for, and they *just left her*.

They just… left her. The sugarwitch. The rubbish one.

What a horrid day.

She feels something tickly on her neck. Trevor is on her shoulder, gently patting her in a placating manner.

'Hey, now,' says the spider, and Buttercup is, not for the first time, so very glad that the tiny talking arachnid chose, out of all the options available to him in the forest, to be her familiar. 'First things first, let's go back to the village with the others. As a very dear friend of mine often says, "everything feels a bit better with a roof, a hearth and a nice cup of tea".'

Buttercup manages a smile at that, and lets Hansel lead the way back towards the village.

'OK, fine,' calls Charles the Magnificent, following them at a limp, 'but to pre-warn you, I shan't be lending my natural splendour to your Citadel mission. It's too far, and cobbled streets play merry wossname on my majestic hooves.'

Due east, Gretel just about manages to keep up with Snow's long-legged striding pace. Occasionally they'll have their path blocked by a thicket too dense even for one of Snow's axes to make quick work of, so they wait a moment for Jack to catch up and rot the greenery away.

Snow is pensive and unusually quiet. Her expression is determined, but sad-looking. Gretel's pretty gutted about the cottage too, and she only stayed there for a few months. And then there's the guilt over leaving the others behind. Especially Buttercup. Gretel hates to think of Buttercup's soft, sweet, round face crumpled with hurt and distress. It must feel worse for Snow, considering their relationship. Every time Jack and Hex catch up to them, usually still holding hands, Snow casts her eyes down a little at the reminder that her own significant other has been left behind, disappointed and betrayed.

Jack and Hex trot up to them once more, while Gretel gets her breath back next to a thick tangle of thorns. Hex really doesn't look happy about this whole excursion, either. Gretel is putting this mostly down to his whole 'terrified of going back to Ashtrie' thing, but the occasional raven's mood can't have been lightened by the fact he's now having to wear Snow's spare tunic and breeches, after ripping his own clothes in the fight against the flying machine. Snow may be large for a woman, but her clothes still don't quite fit Hex, especially considering his wing, and her penchant for practical, figure-hugging tunics does not sit well at all with a man so utterly uncomfortable with his own body. Hex hangs back, tugging at the tunic's hem self-consciously, as Jack withers the thorns away.

'I feel bad,' says Gretel, after a while.

'Yep,' grunts Snow.

Hex tugs at the tunic some more, trying to cover up the top of the breeches, where the outfit is at its most uncomfortably obvious that it was designed and cut for a woman to wear.

'Hope Gilde's all right,' he mutters. 'Suppose she's got Scarlett to keep company.'

'And Buttercup and Trevor.' Gretel tries to strike an upbeat tone, but she's started finding it harder to see the positives like she used to do. 'And we can get back to them soon enough, can't we?'

'Yep,' says Jack, as the thorns collapse into a soggy, stinking heap. 'Get into Ashtrie, get this meddling witch to pack it in, get out again, quick and quiet as the night. Just like my old thieving days.'

He gives her one of his Jack grins, one of those bright, confident ones that look like they've been painted onto his face. Gretel wonders briefly why he still bothers using that thin disguise of self-certainty with her, or anyone, in fact, who's had a glimpse beyond that veil, of the deeply troubled and haunted young man underneath. Perhaps it's an automatic thing, like Buttercup wringing her hands or Snow's penchant for looking down her nose at absolutely everyone – including creatures several feet taller than her, which involves a lot of neck flexibility and truly must be seen to be believed.

'Best crack on, then,' announces Snow, and strides on through the rotten remains of the thorns.

The others follow, Jack carefully growing the wall of thorns back once they're through. Gretel checks the map. They're close to the eastern edge of the charted forest already. They should make it over the border to Ashtrie by nightfall.

And then what?

She notices that Jack has slowed his pace. He's frowning upwards.

'What?'

'Anyone else hear that?'

She and Hex listen carefully, along with Jack. All Gretel can hear is the forest, and the purposeful clanking of Snow, ahead.

'Hear what?' Hex asks.

Jack pulls an odd expression, and shakes his head. 'Nah. Forget it. Imagining things. Nerves just probably still a bit shot from having my house blown up today.'

'Hmm.' Gretel continues to keep an ear out as she walks, but hears nothing unusual.

Above and around them, hidden by the trees, the air sparkles like fractured crystal.

8
Night Lights

Night falls over Myrsina, Ashtrie and the forest in between. In Myrsina's Citadel, the hustle and bustle doesn't stop. People have started to put up little sparkly lights as early preparations for the coming Midwinter festivities. It looks pretty. They weren't allowed under the old, strict regime, but the new Head Huntsman rather likes them. She thinks it best to let the ordinary, decent folk of Myrsina have their little pleasures, their little freedoms, especially if it helps keep them on her side regarding the whole 'killing all of the magicals' business, which could potentially get a bit messy, otherwise. No. Give them treats from time to time, show them what happens if they do disobey, and the normal people will be good as gold. Besides, she thinks as she sits with her dog in the cosy firelight in the castle, the Midwinter lights really are terribly pretty.

'Morning?' calls a huntsman lieutenant, even though it's evening. She does this because the Head Huntsman's name is Morning Quarry. Yes, it does make things confusing, sometimes.

Morning smiles a big, warm smile. It's the smile of a lovely, slightly scatterbrained art teacher. It makes people feel all fuzzy inside. If smiles were clothes then it would be an oversized cream-coloured cardigan. She's worked hard on that smile, making it just so. One of the reasons she got huntsmen to modernise their uniforms and stop wearing those creepy old masks was so that people could see the smile. There's a lot of things she can get away with, with that smile.

'Yes, Fennel?'

'The witches destroyed the new airship, I'm afraid,' says Fennel the huntsman.

Morning shrugs. 'It was only a prototype.' She pauses, for possibly just a fraction too long, before remembering to ask after the huntsmen who were piloting it.

'Walking wounded, but they'll be OK. They made it to one of our outposts; the messenger just arrived. They got further in than we'd hoped. Morning…' Fennel grins. 'They got Little Cottage.'

Morning blinks, impressed. 'The witch HQ? Goodness, how clever of them. Did they take out any undesirables?'

Fennel's expression becomes more sympathetic. 'None confirmed, but they did have to bail quickly.'

'Probably shouldn't have bailed then, should they, Sausages?' asks Morning to her dog, who is inexplicably named Sausages. Sausages raises her ears at the mention of her name. 'Do you think Fennel should make it known to the others not to bail out until the job's finished next time, Sausages?'

Sausages thwacks her tail and lets out a soft *woff.*

Fennel opens her mouth for a moment, then closes it again, and gives Morning a friendly smile. 'I'll let them know.'

'Thank you so much.' Morning beams. 'Have a great evening, you.'

'You too.'

Fennel leaves Morning to fuss over her dog by the fire, as pretty little lights go up around the Citadel.

The people of Myrsina have never had it so good. Morning Quarry is no tyrant. Tyrants don't have dogs called Sausages.

In the village of Nearby, there are no midwinter lights up yet. Nobody's had the time or the resources. Buttercup finds there that things only feel slightly better for a hearth and a nice cup of tea. The villagers are compassionate hosts, and welcome the new set of refugees readily and unconditionally, but Buttercup can see that space and resources are getting squeezed. Nearby is, after all, the only place any homeless Darkwood residents can safely go.

Buttercup knows about taking in waifs and strays. She knows about sheltering and feeding the lost, scared, tired and hungry. She knows that 'always plenty of room' comes with certain practical concerns. She knows that if the huntsmen keep making areas of the Darkwood unsafe and uninhabitable, bit by bit, drip by drip, the sole safe haven of Nearby will become harder and harder to maintain, and to defend. She sees the faces of the villagers as they bring her and the others hot drinks and blankets, and she sees that they know this, they can see it coming too, and that their solution to the problem will never, ever be to turn the needy away.

'You're right,' she says softly to the Ghost in the shadows. 'We don't have time. We need to go to the Citadel.'

Miles east, in the dark, Snow stops by a stream.

'This is it,' Gretel tells her, walking up with her torch and map. 'The border between Myrsina and Ashtrie.'

'Such a little thing,' mutters Snow, looking at the thin stream. 'You know, I've never been outside my country?'

'Until this summer, I'd never gone into the woods,' Gretel replies. 'Never even gone further than Miggleham.'

Snow gives her a small smile, and surprises Gretel by holding out her hand. Gretel takes it, and in one large stride, they step over the stream together.

'And, just like that, we're foreigners,' says Snow. 'Let's rest here till dawn; that torch thingy of yours is making the trees look weird – it's giving me a headache.'

Gretel shrugs. The torch isn't making the trees look weird at all, but any excuse for a few hours' rest.

They don't dare start a fire, but Gretel has some dried rations and lightweight blankets of her own invention packed. They eat quietly, pensively. Jack and Hex join them, lagging behind as usual, but Snow stops short of making any caustic comments this time. Hex's expression of cold terror as he hops over the stream is nothing to be made fun of. Neither is his quiet determination in the face of that fear.

'You all right to stop here?' Snow asks him, quietly, without judgement.

Hex nods. 'It'll be better in daylight.' He sounds as if he's trying to convince himself.

Jack cocks his head, listening to the forest, then raises both hands in a sweep. Giant ferns unfurl in a low canopy over their little camp.

'That really necessary?' asks Snow as Jack crawls in with them, beneath the leaves.

'It's going to rain soon,' Jack explains.

Snow quirks an eyebrow at the others. 'Hark at the weather witch, all of a sudden.'

'Do you not hear the thunder?'

Gretel has not heard any thunder, and from the expressions of Snow and Hex, neither have they.

'It's been rumbling away for hours,' Jack tells them. 'Still miles off, but better safe than sorry.'

They settle down for some sleep, Hex's feathers tickling Gretel's nose as he drapes his wing over Jack, 'for warmth'. Not a drop of rain falls all night.

Gretel has spent her whole life attuned to her twin brother's magic. For as long as she can remember, she's been able to feel it – a vibration, a fizz of static in the air. After they were separated in the summer, she found herself capable of receiving messages from Hansel, projected magically, directly to her brain, usually while she sleeps. He doesn't send messages in this manner often, so usually when he does, they're an urgent warning. So, when she senses Hansel's magic as she sleeps under the fern canopy, it's almost enough to shake her awake.

She doesn't completely wake up, though. A part of her still clings to sleep, even as her mind struggles towards consciousness. The result is a lumpen half-sleep, her body leaden and motionless as her mind spins with anxiety. In her dream, she gets up, heavily, crawling out from under the leaves, but every inch she manages on hands and knees becomes a mile, and now she's crawling out of Mudd Farm as her brother calls to her. The farmhouse's doorframe is so low; why is it so low? There's mud everywhere, and the doorframe is scraping her head as she crawls, and she feels the farmhouse sinking into the soft earth. She scrabbles to get clear of it just as her childhood home disappears into the ground with a disgusting squelch and plop. She looks around, at the rest of the village, and it's gone, all gone, sunk into the mud.

She hears a voice.

'The witch problem is a threat to our way of life.'

Great shadowy tendrils fill the sky, blotting out the sun. They solidify into a huntsman's dark robes.

Morning Quarry.

Gretel wakes up.

She can't get up. The ground is sucking her down.

'Help,' she mutters. She reaches out to Snow, but as she touches the armour of the White Knight, it falls apart, filled with nothing but rats and sparrows.

'Help,' she tries again, turning to the sleeping men, only they're not there any more either. Just a length of rotting beanstalk shaped like a skinny young man, and a terrified, flapping raven.

She tries to crawl, but the ground trembles and sucks, and she is not a part of this world, this magical world; she's ordinary. A drab human child, a nothing. What can she do in the face of such magical splendour? How could she possibly stop the flow, the push and pull? Humans will always resent witches, and witches will always know themselves to be superior. To try to stop that ebb and surge is like trying to stop the tides. The hatred is energy, and the energy is life, and soon the tide will turn and begin flooding back over all the ground these humans think they've taken. Their destruction will be reflected back upon them so many times over, and there's nothing she can do, because she's *the wrong twin.*

They went after the wrong twin. She's a mistake, a silly little insignificant error, soon to be forgotten.

She tries to crawl. The ground slips and slides. A house-worth of crumbs oozes past her. Dead wolves. Dead bears. Dead spiders. Ghosts wail, towns sink. The sun goes out.

And there, amongst the sinking wilderness, she finally sees it, rising from the quagmire. The most beautiful palace, all made from sparkling crystal. Breathtaking as a sob. Elegant and cold as a mausoleum. On its throne, a queen, her face always shifting, as if it's moving behind shattered glass. And at her feet…

At her feet, the earth itself. The Mudd Witch, no longer a boy but a plume of raw power, rooted to the ground, tendrils of dark, crackling magic choking the sky.

'The witch problem is a threat to your way of life.' Only it's not Morning saying it this time, it's Hansel. And there's no shame or distress at this statement in his tone, just a flat matter-of-factness. This is just how things are. The huntsmen hate witches because beings like Hansel are an existential threat to humans. Too powerful; much too powerful and destructive.

It's hopeless. It's hopeless, and she's nothing. The wrong twin, the nobody, no power, nothing. And her brother has so much power that he can't possibly keep it all in; it's going to explode and leave nothing left of him but writhing tendrils of magic and people; so many people are going to get hurt, and a voice somewhere out there in the palace of crystal is laughing, like that's a good thing, like they deserve it, and Gretel feels so small and unwanted and helpless, like vermin, like a weed, like a little bird, and the terror fills her, transforms her, and…

'...no...'

'Hex!'

Gretel is shaken awake – properly awake, this time, by half of a very large bird in their canopy.

'Hex?' Jack is crouched low, shuffling tentatively to approach Hex, who panics and flaps and croaks, shifting wildly between human and bird forms.

Snow too snorts awake, and blearily takes in the situation.

'Stay back, Trott, I can grab him.'

'Please don't,' begs Jack, meeting her eyes. Something about his tone gets through to Snow. She nods at him, and shuffles backwards out of the way.

'Anything I can do?' asks Gretel, but Jack shakes his head.

'He warned me about these.' Jack crawls towards Hex a little more, shielding his eyes from Hex's gaping, thrashing beak. 'Hex. It's OK. It isn't real.'

Still, Hex flaps and flounders, a confusion of feathers and skin and hair. Whether bird or man, his eyes stay the same: wide open yet blind to his surroundings, focused on something beyond – something that clearly terrifies him.

'It's just a dream,' Jack tells him gently. 'Bad dream, that's all. You're safe. I'm here.'

Hex blinks. His eyes find Jack, in the pre-dawn gloom. His form stabilises in its usual, mostly human shape.

'Jack,' he mutters. 'You're OK.'

'Course I'm OK, I always am.' Jack grins at him. 'We all are.'

Hex rubs at his face and looks around the group still huddled under the leafy canopy. He cringes, embarrassed. 'Sorry, did I wake you all?'

'It's fine,' huffs Snow, 'I wasn't sleeping well anyway.'

'I should actually thank you for waking me; you pulled me out of a nightmare of my own,' Jack tells him. 'Think it's this storm that keeps trying to happen out there – it's been bothering me all night.'

Gretel glances up at one of the small gaps between the leaves on the canopy. She still sees stars through it, and the light of a bright moon in the completely clear night sky.

'I'm sorry,' says Hex again. 'The full moon doesn't help; all transmorphers have a weird few nights around it. Me and Scarlett used to drive Gilde to distraction every month.'

Gretel thinks about the unusually bright moonlight, and the continuing claggy discomfort in her belly, and concludes that nature's various monthly cycles mostly likely explain her own horrible dreams as well.

They decide that they might as well get up and continue east. It's close to dawn anyway, and the moonlight is particularly bright, so they have plenty of light. The moon looks strange, notes Gretel. Was it even supposed to be a full moon tonight? She's sure it looks bigger than usual, and its light throws strange patterns of shadow amidst the trees. Perhaps she's just tired. Being a new woman continues to ache, and make her feel wrung out and weary.

She's surprised when Snow fishes into her backpack, pulls out a full gourd and hands it to her.

'I recognise that stance,' grunts Snow. 'It'll only ache for another day or so. Brought some of that disgusting tea. It's cold, but…'

Gretel sniffs the liquid within. It smells of feet. 'You brought this for me?'

Snow nods curtly. 'Somebody had to. And Buttercup's not here.'

9
The Witch of Making Things Better

'The Citadel, are you sure?' Hansel looks worried, although Buttercup has realised since finally meeting Gretel's brother that Hansel usually looks worried. She knows the feeling. 'I thought the plan was…'

'That plan was made before the huntsmen came back and started blowing things up again,' Patience snaps. 'There's no time. It's all at risk now. The forest, the village—'

'The mountains,' Gilde says over her, 'my bears…'

'You're going too?' Hansel casts a concerned glance over the Bear Witch's tiny, elderly frame. 'I thought you needed to hibernate?'

Gilde shrugs. 'Well, I'da *liked* to, but every time I've settled in a cosy lil house so far this winter, someone's knocked it down or blown it up. Anyhoo, I'm awake now, may as well make the most of it.'

Hansel turns his gaze back to Buttercup. 'And you'll be all right, will you? Just, Gretel and the princess were concerned about your safety…'

Buttercup sighs. Snow's concern for her can be sweet, and flattering, and make her stomach flutter a little, but ever since the huntsmen started taking the fight to the forest, those butterflies in her tummy have turned into miserable, heavy slugs. It was different before, in those relatively peaceful years hiding out in her cottage. She felt like an equal part of something. The lighter of fires, the putter-on of tea, the one who took time to reach out to others in a softer way, when Snow's gruff orders and Jack's superficial charm didn't work. But now? It's all gone. There's nothing left but a cold, hard battle and there's no place for people like Buttercup in that. And Snow knows it. Even Jack and Gretel know it. That's why they left her. That's why even this troubled boy isn't sure she's up to an undercover mission to the Citadel. She's the weak one. The rubbish one. To be carefully wrapped as if she's made of glass.

She puts on as confident a smile as she can muster. 'I'll be fine. We've got a guide...' She indicates to Patience. 'And a spy.' She points to Trevor, on top of her head. 'And' – she gestures towards Gilde – 'someone who's very good at getting other people to do what she wants them to do.'

'I'm a manipulative lil minx,' says Gilde proudly.

Hansel sighs. 'OK, well, I'll keep watch on you all through the Mirror. If anything goes wrong, I'll get you out of there. I can just pull whatever bit of street you're standing on back to Nearby if needs be.'

Buttercup tries to keep a cheerful face. She really doesn't like the sound of just getting magically yoinked back to base if the mission starts going awry.

'Psshh.' Gilde flaps a hand in Hansel's face. 'If we run into trouble, I can always call my bears out of hibernation to help out. Although they'll be mad as a bag of cats over it, and twice as hungry.' She nudges Buttercup. 'Got everything you need there, sugarwitch?'

Buttercup hefts her bag onto her shoulders, having been very easily persuaded she should be the one to carry all the provisions for herself and Gilde, as well as Trevor's latest box of disguises.

'No time like the present, then.'

Buttercup is only able to half-turn away from the concerned Mudd Witch, before her attention is caught by Scarlett, calling them and running over.

'Hey! Hey!' The Werewolf's face is doggish; her anxious cry is close to a bark. 'Wait for me!'

Buttercup dithers, torn between Scarlett and the now resolute-looking Gilde.

'Wolfie', says Gilde, 'me and the others were thinking maybe these good village folk who've been so kindly as to take us in would be needing a strong set of hands and paws more than we need a fifth wheel in the Citadel.'

Scarlett stares at them all. 'What?'

'We're goin' undercover, puppy,' continues Gilde in sugary tones. 'Yer six foot one, and bright orange even in human form, *and* you always have to wear yer granny's very old, obviously magical cape, *and* with the moon gettin' fat fer the month, you're going to have more prickly a time keeping yerself from turning full wolf – you always do.' Gilde pauses and regards the Werewolf, who has started to emit a quiet, high pitched, doggy whine. 'Remember a few springs back, for three nights each side of full moon you changed every time you sneezed?'

'I'll be fine.' Scarlett cringes clumsily, barely keeping her human form together in the face of the humiliating reminder. 'It's not even hayfever season.'

'You ain't coming with us.' Gilde pauses. 'You'll hold us back.'

Buttercup desperately wants to say something, but she too has noticed how much trouble Scarlett's been having retaining her human form in the past couple of days as the moon has waxed gibbous. It still feels horrible, though.

'Sorry,' Buttercup manages. 'If it helps, I know exactly how you feel, what with...'

Scarlett whines and shakes her head, her shoulders hunched.

'Hey,' Trevor tells her. 'I'd cheerfully swap with you, but how much use would *I* be, defending a refugee camp, or building one of Gretel's weird inventions?'

'I can't build machines,' whimpers Scarlett.

'You used to be a woodcutter, didn't you? Back in the day? I've seen some of those blueprints and they are going to need wood, and lots of it.'

'That's true,' admits Hansel. 'And to be honest, we could do with as many fighters as possible, in case there's a ground attack.'

'It must feel weird splitting off from us, because you're a pack animal,' Trevor tells her kindly. 'I get that: spiders are notoriously solitary; I had to learn to work in a team with a bunch of bipeds. But the good news for you is, by staying here, you get to be part of a bigger pack. And they need the protection of an alpha wolf.'

'I'm not an alpha.'

'Like I said: spider. Don't really understand pack hierarchy or mammals in general. Just do your best, eh, mate?'

Scarlett nods resolutely. 'OK. I'll try. Thanks, Trev.'

Buttercup gives a small smile to the spider, even though, from his perch atop her head, Trevor can't see her. She wonders, not for the first time, if he knows how good he is at this sort of thing – gently talking people round. In any case, she's very glad to have him with her, as well as Patience, the invisible guide to all things huntsman, and Gilde with her unstoppable willpower and ursine back-up force. And Buttercup... well, Buttercup is good at carrying the bags, as long as she doesn't get distracted and turn the straps into pastry. So she's got that going for her, she supposes.

The condition of the road from Nearby to the Citadel is terrible, even by the standards Buttercup's used to, and she's used to forest pathways. The road is falling apart, with a long, wide gouge running along the centre.

'So,' says Buttercup as they trudge along. 'When we get there, I should find us an abandoned shop or something and set up a bakery.'

'Don't get that many buildings just left abandoned in the Citadel,' Patience tells her. 'Real estate's through the roof, up there.'

'They've got estates in their roofs?' Trevor asks, confused.

'It's a figure of speech.'

'But you just said they were *real* estates.'

'We'll need a base though, surely?' Buttercup asks, if only to derail Trevor. 'Somewhere for... well, for me to be. I need a hearth.'

'What for?' Patience asks.

'For starters, so that I can pretend I'm baking all the cakes that'll keep appearing around me. But also... I don't know, it's just what I do. Or what I did, before my cottage...' She trails off, trying not to think about being showered in the stale crumbs of her once content life. 'I thought you lot could go out and find underground witches and things, and then I'd help win them over, with a cosy fire and something to eat?'

'I guess there is a lot to be said for offering a shelter from the cold, a bowl of porridge and a cup of sweet tea to bring folks on side,' mutters Gilde, 'but there's more to it than that.'

'Well, yes,' Patience tells Gilde, 'you also used manipulation, intimidation, emotional abuse and really, really big bears.'

Gilde chuckles warmly at the memory. 'Yeah.'

'Well, I can't do any of those things,' replies Buttercup. 'I just do cakes. That's it. That's all I can offer here. So I'm going to need a bakery.'

'Buttercup, come on, now.' Trevor tickles a leg over her hot cheek. 'That's not all you can offer.'

'It's my only power, and it's a stupid power, and that's why Snow and the rest went off without me, and I'm sorry but that means either you're stuck with my stupid cake hands or I turn around now and go back to the village and—'

'Woah, woah, woah! You're on this team because we need you on this team.'

Buttercup shoots the spider a look. 'You don't need cakes on this team.'

'Will you stop going on about cakes?' asks Trevor. 'This has nothing to do with cakes. Look at me – I went from being a scared little spider who didn't understand why he could think and talk, to being a valued member of your gang, *and* your best mate. You did that. And I don't even eat cake. Can't digest the stuff. Patience can't eat, either, and you helped her. Just like you helped Snow and Jack and Gretel and all the others, with or without a jam sponge to hand. You're not the Cake Witch, not really. You're the witch of making things better. And we need one of those.'

'They still do call me the Cake Witch, though.'

'Yes, well. That's a bit easier to say than "The Making Things Better Witch".'

Buttercup thinks about what Trevor's said, and feels a bit better.

'I do still think we'll need a base, though.'

'Fine.'

'And I still feel horrid about poor Scarlett,' she says, after a while. 'I know what it's like to be the one left behind.'

'Kindly don't compare what I did for Wolfie to what your princess did to you,' replies Gilde curtly. 'I *know* Scarlett couldn't manage in the Citadel. I *know* she'd fall apart and go full wolf. With you and Majesty it's different, because you're courting, and she wants to play the big, tough White Knight, always running to her sweetie's rescue, impressing you so. Keeping you in a high tower out of harm's way until you start to believe that's where you belong.'

'I'm not sure I care for what you're implying,' retorts Buttercup.

'I really don't give a hoot whether you care for it or not. It's the truth. It's perfectly possible to love someone to the hills and back, and not think much of their capabilities.'

'I'm sorry, Gilde, just because you feel that way about Scarlett, that doesn't mean—'

Patience wafts in between them, like a self-righteous draught. 'You're both right, and you're both wrong. Gilde and Snow are *both* stuck-up and underestimate the rest of us.'

'I do not,' snarls Gilde at the exact same time that Buttercup defensively cries, 'She does not!'

'Sorry, guys.' Patience doesn't look even a bit sorry. 'Telling uncomfortable truths is part of the whole Ghost deal. Buttercup, Snow's a witch queen in waiting, she's had it drummed into her from birth that everybody else is less capable than she is. And Gilde, we've seen you talking down to the others. Don't tell me for a second you wouldn't have kept Hex in the village as well, if you could.'

Gilde sighs. 'I was trying not to think of Sweetiebird. You don't really think he's gone east with that Jack-the-Lad swindler of his, do you?'

'They seemed pretty attached at the hip last time I saw them,' admits Trevor. 'I think probably wherever Jack's gone, Hex will have gone too. Early stage of the human mating ritual, innit. Sounds a lot more complicated than the spider way – waiting for a female to shake her front legs at you and hoping she doesn't eat you afterwards.'

'Trevor's right,' Buttercup tells Gilde. 'About Hex and Jack,' she adds hurriedly; spider dating sounds horrific – she's actually quite glad that Trevor seems to fall flat with the spider-ladies. 'And Jack was keen to follow Gretel and Snow.'

Gilde sighs. 'Silly, lovely bird. He don't know what he's doing. Him and his loverboy are gonna get each other killed. Or worse. In Ashtrie, it can always be much, much worse.'

10
Fee Fi Fo Fum

In the eastern forest, bright moonlight turns into a dawn that brings no warmth with its wintry rays. A light frost shimmers on leaves and silvery bark in the early sun. Even the clouds of vapour issuing from the mouths of the four interlopers seem to sparkle and dance in the dappled light. This part of the forest may be eerie, but at least it's pretty.

They walk on, in silence. The sounds of their feet crunching on the frigid ground and Gretel's pencil filling in the blank spaces of the map seem amplified, in the surrounding quiet. They remain in a tight group – Snow no longer striding ahead, Hex and Jack no longer deliberately falling behind to snatch alone time together. Jack keeps looking over at the skyline, frowning, as if trying to make out something faint in the distance. Even Snow seems edgy. Once the sun is up completely, she stops in her tracks, one finger held aloft in a silent signal for the others to do the same.

'You guys hear it too?' breathes Jack, still gazing out at the sky.

Snow shakes her head. 'Nothing,' she whispers.

'Nothing,' echoes Hex warily.

Gretel notes Snow's troubled expression, and realises what the princess means. Usually in the forest they wouldn't be able to hear their footsteps, or the gentle scratch of pencil on paper. Not at this time of day. Usually at dawn, the forest would be annoyingly noisy with rustling, flapping, twittering, skittering life.

'I thought last night they might just be asleep.' Snow frowns, concentrating the way she always does while trying to find a bird or rat to use as a spy. 'But they should be awake by now.' She looks to Hex. 'Why aren't the birds singing? Why aren't *any* of the animals doing *anything*? I know they're out there, I can feel them, but they're... I don't know. They're not right. They're... *thinking*. Not about hunting or mating or fleeing, but something else, something I can't work out. It's like they're not properly animals.'

Gretel notices something else. 'All the trees still have their leaves, here,' she points out. Indeed, they are surrounded by multiple oaks, ashes, beeches and chestnut trees, all with fat, lush green leaves sparkling with frost. 'No leaves underfoot at all, they haven't even started going brown – it's practically winter.'

'All of this is hers,' Hex says quietly. 'The birds and the mice. The trees – definitely the trees. They were all on her side before she took power, so it's said. They helped her to do it. The trees shook their beauty down from their boughs onto her, and she charmed the mice and the birds and the lizards into becoming anything she wanted them to be. They're keeping things the way she likes them. Nice and pretty. Nice and obedient.'

'Hmm.' Snow looks about herself, at the deathly quiet, glittering forest. 'My powers won't work here, then.'

'Of course they won't. Other witches are a threat to her; if all she does to neutralise you is make sure you've got no critters to control, you will be incredibly lucky. As far as I know, the last witch to try to stand up to her was my sister.' Hex flaps his wing self-consciously. 'And look how that turned out.'

Snow takes in a deep, controlling breath. 'OK, well let's have our wits about us. Keep a close formation, watch each other's backs. After all, I'm not the only witch in our... oh trousers, where's Jack wandered off to?'

Jack has indeed disappeared somewhere off into the trees.

'Jack?' Gretel calls after him. There's no response from the silent woods.

'Oh, no.' Hex takes a couple of steps towards the trees, then stops, thinking better of it, and tries to remove the spare outfit Snow gave him so as not to rip his last available clothing. 'Stay there, I'll look from the air... gah, these hook and eye clasps aren't designed for one hand...'

Not one to do as she's told, especially when told to stay put while somebody else does the rescuing, Snow heads straight off into the trees. Gretel shoots Hex a quick, apologetic glance before hurrying after her, leaving Hex trying to keep up while toeing off boots and struggling to remove a fiddly leather tunic singlehanded. It takes a miserable series of increasingly desperate and sweary entreaties from Hex telling them to wait for him before Snow furiously doubles back.

'Fine,' she shouts. 'Jack, wherever you are, I hope you're happy; apparently the first thing I need to do to rescue you this time is help your ridiculous boyfriend get my britches off.'

Wherever he is, Jack is not happy. Wherever he is – and right now, he doesn't know exactly where that is, besides 'surrounded by sparkly trees' – he is only driven by finding the source of that trousering noise, that thundery rumble that's been driving him to distraction since last night. It's closer now, he can tell, but the sky remains cloudless. It can't be a storm, surely. Besides, now that it's nearer, it sounds as if it's coming from much closer to ground level. Maybe somewhere in the treetops, but certainly not from the sky itself. He tries to follow the noise, wilting a path for himself. The closer he gets to the source of the rumbling, the more rhythmic it sounds – almost organic.

There's something faint behind it, too... sounds like his name. Is that Snow calling for him? And Gretel, and Hex? A part of him feels bad, but a much more insistent voice in his mind is urging him to find the source of that noise. It's suddenly deadly important to him that he does so. He'll join the others really soon, once he's found out what the rumbling is. Maybe it's an important clue to all of this. Maybe whatever it is will help them, help them win over this witch of the east... help them win the whole thing, maybe. Help them finally put an end to thirteen long, miserable years of violence: a lengthy, one-sided war that started when...

When he...

There's a shape up ahead in the trees. Jack can't make it out between the silvery trunks and shadows. It's some sort of steep hillock, perhaps, or a lumpen, rounded building, some sort of cottage... whatever it is, Jack is sure the noise is coming from the top of it.

He peers at the gloomy, rumbling shape.

'Hello...?'

Gingerly, he steps towards it, encouraging the trees to gently part.

Not a hillock, or a building. Something grey and meaty, sitting with its back to him. Something man-shaped, but much, much bigger. Bigger even than an Ogre.

For a moment, Jack is rooted to the spot, unsure what to feel – wonder? Fear? Sorrow? Joy? He hasn't seen one of these since he was a little kid. Hasn't seen one of these since they came after him, accusing him of murder. Hasn't seen one up close since the horrible day he robbed one, and accidentally collapsed a beanstalk during his escape, starting off a deadly chain of events that resulted in the huntsmen waging full war against magical beings.

A Giant.

Slowly, the huge creature turns. It spots Jack, and peers down curiously at him, sniffing deeply. Jack finds himself welling up with tears. He had forgotten how gentle they look when they're at peace, just getting on with their lives. He had forgotten about the way they sniff and snuffle, their soulful eyes too weak to make out fine details all the way down on the ground. He remembers now how much they have to rely on their sense of smell to get about when not in their great sky-nests.

The Giant takes in his scent. 'HUMAN,' it rumbles.

He holds up his hands slowly. 'Yes. Human. I'm not going to hurt you. I just wanted to…' He pauses, feeling stupid. He just wanted to do what? What could he possibly say or do to make this right? The deaths of all those Giants are still mostly his fault. 'I just wanted…'

The Giant huffs again, and this time, the gentleness starts to ebb from its eyes.

'IT WAS YOU.'

'No! No! Well… yes, but…'

'THIEF! KILLER! COWARD! IT WAS YOU!'

The Giant gets to its feet, causing the ground itself to grumble. Trousers, it's huge.

'I didn't kill him,' Jack shouts. 'Not… not directly, at least. If you'll let me explain…'

'NO EXPLANATIONS. IT WAS YOU.'

Jack starts taking steps backwards, even though he's painfully aware that the Giant could lash out a single arm or leg to crush him within seconds.

'What do you want from me?'

'JUSTICE,' booms the Giant. 'AT LONG LAST, JUSTICE.'

Criminal. Coward. Yes, he is both of those things. Jack turns, and runs, as fast as he can. He doesn't even bother to block the path behind him with trees; they wouldn't stop this Giant. A massive foot crashes down in front of him. Jack skids to a stop in front of it and turns a full one hundred and eighty degrees, sliding down to hands and knees in the frozen dirt and pushing himself back up again to spring away in the opposite direction, leaving filthy grazes on the heels of his palms. The Giant takes a while to turn, but Jack knows it will be able to catch up with him soon enough. His hands hurt, his legs hurt, his lungs are on fire and his eyes sting with tears. The Giants are gone and it's his fault. And when this last Giant finally catches him, he'll be torn limb from limb, and it will be all he deserves.

He runs, without daring to look behind him to see how close the Giant is. He can hear voices behind him, calling his name. The Giant? The forest itself? He doesn't know, and he isn't about to stop to find out. Something's close behind him – he can feel it prickling the back of his neck. Desperate, he grows a beanstalk. Like all of his beanstalks, it's fast and hefty enough for him to grab on to the stem as it shoots from the ground to propel him along through the whipping, stinging foliage as it grows, moving him faster than his legs possibly could. Also like all of his beanstalks, it's incredibly unstable. It begins to rot, only a few seconds after it sprouted. Jack grows another, dropping from the old, withered stem to the fresh one shooting from the ground. He grows another, when that one also quickly withers, and another, and another. He knows he's exhausting his magic, but he needs to get away. Multiple voices are calling his name, now, ordering him to come back. He can't. He can't. He…

He tries to grow another beanstalk, but nothing comes. The ground is too frozen, and his magic too depleted. He tries again. Nothing. He's left holding on to a beanstalk that is rapidly turning brown and wet with rot, with nothing beneath him but several dozen feet of air, a rock-hard forest floor and painful, messy death.

What's left of the beanstalk turns into stinking slime. It slithers wetly through his fingers. He falls…

And is caught, mid-air, by something big and black and warm and feathery.

Bewildering, battling thoughts besiege his brain. Part of him tells himself that he's been captured, while another voice within him tries to calmly tell himself that he's safe now. He knows these feathers. He knows this warmth.

Before he's able to react, he is gently deposited onto the ground. Strong hands grab his shoulders.

'Jack. Snap out of it.'

He focuses onto a haughty, dark-eyed face. 'Snow?'

'What the fruit was all that about?' Snow demands. 'Running away from us like that. Could have got yourself killed.'

'There's a Giant…' mutters Jack, gazing off into the trees for some sign of the enraged behemoth.

'Think we'd have noticed a Giant, Trott,' retorts Snow.

'You must have been seeing things,' Gretel adds, still out of puff. 'When Hex led us to you, you were running scared from… well, from nothing. We tried calling to you, but that just made you more frightened.'

Jack frowns, still confused. It was there! It was real! It rumbled and snuffled and shook the ground and looked down at him with those eyes, those eyes, usually so soft and gentle, so full of rage and grief and hatred. It had to be real.

'There *was* a Giant. It spoke to me…'

'There've been no Giants in Ashtrie for years,' Hex tells him, softly, and yes, that's the warmth he remembers, those are the feathers he knows, black and sleek, tucked in as Hex tries to dress with a sweet clumsiness. 'She didn't like having them around, and after she was deposed, Ashtrie still wouldn't have them. All the ones who escaped the huntsmen in Myrsina went north, beyond Bear Mountain. They're long gone now. I'm sorry.'

'It's me who's sorry.' Jack breaks away from Snow's steadying grasp, and helps Hex with his clothes. 'It felt so real. Do you think it might have been…'

'The Glass Witch? Definitely. This is what she does… *some* of what she does, anyway.' Hex gives Jack a small smile of gratitude at his help with the fiddly fastening on the tunic.

'This is not the most practical outfit,' mutters Jack.

'Oh for pity's sake,' barks Snow, 'would you both stop whining about *my* spare tunic which I lent out…'

Gretel reaches over to Jack's sleeve and tugs at it insistently

'…out of the goodness of my heart? I mean, I've got no casualwear option now that he's wearing it, but do you see me complaining?'

Jack follows Gretel's gaze and notices that she is staring at something off in the trees. His insides clench. 'What? What is it? The Giant? Do you see it too? In the trees? I said it was real!'

'Not a Giant.' She points into the trees. Jack can make out something glinting.

He follows the glint of light upwards. It continues, above the treeline. It's practically transparent, but he can make out exquisite lines and shapes shining in the early morning light.

It's the ornate towers and ramparts of a palace. Made entirely out of cut glass.

'It's her,' breathes Hex, gazing at the palace with a mix of wonder and terror.

'She lives in a castle made out of glass?' Snow snorts. 'In the middle of the forest? How is that practical?'

'You live in a cave,' Jack reminds her.

'And we used to live in a house made of cake,' adds Gretel.

Snow huffs. 'Still, though.'

11
A Proper Pickle

By the time Patience and her friends reach the Citadel's main gate, they've managed to agree on a cover story, and have practised staying in character as much as possible. Buttercup is to be a starry-eyed young baker, here to try to make her fortune in the big city now that the laws regarding women's careers have been relaxed under the new huntsman regime. Gilde is to be her poor frail old granny, who couldn't possibly be left behind, not with her lungs the way they are. Gilde has practised her Frail Old Lady Cough considerably, and has managed to get it to a really annoying level now. Trevor has thought up a way to stop huntsmen recognising Gilde and Buttercup. It involves hats.

For himself, Trevor can easily hide to avoid detection. And Patience – Patience can simply fade from view and go undetected, nothing more than a minor prickling shiver as she passes through people, the sense of something being very slightly wrong. She shouldn't mind being invisible, really she shouldn't. It takes up much less energy. It's the closest thing her wandering spirit gets to rest, these days. Back in life, only a few months ago still, she always went unseen, beneath her huntsman robes and mask. She would think nothing of it. If anything, she found it comforting, liberating, even, knowing that nobody could see her face. But that was then, and Patience has become a whole different person since those days. Not simply because back then she was a very alive young human woman, and now she's dead, her Ghost pulled from what was left of her body by the magic of the Darkwood. Death has given her a new perspective. Death returned her true face to her, and now she actively enjoys showing it to others, either in friendship, or in order to scare them. She can do some simply terrifying things with her face, these days. Haunting really is great fun, but now is not the time.

Now is the time for her to vanish, a wafting shape made out of nothing but memories. Now is the time for her to go undetected. Now, as they approach the gate that in life she always dreamed of passing through as a hero of the huntsmen's cause. Now, as the guards nod at Buttercup's story, accept her bribe and let her and Gilde through, Patience passes through the gate too, an invisible shade, a shudder.

What she hasn't told anybody is that despite spending her years as a fledgeling huntsman studying the Citadel on paper, she's never actually been in person. In life, she longed to march through the cobbled streets, her boots and mask hard, her heart proud, watching eyes turn towards her cowled figure, seeing only the uniform but understanding that beneath it was somebody important, somebody in charge. Now, she floats in the others' wake. She has no feet as such, only the memory of feet, and they do not touch the cobbles of the street. No eyes turn towards her. She doesn't even cast a shadow.

Whispering in Buttercup's ear, she directs the witches over to the poorer southern quarter of the city, where they might be able to afford to rent a small base with the money and gold donated to them by the villagers and Dwarves respectively. She steers them away from anyone who looks particularly likely to mug or kill them, as well as keeping them away from the areas she understands to be huntsman hotspots. Buttercup and Gilde's large hats may do a good job of shielding their faces, but wide-brimmed floppy hats like that haven't been in vogue outside of the provinces for years now, and frankly they're attracting more attention than they deflect. She locates an available basement room beneath an inn. It's a good size and has a stove for Buttercup to run her 'bakery'. She whispers advice to Buttercup throughout the rent negotiation with the inn's landlord, but ultimately it's Gilde's interjections, in her treacherously sweet and frail little old lady voice, which result in their hefty discount. Gilde truly is a shockingly manipulative little minx.

As the rest of the party trudge down the steps to get set up in the basement, Patience tells them she's off to scope out the Citadel, see if she can pick up any leads. When she slips away from them, it isn't that she's not trying to find leads as such, it's just that also she would really like to get to see the Citadel, at long last.

She floats unseen through narrow, high-walled alleys that open at surprising intervals into complex public squares, with multiple alleys leading off like a spider's legs, shops and cafes and specialist workshops lining every side. A lot of the walls have faded patches of brick and scraps of ripped paper where the edicts and abomination lists that used to brutally control civilian human lives must have, until recently, been plastered. All must have been torn down in the days since Morning Quarry became Head Huntsman. Instead, large, bright posters depicting Morning herself grin affably down on the artisan markets and bustling throngs of the squares, along with upsetting slogans such as 'Let's Have a Purge!' and 'Burn Them All!'

Besides the newer posters, almost every public square has a feature in its centre, such as a fountain or a tiny community garden or, most commonly, a statue. A lot of the statues are to huntsmen, so they're pretty samey. Patience is just about to inspect one when something catches her attention. It's an odd whistle, coming from down one of the many meandering, spindly alleyways. In her old life, she'd have thought nothing of it – just the slightly annoying, repetitive whistle of someone busy at work. What now marks it out as significant isn't any sort of psychic vibration that she's able to pick up on now that she's a Ghost. It's simply that the whistle sounds almost exactly like Snow's. It's the same cadence Snow uses when controlling squirrels or mice, but at the same time it isn't quite Snow herself. Patience frowns, and drifts in the direction from where it came.

She floats through a damp, algae-spattered wall, and into a dark workroom. It's no bigger than the basement she and the others have just hired, and is crowded in on every wall by shelves full of jars. Several barrels of vinegar litter the floor and at one end of the room is a range with large, bubbling vats. Baskets of fresh onions, beetroots, cabbages and courgettes lie around wherever there's room. It's a pickling plant.

A solitary man flits from the bubbling pots to the jars. Patience has no sense of smell any more, but from the spices he's adding, he seems to be making a batch of pepper chutney. As he works, a rat creeps from a crack under the door. Emboldened by a life scavenging the urban streets, the creature heads straight for one of the baskets of fresh produce. The man doesn't even look at it, but whistles that particular cadence once more. The rat stops, an oddly familiar look in its eyes. It's the expression of the creatures Snow manages to control. The rat turns and leaves, without a fuss.

Another vermin witch! Just like Snow. Well. Not like Snow, because Snow is a tall and haughty princess in hand-beaten, skull-adorned silver armour, and this man is a small and mousey middle-aged pickle maker in shabby, patch-covered clothes. She tries to float off to tell the others, but in her haste, mistakes a harmless cask of vinegar for one of salt. The salt is like glue to her. Only one of her hands has passed through into the cask, but the salt sticks it fast. She can't move. She struggles to pull herself away from it, her frustration turning the air around her frosty, and sending a nearby spoon sliding to the floor.

The man turns, shivering. 'Is someone there?' His breath becomes vapour. 'Hello?' He looks terrified, and Patience isn't sure it's just at the prospect of a possible Ghost in his workshop.

Patience struggles harder to free herself. Some of the glass jars nearest to her begin to rattle with her vexation.

'Go away,' quavers the man. 'We're not interested, leave us be!'

At the sound of his voice, a woman hurries into the workshop from upstairs.

'We'll have no trouble here—' she starts, then breaks off suddenly, scanning the gloomy workshop.

'Where are they?' she asks the man.

'Invisible,' replies the man, grimly.

'Trousers,' breathes the woman. 'That's just asking for a knock from huntsmen.' She raises her voice. 'We said no! You're just going to get us all killed or carted off, like the others.'

Patience tries calling out to the couple to explain, tries manifesting, but the salt won't let her. She concentrates as hard as she can, and with one draining burst of energy is able to yank her hand out of the salt. The salt topples over one way and Patience is thrown from the workshop the other way, out through shelves of pickles, causing the pickles to freeze so suddenly that they crack the glass of their jars.

She hears the man cry, 'Rose, the produce,' and sees the woman hurriedly raise a hand in the direction of the broken jars, but then the momentum of her psychic energy burst hurls Patience through the wall, and another wall, and another, until she lands, weak and diminished, in a new alleyway.

Well, that could have gone much, much better. Hoping that she hasn't now scared these leads off before the others can so much as approach them, she tries to find her bearings. After a few different spindly alleyways and closed-in squares, she feels self-doubt begin to set in. She's still too diminished to just lock on to Buttercup, and it's taking longer than usual to regain energy, away from the magic of the Darkwood... or maybe it's taking her longer than usual because she's growing worried, which, considering the main thing that's worrying her is that she's lost and drained, is quite the vicious cycle. She can't be lost in the Citadel; she's supposed to be the group's insider informant on all things Citadel and huntsman-related. That's the whole point of her being here. She's no good at winning people over, like the other three are. Life as a huntsman didn't exactly train her in the art of gentle persuasion. When you were a huntsman, you just let the threat of violence do all the persuading for you.

She stops, glaring reproachfully at the back of yet another huntsman statue. She's in a slightly larger, more open square now, and she can just about see the ramparts of the castle above the rooftops, so it should be easier to point herself in the right direction. One downside of being in a bigger square, however, is that there are more people milling about. Another downside is that this particular huntsman statue is needlessly huge. It's recent, too, she notes. Probably in honour of John Rosier, the former Head Huntsman, after his grisly death in the Darkwood. Eurgh.

She's utterly trousered off by now. The dream trip she's always wanted to take, ruined by death and salt, but mostly by huntsmen. Those bullies, those tyrants... that she herself followed, to her own death. And for what? She allows herself to become angry. Angry at the huntsmen, and angry at herself. The rage energises her. She floats around the statue, leaving a furious trail of frost.

'I might have known they'd still be worshipping *you* here,' she sneers quietly at the statue of Rosier. 'Satisfied, are you? Was it worth it? Was it worth dying all alone out in that forest...?' She stops. The statue isn't of Rosier. The figure underneath the cowl is slight and feminine.

It's of her.

'No...'

Swirls of ice paint intricate silver patterns under where her feet would be, were she still alive. She notes the inscription on the pedestal: THE FALLEN SISTER.

They didn't even use her name. Not at first. Because under the inscription is something even worse. A plaque has been bolted on. It reads:

Her name was Patience Fieldmouse.
She died at the hands of the Darkwood monsters.

She died protecting you.

When we neutralise the Darkwood, we do it for her.

BE MORE PATIENCE.

– Morning Quarry

'No.'

They're still using her death. Still using it to kill. And now they're doing it in her *name*.

'No!'

A few of the civilians in the square frown, trying to find the source of the distressed voice. A couple of them rub their arms and shiver in the sudden pocket of freezing air.

People have left offerings of flowers and sweets by the statue's feet. With a scream of anguished rage, Patience sweeps the whole sorry, wilting, sticky lot off the pedestal and onto the frosty cobbles below.

'Did you see that?' exclaims a passer-by.

A nearby tinker nods, ashen. 'Did you *hear* that?'

'Witches,' says a third person, doing up the buttons on a particularly fancy coat. 'They killed that poor girl, and now they mock her memory.'

'Witches?' The tinker trembles. 'But not in the Citadel, surely?'

Fancy Coat Man narrows his eyes. 'Ohhh, that's what they *want* you to think, but I've heard of underground cabals, all sorts of horrifying stuff. You ask me, we need a good purge, and it needs to happen right here, as well as in that stinking forest.'

A fresh burst of rage finally energises Patience enough to be able to lock on to Buttercup in the basement and transport herself there. She does so with a miserable feeling that she may have only made matters worse. She doesn't even get to see Fancy Coat Man slip on the patch of ice left in her wake only seconds later, landing in a filthy puddle and utterly ruining his coat, which would at least have cheered her up a bit.

12

The Glass Witch

Nearby Village is a friendly bustle. Scarlett isn't used to being around so many people all the time, and she doesn't particularly like it. She's spent her whole life so far hiding away – first in her granny's cottage and then up in the mountains with Gilde – and being part of a village, even one as accepting and as full of other magical creatures as Nearby is, makes Scarlett feel uneasy. Werewolves aren't supposed to help out at the local woodshop in return for friendly smiles and a nice hot bowl of stew at lunchtime, are they? They're not supposed to muck out stables while the old man feeding the horses cheerfully reminisces about visiting the old Little Cottage. Werewolves aren't supposed to integrate into human society, are they? Humans aren't supposed to want them to. And yet, here she is, even with her face stuck in a slightly wolfish shape, so close to full moon, her ears a little too big, her teeth a little too sharp, her tongue tripping over complicated words, and the humans are still giving her smiles and offers of refreshments as she works.

She finishes off at the stables, and hurries over to Daisy Wicker's house, as she has done after every job so far. Hansel and Daisy have set the Mirror up in Mrs Wicker's kitchen, and Scarlett is, as ever, anxious to find out how Gilde's doing out there in the Citadel and, even more worryingly, whether Hex is OK out east.

'They're fine,' announces Hansel, as soon as Scarlett comes into the kitchen. 'They just got themselves some board, we lost Patience for a bit, but she's back now. You know Ghosts, always floating off.'

Scarlett nods, regarding the Mirror's image of Buttercup and the others conversing in some dark, low ceilinged room. 'And Hex?' she asks.

'Nothing yet.'

Scarlett whines, despite herself. 'What if they're in trouble?'

'I haven't felt anything yet,' Hansel tries to reassure her, even though his face is nothing but a reflection of her own worry.

'But the Glass Witch can block things from you!'

'...yes,' Hansel admits.

No word, no anything, since the cottage was blown up and her friends went off east into danger. And Scarlett is just... chopping wood, and shovelling muck.

'Glass Witch,' she barks at the Mirror. 'Rhymey rhymey rich, just how dangerous is the Glass Witch?'

'Scarlett,' sighs Daisy, 'it's not that we haven't been trying.'

'I still can't see into Ashtrie,' the Mirror tells her apologetically. 'But... but there is one thing. When the sky cracked? Just as we saw the flying machine? I was able to catch hold of a fragment of a memory. At least, I think it was a memory. It could just be another trick. I didn't want to tell you about it until I'd pulled at the thread enough to be sure it was real.'

'So, are you sure now?' Daisy asks.

'No,' admits the Mirror. 'But maybe you should know about it anyway. Just keep in mind, the only thing you can truly be sure of regarding the Glass Witch is that you can't be truly sure of anything.'

'Must you always speak in riddles like that?' asks Daisy.

'Sorry. I'm a magic Mirror. It's sort of what we do.'

The Mirror's image of Buttercup's team in the Citadel fades. Its surface becomes a crackling magical static.

'Here's what I remember. Or, possibly, here is what the Glass Witch is making me *think* I remember,' says the Mirror. 'Once upon a time, Myrsina and Ashtrie were friendly neighbours. Wealthy merchants and artisans would pass safely from border to border, through both countries, buying and selling, happily taking caravans along the road through the forest. As in Myrsina, the royal family of Ashtrie would employ and consult magical courtiers; in fact, many minor nobles were themselves blessed with witch powers. One such magical Ashtrian noblewoman tragically died in childbirth, and her widower fell into a great sadness. A governess was installed for the baby – a widow herself, with two young daughters of her own. Considering the obligation of care to his motherless child fulfilled, the nobleman turned his back on the world, on his hearth, on his own daughter. He turned only towards the oblivion of the bottle. He barely surfaced from the drink in order to marry the governess at her suggestion, for sake of "stability". He died soon after.

'Little more was heard of the nobleman's orphaned child for many years. The mansion fell to disrepair under his second wife; rumour spread that the family fortune was all gone, along with whispers that the orphaned girl could sometimes be seen out foraging, in rags. And then, one night, she reappeared at the prince's Coming of Age Ball, dressed in impossible finery. They say she cast a glamour over every soul who set eyes on her. There was no mistaking that she, like her mother, was a witch. There was also no mistaking that the young prince was enraptured. When he searched for her the following morning, he could barely believe that she was the product of such a dilapidated and shamed household, less still when she appeared from behind her two common stepsisters, bruised and dirty and dressed in scraps, but it truly was her – apparently, the prince could tell from her feet. I actually attended that wedding as King of Myrsina, or at least I think I did, and the prince went on about her feet a *lot*. He might have had a thing about feet in general. The part where I doubt that this memory is real is, I can't picture the bride, at all. All I can tell you is that she was beautiful. All the details about *how* she was beautiful remain out of my reach. Like a half-forgotten dream. Her dress was the colour of the sky, but whether that was a bright blue sky or a twinkling night sky or a moody dawn or a stormy sunset, I cannot say.

'I can remember her name, though. Lady Ella Hardup. Then, Princess Ella, and then, following the mysterious death of the king, Queen Ella.'

'Too much power,' says Hansel softly, frowning at the static in the mirror. 'When there's too much, it can eat you up. It makes you feel invincible, a mighty monster. When it crackles through you, you can't help but think about how easily you could take revenge on the people who've hurt you, with no regard for innocent bystanders. That sort of power, in the hands of a young queen, one who'd had a horrible start in life…'

'As king, I received reports that the new princess's family had been found guilty of neglect, and exiled as punishment,' says the Mirror. 'Other rumours abounded, that they had been subjected to horrific punishments. After that came other worrying accounts. It started to become clear that she was in charge of Ashtrie, and was ruling with increasing tyranny and paranoia. Coming down hard on anyone she even considered a threat to her supremacy, including other witches…'

Hansel was still squinting into the Mirror. 'That sort of power thrives on rage. Unchecked, it tells you to swallow the sun, to parch the ocean, to drown the land. It wants you to be the only one; it tells you that if you can find peace, cold and alone, if only you can silence everything else. Everything.' He pauses, his eyes still fixed on the Mirror. 'I see her.'

'What?' says the Mirror. 'No you don't.'

'I do. Just a shape, but I see… she's no monster, she just never got the magic under control, she fed it too much fury, and now she's…'

The static vanishes. The Mirror's surface shows a normal mirror image again, leaving Hansel staring at his own, close, slightly cross-eyed reflection.

'What did you do that for?' Daisy exclaims. 'Hansel could finally see her!'

'Could *you?*' the Mirror asks Daisy.

'No, but…'

'Could you, Miss Wolf?'

'Oh, no,' admits Scarlett truthfully, 'but my vision always goes to flip this time of the month anyway – not easy to focus when your synap… synassess… brain-wires are part dog.'

'Well,' continues the Mirror, 'neither could I. With the Glass Witch, we need to be careful. And whatever it is you think you saw in there, Hansel, it wasn't coming from me.'

They need to be careful. Everything about the delicately pointed glass spires shimmering ahead tells Gretel that they need to approach them with caution.

Unfortunately she's not able to mention this to Snow before the princess strides off in the direction of the glass towers, with her usual sure-footed stomp. Gretel hesitates, eyeing Hex worriedly.

'You going to be OK in there?' she asks him.

Hex nods briskly, with an unsure expression. 'I've come this far. I owe it to myself now to look that woman in the eyes, at least. Show her I'm not scared of her any more.'

Everything about his body language screams that he is very definitely still scared of her.

Jack squeezes his good shoulder. 'Well, you won't be alone, this time.'

They set off in Snow's wake, jogging to catch up with her, and Gretel doesn't mention out loud that, according to Hex, he wasn't alone the last time either, and the Glass Witch destroyed his family on a whim anyway.

The castle actually gets harder to see, the closer they get to it. Trees mask the spires whichever way they move, and when they're able to spot the twinkling towers again, they're never where they're supposed to be. Gretel could be absolutely certain that they're heading in the correct direction, and the next time she spots the towers, they look further away than they were before, or they're suddenly over on her right. She consults her compass almost constantly, until Snow snatches it off her, declaring that it clearly isn't working and that they should just use, in Snow's words, 'simple common sense, you ridiculous child'. Jack offers to wilt the trees so that they can see better, but Hex tells them that it's probably a good idea to completely eschew magic on approaching the Glass Witch's palace, if they've any hope whatsoever of keeping things civil. There is a chance, he says, that all of this is a test, to gain her favour.

There is also the chance, he adds quietly, as they push on through the maddening silver trees, that she is simply toying with them, because she's bored.

They come to another clearing and crane their gazes up to look at the visible patch of sky, only to find that they now cannot see the towers anywhere at all.

Snow punches a tree, growling in frustration. 'She's laughing at us!'

'Oh, almost certainly, yes,' Hex tells her.

'If this is a test,' reasons Gretel, 'or her idea of a joke, then shouldn't the towers disappearing from view altogether happen when we're very nearly at the palace? To see if we give up now, or to make us think we've got completely lost...'

'Or maybe we *have* got completely lost,' grunts Snow. She starts marching off again. 'I don't see any sign of a...'

She smacks into an invisible wall. Her breastplate takes most of the brunt, but her uncovered face manages to make a fairly forceful impact as well.

'Ow!'

'You all right, Snow?' calls Jack, in spite of the evidence to the contrary.

'Yep, fine,' shouts back Snow, again, in spite of the evidence to the contrary – in this case, the gush of blood now coming from her nose.

Gretel approaches the invisible wall carefully, and runs a finger over it. It's glass. Surprisingly tough glass; it hasn't even cracked under the impact of a large woman in full armour striding full pelt into it.

'This is it,' she breathes, running her hand along the glass. It seems to stretch on and on. 'Now we have to find the way in.'

'Do you?' comes a harmonious voice from somewhere above them. 'Or do you need to find the way out?'

Gretel looks up, searching for the source of the voice. It's hard to pinpoint. She knows it's come from *somewhere*, she's just not sure where, exactly. She knows that the voice is lovely, beautiful, like a half-recalled lullaby. She knows that this is the voice of a true ruler, an eternal queen, to be utterly adored and utterly feared.

She looks to the others. Snow is scowling, clutching her bloodied nose. Jack looks as entranced and perplexed as Gretel feels. Hex looks more terrified than Gretel has ever seen before. He clutches tightly on to Jack's sleeve with his good hand, and he has raised his trembling wing as a rudimentary shield for himself and Jack.

'She let us in already,' Hex whispers shakily. 'Somewhere back there. We're already in her palace. Look.'

Gretel looks. Hex is right. They're not in the forest at all; this is a beautiful palace of shining crystal. She can still see the silver forest beyond, but mostly what she sees are angular reflections and shards of light beaming off the shapes in the cut glass. Gretel sees herself reflected in the transparent splendour over and over again – a brown, scruffy little thing, in a dirty, farm girl's dress, carrying a lumpy knapsack. A creature of the mud and the twigs. An ugly little sparrow, fluttering in the finery, looking for crumbs. She doesn't belong here. She never did. She belongs in the dirt; what is she doing here, what was she thinking?

'The queen has granted you an audience,' sings the voice, and oh, it's like a nightingale's song, so lovely, so rare. A beautiful vision moves through the shifting angles of glass. Gretel can't make the figure out properly, but she can see that it's wearing a gown that shimmers with every colour in the spectrum. 'Princess Snow of Myrsina, is it? I was at your naming ceremony. I remember asking your mother at the time whether naming such an... indelicate child after the snow might be some kind of joke.'

Usually, Snow would have some huffy comeback to that sort of insult, but she just clutches at her bleeding nose and mutters, 'Mum...'

'But of course, where are my manners?' adds the melodious voice. 'You're not a princess any more, are you? You're queen. So sorry for your loss; I'm afraid that's subjects for you. You should have been firmer with them from the start, it really is the only way they learn. It's a kindness, really.'

'We came to ask something of you,' begins Snow, but she seems forgetful. Gretel herself has to wrack her brain for why it is they dared to encroach upon the Glass Witch's domain.

'You ask a favour of the Glass Witch?' The figure, resplendent in her gown of rainbows, smiles. So lovely. So lovely. 'Is this why you bring me gifts, Queen Snow?'

'Gifts...?'

The Glass Witch gestures towards Gretel, Jack and Hex. 'Queen Snow, I must humbly refuse these. They do not please me.' She runs an exquisite hand down Jack's frozen face. 'What use have I of a plant charmer when all the trees already bow to me? I found the skills he demonstrated to be lacking; he's too distracted by his crimes against the Giants. I shall see to it that the plants of Ashtrie cooperate with him no more.' She turns her attention to Hex. 'And you brought back one of my old spells – how dreary. Ugly thing.' She turns to Gretel, and Gretel feels even smaller and filthier and more unworthy than before. 'As for this one, nice try, but it's the wrong twin. Everyone knows that. This one's useless.'

'They're my friends,' manages Snow.

The Glass Witch raises an eyebrow. Gretel swears she can hear cracking glass as she does so.

'They're not the gift,' continues Snow, blood dripping over the silver of her armour and the ebony of her hair. 'The gift is our alliance and our help, if you accept it. You're in terrible danger…'

'You do not know danger.' Now, the Glass Witch's voice is cold and sharp. Her gown no longer shimmers with colour. Now, looking at her… hurts, somehow. '*You* are in danger. I am exactly where I need to be. I always am. How *dare* you threaten me!'

'It's not a threat,' continues Snow, 'it's a warning. You know we have a point. That's why you allowed us in, why you gave us an audience.'

'I allowed you in,' says the witch, her voice like splintered shards, 'because of your links.'

'What, just because I'm royalty too?'

The witch laughs, with a noise like a vase being dropped into a bucket full of bottles. 'A smidge. But you have more important links. Your links to the Looking Glass.'

Suddenly, she is right in front of Gretel, looming over her, her smile too wide, like her face has cracked in two. She reaches her hand out to Gretel's face. Gretel is aware that there's something in her eye. There has been for some time.

'And your links,' continues the Glass Witch, 'to the land.' She puts sharp, cold fingers on Gretel's eye and pulls out what was stuck in it. It hurts. Gretel screams, and brings her hands up to her face automatically.

They're all screaming. All four of them. The pain…

'Stay awhile in Ashtrie, Queen Snow.' The melody of the Glass Witch's voice soars above the backing harmony of their screams. 'You will find me a gracious host.'

And then the voice and the pain are gone, and there's just a cold emptiness.

Gretel opens her eyes.

The shard of whatever it was in her eye has disappeared.

So has the Glass Witch.

So has her palace.

So has the forest.

They are in a patchy scrubland.

'What...' Jack rubs at his face. 'Did she just put something in my eye?'

'She took something out,' replies Hex, his voice dull and defeated.

'Where are we?' Snow asks Gretel.

Gretel scrabbles for her map and compass, even though she already knows that neither will be of much help to her; they clearly aren't in the Darkwood any more.

'We're in the badlands,' Hex sighs. 'It's where she sends you when she's done with you. It's where she sent me, and my brothers. That palace, it was an illusion.' He nods at Snow's nose, which is no longer showing any sign of the impressive nosebleed from only moments ago. 'All of it was. She muddles you, misdirects you, and when you can finally see properly, you find yourself out here, left to rot.'

'Well,' reasons Gretel, with as much cheer as she can muster, 'if we got here in the matter of a few hours, we can get ourselves back on track easily enough.'

'That's what we thought too, at first,' Hex replies. 'And we were ravens; we thought we could just fly out... but we were stuck out here. We were stuck out here for six years.'

13
A Load of Cobblers

Buttercup has only had the 'bakery' in the inn's basement open for a day, and she's already sold five pies and thirteen pastries, which is lovely, honestly, but that really isn't what she came here to do.

She worries about the others. Well. Maybe not Trevor, who seems absolutely in his element sitting in his corner watching the customers coming in and out, listening carefully for any sort of lead. Gilde is a concern, though. Buttercup was rather hoping that as the natural alpha witch amongst them, Gilde would take the lead on this one, but having helped secure them the basement, Gilde has taken a step back, sitting quietly and leaving Buttercup to deal with everybody who follows the smell of fresh baked goods downstairs. Buttercup knows she needs to start quietly asking around about underground witches, without arousing suspicion from anyone unsympathetic to their cause, but truthfully she has no idea how to go about doing that. She can't even tell which of the Citadel customers might be on their side, and which might not. She is only too aware that her many years in the forest have left her rather out of touch with how to go about interacting as a normal human. As she thinks about this, she understands why Gilde has grown so quiet and reserved. Buttercup has only spent thirteen years in the wilderness, and has always been amongst friends even then. Gilde was in the mountains for maybe sixty years, and spent most of those completely alone, besides her bears. When they were negotiating the lease of the basement, the landlord of the inn frowned and cocked his head at her old-fashioned turns of phrase. Gilde ploughed on, unfazed at the time, styling it out as just being the weird old lady who says weird old lady stuff and, honestly, Buttercup barely even notices the antiquated utterances any more. Whole sentences full of phrases like 'jumpin' jellyfish' and 'dern tootin'' and 'ain't nothing but a hill o'molasses' simply wash over Buttercup after less than a fortnight of knowing Gilde. But they're in the Citadel now, the home of the huntsmen, the home of the very idea that a weird old woman doing weird old woman stuff is to be treated with extreme suspicion. Gilde probably can't get away with talking the way she does, without attracting the wrong kind of attention. Besides, reasons Buttercup, Gilde may be feeling overwhelmed by all the people here, and missing her bears. The Bear Witch seems lost, in the big Citadel. Lost and obsolete: more of a Ghost than Patience.

Actually, no, Buttercup tells herself, that's wrong. Nobody is more of a Ghost than Patience. Since tumbling in last night, a mere cold, angry smudge, almost entirely out of energy, Patience has been at her most Ghostly. She was almost completely invisible when she came in; only Trevor noticed her at first, she was so depleted. They then spent a frustrating twenty minutes or so trying to work out what Patience wanted to tell them, even though nobody could hear her, she was too weak to write telekinetically and her image was too thin to be able to read her lips. In the end, Buttercup had to let her know that whatever it was was simply going to have to wait until the Ghost had recovered enough energy to tell them properly. Patience threw the wafts of faint shadow that passed for her arms in her weakened state up into the air and vanished in a chilly huff.

It isn't until Buttercup closes the bakery for lunch the next day that Patience manifests again, fully visible, audible and crackling with cold impatience, right in front of Buttercup, making her yelp.

'As I was *trying* to say,' snaps the Ghost.

'I *wish* you wouldn't do that,' mutters Buttercup, prising her fingers out of the Closed sign, which she's accidentally turned into baklava in alarm. 'Gilde, could you make me a new Open and Closed sign, please?'

Patience wafts out of Buttercup's face a little. 'As I was trying to say,' she continues in a deliberately calmer tone, 'I have a lead. Picked it up last night, but then I got stuck in salt and got lost and then there was this statue of me... it was a whole thing.'

'A lead?' says Trevor excitedly.

'A statue of *you*?' asks Gilde, over him. 'Fancy.'

'It wasn't fancy, it was awful,' Patience tells her. 'And yes. A lead. In a pickling plant down one of the side streets. I think the labels on the jars said something like Pike's Pickles? Or Percy's Pickles?'

'Well, none of *us* ain't got no highfalutin statues to us in the big city,' mutters Gilde.

Trevor abseils down onto Buttercup's head, excitedly. 'Piper's Pickles, maybe?'

Patience's eyes widen. 'Yes, I think that's it!'

'One of our customers was carrying a jar of Piper's Pear and Pepper Piccalilli; I remember seeing the label and thinking about how much fun it must be to say out loud and now that I have said it out loud I can confirm that yes indeed, it is tremendously fun to say out loud. Piper's Pear and Pepper Piccalilli!'

'The man there was a vermin witch, like Snow,' Patience tells them. 'Peter, I think his name was... he could control rats by whistling, just like she does.'

'*Peter* Piper's Pear and Pepper Piccalilli,' says Trevor, delighted.

'Just like Snow?' Buttercup isn't sure what to do about this information. There's another witch with exactly the same powers as Snow, out there? Like her special, one-of-a-kind Snow? The actual princess? And there's some fellow making pickles down a side street, with exactly the same abilities as her? Does... does that mean there are other witches out there who turn things

85

into cakes? Does she want there to be? Does she want there to be other witches like Snow? She honestly doesn't know. She tries to mentally shake away the thought. Whether she wants there to be other witches with the exact same powers as her and her friends is neither here nor there. What matters is that Patience has found another witch, living right under the huntsmen's noses in the Citadel, and they need to go and see what they can do to help him.

And what this Peter Piper might be able to do to help them.

'Oh, he really doesn't want to help or have anything to do with any other witches, by the way,' says Patience, and frankly it would have been more helpful for her to have done so before Buttercup had gone to the trouble of finding Piper's Pickling Plant, going there with Gilde and Trevor and knocking on the door. 'He knew I was here yesterday, kept going on about leaving him and his wife alone – I think she's a witch too, but I didn't get to see her power – anyway, he knows about some sort of underground movement, they want him to join up, whoever they are, but he wants absolutely none of it.'

Buttercup gives Patience her best attempt at a withering look. It's about as severe as a kitten trying to stare down a Rottweiler. And the kitten's in a cute little hat. And the Rottweiler thinks the kitten is her pup. And it's in a field full of daisies. And marshmallows. It's that withering.

'What?' asks the Ghost, unabashed.

The door opens. The middle-aged woman on the other side of it looks poor, and perturbed. Her pinafore is patched. Plainly, the pickling profession isn't particularly profitable.

'Yes?' asks the woman. 'You want to make an order? We're doing a nice rhubarb and ginger pickle for Midwinter Feast…?'

'It's not that.' Buttercup gives her the sort of smile she usually saves for anxious creatures and lost folk of the Darkwood. 'Might we come in, Mrs Piper?'

Mrs Piper frowns. 'We already gave the huntsmen a considerable donation for their continued protection, only the other week. You can't be here for another already? We just don't have the silver…'

'We're not from the huntsmen. We're… friends.'

Mrs Piper casts a wary eye over Buttercup and Gilde, while Trevor hides up Buttercup's sleeve and Patience remains invisible. Even without the Ghost and spider in view, something about them clearly clicks in Mrs Piper's mind. Her expression hardens.

'No,' she whispers. 'No, we have *told* you people, time and again. We'll have nothing to do with you.'

'Nothin' to do with who now, sweetie?' asks Gilde in her dangerously syrupy tones.

'Begone!' Mrs Piper looks across at something in the alley behind Buttercup, and scowls. 'Might have known. I *told* you, no!'

Buttercup turns her head to see what Mrs Piper is looking at. There's a woman of about thirty lingering in the alley, watching. She's half hidden in shadow and wearing a headscarf, but Buttercup is positive that in the few seconds that she sees her, the woman grows her hair.

This in itself isn't a surprise; most people are growing their hair all the time, but not quickly or dramatically enough to be observed over a handful of seconds from the other side of a dingy alley. A glossy fringe slides down the front of the headscarf as Buttercup watches, only for it to be swiftly tucked away when the woman turns to hurry off. As she does so, Buttercup notices a good six inches of hair visible underneath the bottom of the scarf, which she is sure wasn't there before.

'See that?' breathes Buttercup.

'On it,' says a quiet little voice by her ear.

Trevor leaps from her shoulder to the alley wall, where he scuttles at speed in the direction of the departing woman with the mysterious hair.

'Sorry to bother you,' Buttercup tells Mrs Piper, also setting off to follow the scarf-covered stranger at a brisk walk.

'And don't come back,' Mrs Piper tells them, shutting and bolting the door.

'Reckon as we *should* come back to the Pipers',' Gilde tells Buttercup, struggling on her little old legs to keep up with the younger witch's stride, 'if'n only ter get some of that pickled rhubarb. The wife had powers, too. Strong 'uns. Could feel 'em.'

Buttercup nods at the mysterious woman taking a sharp turn at the end of the alley. 'And that one?'

'Hair don't grow like that natural, and she ain't no kind of Werewolf, not with her keeping her face so nice and neat under a full fat moon.'

'So it's a good thing that we're following her through this alley? And not... sort of creepy?'

'Well, we've committed to following her now, ain't we? Think I saw Trevor catch up and jump on her coat 'fore she turned the corner. So it don't rightly matter one way or t'other if it's creepsome or she's leading us a merry jig into a mean ole trap.'

Buttercup and Gilde turn the corner, which opens up into a square. She can just about see the scarf-wearing woman duck down another alley. A thin trail of frost on the ground shows that Patience is also following the woman, invisibly.

Buttercup does her best to keep her expression neutral while they stride through the crowd after the woman. 'You think I might have just sent Trevor and Patience into a trap?'

'Not as such, since we're tailing her too. There's a mighty chance yer leadin' us *all* into a trap, if that makes you feel any better, little sugarwitch?'

'Not really, no.' Buttercup breaks into a jog down the next alley, following Patience's icy trail. It suddenly stops, halfway down the alley.

'Trousers. Where did they go?'

There are no doors, no windows, through which the woman might have slipped. No stairs leading to basements or rooftops. No manholes into the sewers. Nothing but high brick walls, everywhere she looks.

'Trevor?' she whispers, growing anxious. 'Patience? Trevor!'

Most house spiders don't come when you call them, but Trevor isn't most house spiders. Similarly, most people aren't usually as pleased and relieved as Buttercup is when a spider crawls out from a crack in the brickwork and jumps onto them. That's just one of the reasons why Trevor and Buttercup make such a good pair.

'What happened?' she asks Trevor. 'Where does the trail—?

'Buttercup,' interrupts Trevor, 'I just want to thank you right now for bringing me to the Citadel. I am having the *best* day.'

'Where does the trail go, spider?' asks Gilde impatiently. 'Where's Ghostie?'

'She went in with them to check it's not a trap.' Trevor is bouncing with glee. 'I decided to stay behind to show you guys the *secret knock*.'

'There's a secret knock?' Buttercup asks.

'Yes!'

'To a secret den?'

'Yes!'

'You've always wanted to discover a secret knock to get into a secret den!'

'I know!'

'Aww. Congratulations, Trevor!'

'Thanks, mate, that means a lot.'

'What's the secret knock, then?' Gilde asks, her impatience on the matter clearly not tempered one smidge by the happy news that Trevor's just achieved one of his life goals.

'Oh! Yep! So,' the spider tells them, 'best if Gilde does this, Buttercup; we don't want to cake this up, no offence'.

'None taken.'

Trevor addresses Gilde. 'OK, so the first bit is, you take off your shoe.'

Gilde does so, frowning doubtfully.

'Then you take one of the loose nails out of the masonry here…'

Gilde obliges.

'And then you ram the nail through the sole of your shoe.'

'Yer want me to break my slipper?'

'Yep.'

'That's the secret knock. A lil ole lady pokin' holes in her shoes in the frost of winter.'

'Trust me.'

Gilde rolls her eyes and growls softly, jabbing a nail repeatedly into the sole of her shoe. 'Ain't believe it's come ter this. Should be cosy in the mountains a-nap with my bears, 'stead I'm out here down a jitty in Huntsman City, smashin' up my shoes cause a spider tole me so.' She shows the spider her shoe, now littered with holes. 'Now what? My foot's going cold.'

'Put it down here.' Trevor indicates to a spot right next to the brick wall. 'And then knock twelve times.'

Gilde sighs testily. 'And now I'm s'posed ter count up to a dozen. Will this work never end?'

Still, Gilde obliges, although Buttercup has to tell her when to stop knocking. As Gilde draws her hand back from the twelfth knock, they see that in front of them is no longer a bare brick wall. It's a shoemaker's shop.

'It's a magical moving shoe shop!' Trevor crows in delight.

The door opens ajar, and a wary face peers through it.

'Good day, Mr Rumpelstiltskin,' Trevor tells the face.

The face squints from them to the broken shoe, and back up to them again. 'Who are you,' croaks the man, 'and why do you look weirdly familiar?'

'We're friends of friends,' says Buttercup quickly. 'Um... we spoke to Mrs Piper...'

It isn't a lie, really. And it makes the man at the door raise his eyebrows. 'The Pipers! Are they finally considering joining us?'

'Not yet, but they helped us get here.' Buttercup picks up Gilde's broken shoe. It turns into a soggy, shoe-shaped shortbread. 'We're like you.'

'That was my shoe,' complains Gilde. 'How're they s'posed to fix it now?'

The man opens the door fully to them. 'We can fix any shoe,' he tells them with a sigh. 'Hey, Salad? Two…' He spots Trevor. 'Three more.'

'Four more, actually,' announces Patience, manifesting and making everybody jump.

'Did you vet them?' asks the woman's voice from within the shop.

'Well… no, but they're magicals and they knew the knock. And the password.'

'The password's just your name though, Rumpel; I keep telling you to change it, it's not strong enough.'

'It's perfectly strong,' says 'Rumpel', ushering them all inside with the biscuit-y broken shoe and locking the door behind them.

'Anyone could just guess it!'

'It's a really unusual name; people don't "just guess it", trust me.'

The woman steps towards them from the back of the shop. She's the same woman whom they followed through the alleys, only she's removed her headscarf and is in the process of haphazardly shearing off her by now waist-length hair. 'A decent password should contain some numbers or something. What about "Rumpelstiltskin1"?' She nods at the others as they watch her hack away her hair. 'Oh, it's you, from the pickle place. I did think there was something weirdly familiar about you lot; might've known you'd be magicals. Name's Salad. Want some hair?'

Buttercup and the others shake their heads. Salad shrugs, ties the hacked-off length of hair together in a neat loop and tosses it into a basket. 'All the more for the wigmaker.' She scrapes her fingernails over her new messy crop. 'Trousers, that's so much better. So, what do you do?'

'This one turned a shoe into a biscuit,' Rumpel tells her.

'Well. That is an unusual power. Most transformers do stuff like stone, or gold, like Rumpel.'

Buttercup stares at Rumpel, who looks embarrassed. 'You turn things to gold? That must be so useful!'

'Not as much as you'd think,' Rumpel admits. 'I can only do certain things – straw's the easiest for some reason – and it only works at night, and if I try to sell too much at a time to the city goldsmiths, well, rumours go round these days about where I might have got it. At least it doesn't just... happen, without me meaning to. There's stories of a king from a few centuries back who had my powers, but they weren't controllable. He got very rich very quick, and then... very, very dead.'

'I heard that 'un,' says Gilde, cheerfully. 'King o' one of them hot countries. Food he was tryin' to eat turned to gold as he swallowed it. They say the autopsy was like a treasure hunt.'

Rumpel shudders.

The other introductions are made. Salad's only power is that her hair grows uncontrollably. She has found no use for it whatsoever besides making a half decent living supplying to the wig trade. Rumpel, it transpires, is a quarter Elf and inherited the magical shoe shop from his Elf granny. They're able to remain reasonably safe in it since it moves around, only appearing to somebody who really, desperately needs their shoes fixing. They found out about Mr and Mrs Piper a while ago and have been trying to bring them into their secret underground society ever since.

'They're not safe living like that,' Salad explains. 'They keep having to bribe people who find out about them, and they really can't afford it. Peter's just a vermin witch, those are ten a penny, really, but Rose can freeze things in time. It's how they can bring in produce from all over – she keeps it fresh for the transport.'

'She's got this plan that once she's strong enough, she'll just freeze her and Peter for a hundred years, until all of this has blown over.' Rumpel shakes his head sadly. 'Don't know whether to be worried for her or jealous that she honestly thinks this huntsman mess is something she can just ride out.' He looks across at them. 'And then there's you lot. You must have only just got here. Why?

Nowhere in Myrsina's safe, but it's horrible in the Citadel for magicals. Nobody magical *comes* here, on purpose.'

'Except the Mudd Witch,' adds Salad. 'They say he came here on purpose on election day, with this nefarious plan, but Morning stopped him, and chased him back to the...' She trails off, staring at Buttercup and the others.

'What?' asks Gilde.

Salad's face splits into a wide, bright grin. 'That's why you look familiar. You're them. Aren't you? Or, at least, you're some of them.'

'"Them"?'

Salad digs in a drawer for a bundle of papers. She spreads them on the desk. They're 'Wanted' posters. New ones, at that. They're finally using pictures of Jack as an adult instead of a seven-year-old boy. It's all of them. Gretel, Hansel, Scarlett, Gilde... all of them. 'The Darkwood Insurgents'.

'This is disgraceful,' says Trevor, scurrying along Buttercup's fingers to get a better look at the posters. 'That's a *terrible* likeness of me.'

14
The Wilderness

They were only misdirected by the Glass Witch for a few hours, Gretel reminds herself. They should be able to get out of the badlands quickly and easily.

Should be.

A good first step towards this would probably be finding out which direction they should head in to get back on track, but Snow still has Gretel's compass, and the princess is in no mood to cooperate right now. Snow is pacing, heading one way in great strides, then stopping, scanning the horizon and marching off in a different direction.

'Snow?' Gretel asks.

Snow stops, clawing at her hair. 'What am I doing?' she murmurs, exasperated.

'It's all right,' manages Gretel, keeping her tone as buoyant as possible. 'These things happen, I suppose, when you try to confront a powerful witch who alters perceptions. Yes, we're a teensy bit lost, but...'

'What am I *doing*?' Snow marches off again.

'We're dusting ourselves off and getting right back on track,' Gretel tells her. 'If I could just have my compass...?'

'I thought your compass wasn't working,' grunts Jack. His haunted expression wails silently of the Giants still stomping through his mind.

Jack walks past Gretel, unhelpfully in a completely different direction to the one she was trying to take. Gretel tries to catch Hex's attention as he's dragged by the hand in Jack's wake, but he's just staring at his wing unhappily.

Gretel really wishes they'd brought Buttercup and Trevor with them.

'"Queen Snow",' sneers Snow. 'I'm no queen. I can't be queen.'

'Snow, I know you're worried about that, but we can still win this, you can still…'

Snow glares down at Gretel. 'No! I can't. I *mustn't*.'

'Wait, what?'

'I know you don't want to hear it – nobody does. But think about it, Gretel. Think about that monster in her crazy glass palace, what she did to Hex and his sister; look at this place!' She gestures out towards the vast expanse of scrubby, blasted land. 'This is her kingdom, nothing can grow here, nothing can thrive! Nobody should have that power. Nobody should have that sort of control over a whole country, or be able to spy on their subjects, or manipulate them, or…'

'Are you saying you don't think you should be queen because you have the Mirror,' asks Gretel, 'or that you don't think you should be queen because you have magic powers…?'

'I'm saying I shouldn't be queen, full stop!' Snow thinks for a second. 'No. That's not it. I think… I think I'm saying nobody should have that sort of power at all. I'm saying nobody should be queen. There shouldn't be one. We're born different, but no worse than anybody else, and no better.'

Gretel can see from her face that this isn't the Glass Witch's spell talking. This is what Snow truly thinks. This is the White Knight talking – the woman who hid her name and her title for all those years. This must be why she's been so hesitant to make her move against the huntsmen – everyone's still seeing her as the country's Happy Ever After, and she's desperate for that moment not to come.

'We need something new,' adds Snow quietly. 'I've known it for a while. Living in a cave for thirteen years gives one the perspective one needs to see this sort of thing clearly.'

'I thought you were just scared of the responsibility,' mutters Gretel.

'Oh, I am,' admits Snow with a small smile. 'Just, not for the reasons you think.'

'You know you would never end up like the Glass Witch,' Gretel tells her. 'You're nothing like her.'

Snow nods. 'I would be a different monster. But a monster nonetheless. The arrogance of kings and queens is what started us all down this dark path. If we're to stop it happening again, we need to break the pattern. No more huntsmen. No more royals. Something new. Something fairer. Not just a teetering seesaw of unjust power. That is, if we manage to win, somehow. That is, if we ever manage to get out of here, after I led us straight into a trap.'

'Well, one start would be to see if my compass is working again.' Gretel holds her hand out for the compass.

Snow gives it to her grumpily. 'It wasn't before.'

'Well,' Gretel says cheerfully, 'you never... oh.'

'Needle still spinning round and round like billy-oh?'

'Yep.'

'Told you so.'

Gretel pockets the broken contraption and squints up at the sky instead. 'Maybe I can navigate by the sun...' She fishes in her knapsack for her astrolabe. Obviously she packed her astrolabe; what explorer and adventurer worth her salt leaves home without her own custom designed astrolabe?

'You really don't give up, do you, New Girl?'

Gretel shrugs. 'If there's one thing I've learned since being chased into the Darkwood, it's that wandering about in a tizzy doesn't do much good.' She pauses. 'Also, I've learned a lot about spiders.'

Snow twitches a smile that's very nearly warm. 'Trott, Hex,' she calls to the two men, 'where are you two wandering off to? There's no time for snogging!'

'We weren't snogging,' calls Jack, turning back to Snow and Gretel, still dragging Hex behind him, 'we were getting out of here.'

'Not without us, you're not,' Snow tells him. 'New Girl has a new plan and some sort of sun-charting doodad.'

'At last,' grumbles Jack. 'It's horrible out here.'

'I did say not to go east,' says Hex quietly.

'You went east, too,' Jack reminds him, under his breath.

'For you.' Hex sounds wounded.

'Guys,' mutters Gretel, still trying to concentrate on her astrolabe, 'can we not? That Glass Witch is still in our heads. Turning us against one another, disorienting us.' Gretel looks to Hex. 'Did she do that to you and your brothers too, the first time?'

Hex frowns at the memory, and nods.

'She's trying to keep us lost and bewildered,' Gretel tells them. 'We focus, and work together. We need to get around her magic and confront her properly before we can go back to the others.'

'Why?' Jack's tone has lost its belligerent edge.

'Because she was interested in the Mirror,' Gretel tells him. 'And she was interested in Hansel.'

'Oh,' breathes Hex. 'Why didn't you lead with that?'

'Hmm?'

'You need to protect Snow's dad and your brother from the Glass Witch.' Hex shrugs. 'If there's one thing you know I'll understand, it's family.'

Jack shoots him a proud little smile. 'Well, wherever you lot are going, I'm going,' he tells them. 'See? That was nice and easy; anything else you want to share with the group?'

Snow shrugs. 'I don't want to be queen?'

'Oh my good trousers, we all already knew that.'

'I knew that,' Hex tells her, 'and I've only known you about a week.'

'What?'

'You're not exactly subtle, Snow,' continues Jack, unabashed. 'We all know. Including Buttercup, so I really wouldn't worry yourself about telling her. She doesn't want to be queen, either.'

'Is your brain still scrambled, Trott? Nobody's talking about *Buttercup* being queen.'

'But you want to marry her, right?'

Snow's face takes on the expression of somebody who has realised something incredibly urgent and important, when they're currently in no position whatsoever to do anything about it – like somebody who's travelled a hundred miles from home and only then remembered that they left the oven on.

'Yes,' she says, shocked.

Jack shrugs. 'I'm assuming the wife of a queen regent would also be queen. I dunno that much about royal hierarchy – maybe she'd be a princess or a duchess or something? Anyway, what I do know is that it wouldn't be Buttercup's thing. She likes a cosy fire and a cottage to potter in; she'd feel lost in a fancy castle, and no offence, but she'd probably turn a *lot* of crown jewels into pastries.'

'Right,' breathes Snow. 'Well. Yes. New Girl, how are you doing with that whole "navigate by the sun" idea? Time's wasting.'

Jack winks at Gretel and grins. 'Knew that'd motivate her. Being in love's given me a whole new perspective on the world.'

'Ugh!' Snow groans. 'You two have only been snogging for two days, smug-face. Wind your neck in.'

'We weren't snogging.'

Hex raises a wing. 'Who *would* be queen? Or king? Um... not that I'm dropping hints or anything; I know I'm ineligible, I'm foreign.'

'You'd make a good prince consort though.' Jack smiles, running the back of his hand down Hex's arm.

'Jack, pack it in,' says Snow.

Gretel doesn't look up from the astrolabe. 'Have you started talking marriage already, Jack? You've only started courting. It'll come across as too much.'

'*Thank* you,' Hex tells her, exasperated.

'And Jack's not going to be king either,' Snow tells them. 'Nobody's going to be king.'

'Oh,' reply both Jack and Hex, sounding unsure.

'We're going to come up with a whole new thing. And by "we", obviously I mean "mostly New Girl", but we need to get out of here first.'

Gretel puts her astrolabe away, and points towards a set of barren, windswept hills. 'Assuming the Glass Witch hasn't managed to move the actual sun, the eastern edge of Darkwood should be a little ways past those hills.'

They set off, but Snow frowns as they trudge. 'I don't like those hills.'

'No, they look pretty bleak. But then, this is the badlands, right?' Gretel smiles cheerily. 'Everything here looks bleak.'

'Are those... people, there?' Jack points at a couple of dark shapes set against the desolate hills. 'Looks like two people, watching us.'

'Hmm.' Jack's right. It does look like it could be two people. Gretel takes a telescopic lens from her bag and gives the shapes a better look. She sighs with relief. 'It's just a couple of dead shrubs. I'm not sure there's anybody else out here.'

'OK,' says Hex shakily, 'so then, who just grabbed me?'

Gretel turns, and stifles a scream. Hex looks grey with fear. There are two bony hands on his shoulders, and two strange women attached to those hands, emaciated, filthy faces scabbed with multiple scratch marks. Each has dirty rags around their right foot, and struggles to hold any weight on that leg. They gaze out at nothing.

There are shards of glass where their eyes should be.

Miles and miles away, in a different country, the other side of the forest, the Mirror sits alone in the kitchen of Mudd Farm.

'Hansel?' it says, in an odd voice – not its usual voice. This is not the voice of the former king. This voice is light and melodic. The voice of a great beauty, light and glimmering. Hansel is not there to hear it – not yet, in any case.

He'll come home, in time. He'll come to the Mirror. He'll hear the enchanting voice, calling, calling his name.

15
Nuts in Slippers

Rumpel does a surprisingly good job of fixing Gilde's shoe. Considering how it had been filled with holes and then turned into biscuit, Buttercup isn't entirely sure how Rumpel ends up handing Gilde a leather shoe that perfectly matches the original, unless he has a second magical power besides the whole nocturnal straw-based alchemy thing.

Rumpel shakes his head, with a light shrug. 'Not *my* magic,' he tells them. 'It's the shop's. Elf magic sort of... seeps, sometimes. Gets into the bricks.' He pats the wall fondly, and the room reverberates with a series of knocks.

'They're here,' Salad tells them, tucking her now bob-length hair behind her ears.

Buttercup looks up hopefully.

'Not the Pipers, before you ask. They're a lost cause. But we do have a little group.' Salad opens the door ajar.

Buttercup cranes her head to see out. Beyond, the alley outside has disappeared and been replaced with the bank of a murky urban river. A swan waddles into the shop, with a hurried, agitated gait. That in itself is odd, but it's made all the stranger by the fact there is a tiny little woman, no more than two inches in height, riding the bird.

'A Thumbling!' Trevor cries, delighted. 'What are you doing out of the Darkwood?'

The Thumbling glares at them as the swan helps her dismount. 'Oh, it's the Insurgents. What are *you* doing out of the Darkwood?'

'Let's hear them out, Bellina,' Rumpel tells her, setting a tin bath down with a clatter. 'Sorry about Bellina, she's a bit...'

'Feisty,' says Trevor appreciatively. He sails down to Bellina on a length of web. 'Fancy a lift up to the top of the table, miss?'

Rumpel tips a barrel of rather stale-smelling water into the tin bath. 'There you go, Odette.'

Buttercup has never seen a swan look actively grateful before, but the one apparently named Odette manages to convey the emotion as it flaps over to the stagnant bath.

Gilde sniffs. 'That pond water?'

'Lake water from her home,' Salad tells her. 'And yes, it was extremely difficult to get hold of.'

Rumpel passes the swan a faded sheet. It takes it by a corner in its beak, gets into the bathtub and transforms into a rather lovely-looking woman of around thirty.

'But,' continues Salad, 'you do what you have to, when it's the only way one of your group can take human form.'

'Even if it means importing it all the way from Ashtrie?' asks Gilde.

'How'd you know I was from Ashtrie?' asks Odette in a distinctive Ashtrian accent, modestly arranging the sheet around her newly human body.

'We've seen the Glass Witch's handiwork before,' Patience tells her. 'Poor fellow with a raven's wing. She must really love turning people into birds.'

'Argh!' screams Odette. 'A Ghost!'

The next visitor doesn't knock at the door, but manifests suddenly in the shop soon after Salad places a slipper on the mantel. Despite appearing from nowhere, this latest new visitor is also definitely no Ghost. He's far too corporeal and colourful for that. He's a large, elderly man, with a cheerful face half hidden by a huge white beard, and a large overcoat the colour of holly. Everything about him exudes warmth. He is, if it's at all possible, the opposite of a Ghost.

'Jolly day,' he booms in a thick accent that Buttercup doesn't recognise. 'Many new friends!'

'How do?' asks Trevor, helping Bellina onto the tabletop. 'My name's—'

'Trevor is Spider,' interrupts the old man cheerily. 'And is Gilde Locke, Buttercup Brick, Patience Fieldmouse. Merry nice!'

'Oooh,' coos Trevor, impressed. 'A name-knowing witch.'

'Names are on posters,' explains the old man. 'But yes, am witch! Very special!'

'Ever woken up on Midwinter Feast Day to find nuts and spiced fruit in your slipper?' asks Salad.

'Yes,' Buttercup admits. She has done, every year.

'Are welcome!' thunders the old man happily.

'That's you?' Patience asks. 'I always thought that was my parents.'

'I thought it were my bears,' adds Gilde.

'And I thought it was Jack,' says Buttercup. 'I mean, he always took the credit for it and everything…'

'Was me,' cheers the old man. 'Was Old Nikolas! Am Midwinter Witch! Very special! Merry nice!'

'Your magic power is giving people nuts,' says Gilde, with an arch of her eyebrow.

'Yes!'

'On one solit'ry day a year.'

'Yes! Darkest day. Coldest day. Old Nikolas bring cheer. Merry jolly!'

'But why nuts? Why slippers?'

Nikolas shrugs happily. 'Whyfore bears? Whyfore cake? All are very special! Jolly merry!'

Buttercup notices that the Citadel witches are all still watching the door, waiting for someone.

'Aladdin's late,' mutters Rumpel. 'Anyone heard from him lately?'

The others shake their heads.

'You don't think...' mutters Bellina.

'Could they have found him out?' Odette asks.

'He's one of the hardest of us to spot,' adds Rumpel anxiously. 'If the huntsmen could discover *his* secret, then what's to stop them finding out about me? Or Bellina, or Salad, with your hair...'

'Is this another witch?' Buttercup asks.

'He's just a lad,' Rumpel tells her, worried. 'But he's got this Jinn.'

'A *Jinn*?' Gilde gawps. 'In Myrsina?'

'His dad's a merchant; he found it in a crate full of imported oil lamps.'

'So now he just keeps a Jinn handy in a crate?'

'In one of the lamps.'

'Oh, well, that's *much* safer. Yeesh.'

'The huntsmen were having a big drive on learning to spot magical containment vessels before I died,' Patience tells them, 'including ones from overseas.' She pauses. 'How good was this Aladdin at hiding the lamp?'

'He's a young lad with a whole Jinn to hand,' Bellina tells the Ghost. 'What do you think?'

'Right.' Patience frowns. 'OK, so I don't want to seem too mercenary, but maybe we should go ahead and start without him?'

'You don't honestly think they got him?' asks Odette. 'He's got a Jinn for protection.' She shakes her head, horrified. 'All *I* can do to defend myself is break a man's arm.'

They all watch the door again for a moment.

'Maybe—' says Rumpel.

'Don't say "maybe he just moved",' interrupts Bellina. 'You *always* say "maybe they just moved" whenever someone goes missing.'

'Well, maybe he did!'

Salad sighs, plaiting her now shoulder-length hair as she sits next to Buttercup. 'As you can see, any help you might be able to offer us here would be appreciated.'

'Didn't you have weapons, at the battle for Nearby?' Odette asks.

'Well...' says Patience.

'That's what I heard,' says Bellina. 'And you used magic to break the huntsmen's machines. You made half the village disappear!'

'That was mostly Gretel,' admits Trevor, 'and she's... she's gone on a different mission. But I'm sure she'll be back, and when she is—'

'We don't have time for "other missions",' Bellina interrupts. 'People are going missing! Right now!'

'Didn't you use the Mudd Witch, at Nearby?' Rumpel asks. 'Is he coming back to save us?'

'That lil piggy farmer stayed home,' sighs Gilde. 'Listen, you people got the wrong end o' the lollipop on what we're fixin' ter do here...'

'And what *are* you "fixin' to do", then?' snaps the little Thumbling. 'Do you mean to actually help us out here? At all?'

'This is an undercover mission,' Trevor tells them. The Citadel witches don't look particularly happy about this, with the exception of Old Nikolas, who just seems to look constantly happy by default.

'But there are things we can do,' Patience adds hurriedly. 'Um... we don't have an inventor with us right now, but we can certainly look at the shoe shop's defence systems...'

'I'm not sure what more we can do to defend it,' says Salad. 'It's a magic moving shoemaker shop.'

'With a password,' adds Rumpel.

'Well... I mean, I used to be a huntsman, so maybe I could go back with all of you and show you what sort of things the patrols will be looking out for?' suggests Patience.

'And I'm a super spy, so maybe I can work out some brilliant uncrackable code for us all,' says Trevor.

The Citadel witches all still look unconvinced.

'So, we're still all just to stay in hiding,' says Salad, disappointed.

'Fer now,' concedes Gilde. 'But here's the thing – I betcha all know a few people who you reckon'll be sympathetic to witches and magical types. People who maybe have a touch of magic in their family? All us witches know the power of a whispered word…'

'Whispers!' Bellina spits. 'Is that all you've got, Darkwooders? Some "insurgents". Some "revolutionaries"…'

'Yes,' says Buttercup suddenly, surprising even herself. 'Yes, it's a revolution. And it's already started.'

'That's why we're on the wanted posters in the first place,' adds Trevor, enthusiastically. 'Even though *that* – he points a leg at his poster – 'is clearly a common garden spider, while I am a giant house spider; I mean there's just no excuse for that sort of ignorance.'

'You really think words and whispers can change things here?' Rumpel asks.

'They have done, elsewhere,' Patience tells them. 'I had my mind changed. Gilde, too.'

'…got the abdomen *all* wrong,' grumbles Trevor. 'That's speciesism, that is…'

'Words and whispers got the huntsmen into power in the first place,' continues Patience.

'And violence,' adds Salad. 'Really a lot of ongoing murder, torture and general violence.'

'Well, yes,' admits Patience. 'But behind all of that, they're still just an idea. That's all any of us are, at the end of it all.' She frowns. 'We can be better ideas. We can leave a better legacy.'

'You saw the huntsmen's statue to you, didn't you?' asks Bellina.

'Yes,' sighs Patience.

'I don't want to get killed in a revolution because a Ghost doesn't like her statue,' says Odette.

'We didn't come here fer a statue!' Gilde huffs. 'I ain't even seen this whatchermercallit yer yammering about. And ain't nobody gonna get killed, neither. Hopefully. S'one of them bloodless revolutions. Mostly.'

'"Mostly"?' echoes Rumpel, troubled.

'Guys!' Buttercup cries, already feeling like she's losing the room. 'Yes, they might attack us if we stand up to them. That's true. But we know that they attack us when we don't. So we may as well try, right?' She pauses, gathering her thoughts. 'What if… we don't just hide? What if we start to show ourselves?' She gauges the expressions of the others. 'Carefully, of course.'

'But the others said…' starts Trevor.

'The others aren't here. We are. We have a better understanding of the situation.' Buttercup's voice trembles slightly, aware that she's undermining Snow a little, even a teensy bit excited at the fact. 'What if we started doing small bits of magic, for good? Performing quiet deeds that show up the huntsmen's lies? Look at all of us! We've got a magic travelling shoe shop, we've got all kinds of back-up if things go wrong… we should try to do something bold. Revolutionary.'

The Citadel witches look at one another. It's Old Nikolas who steps forward first, and takes one of Buttercup's hands in his huge, warm grasp. 'Nuts in slippers – is idea. Idea of kindness on darkest day. You get nuts, you think is from family, you give gift in return. Warmth, in the cold. A merry hearth. Yes? Merry nice?'

'Merry nice.' Buttercup nods in understanding.

'We put nuts in slippers, up *here*,' continues Nikolas, tapping the side of his head. 'Lights in darkest day. Yes?' He turns to the other Citadel witches. 'Merry jolly?'

Salad sighs. 'Merry jolly,' she agrees, adding her hand to Nikolas's.

'Merry jolly,' adds Rumpel.

'Will there be cool machines eventually, though?' asks Bellina. 'Once an inventor joins us?'

'If we really need them,' Patience tells her.

'Also, I got bears and a Werewolf,' adds Gilde.

'Then, OK.' Bellina rests a hand on Nikolas's huge coat. 'Merry jolly.'

'Merry... hang on...' The bathtub sploshes as Odette struggles to get herself out while remaining modestly draped in the sheet. As soon as she stands up, feathers begin to sprout and her neck begins to elongate. 'Merry... oh, bo...' The rest of what she was trying to say turns into a silent breath of frustration from an elegant, if annoyed, beak.

16
Ugly

'Unhand him, whatever you are.' Snow has an axe drawn and pointed in the direction of the two wraith-like women gripping Hex's shoulders before Gretel can get a word out.

This isn't ideal, especially since most of the words Gretel wants to say at that moment are along the lines of 'let's not threaten these strangers and escalate an already dangerous situation', 'I don't think they can see your very impressive axe anyway, Snow' and 'Snow, they are already literally holding Hex as a human shield, what good is waving an axe at them even going to do?'

Still, the axe is out now, so Gretel will just have to deal with that.

'Is it one of her men?' asks one of the eyeless women.

'Or one of her birds?' asks the other.

'Neither,' says Jack, stepping slowly towards them. 'Ladies, please. I assume you're here from the Glass Witch?'

'He's one of hers,' coos the woman with her hand on Hex's winged shoulder. 'Come to punish us again.'

'He's with us,' Jack tells them, in his most charming, confident tone, the kind that suggests at any second he'll grab something precious and make a dash with it. 'And he's not here to punish anyone, none of us are, we just got a bit lost…'

'Oh, we're all of us lost,' says the other woman. 'She saw to that.'

'She sends her birds,' says the woman holding Hex's wing. 'They peck.' With her free hand, she points to the scratches on her face. 'Cuckoo. Cuckoo. There's blood…' She giggles a little, darkly. 'You'll see. You'll see what she needs you to see.'

'If she's got you lost out here, then she will have her reasons,' says the other woman. 'You must have been too ugly for her to abide.'

Still frozen to the spot as the women paw at him, Hex looks as if he wants the ground to swallow him up.

'Don't call him that,' says Jack, a tone of genuine protectiveness undermining his practised conman patter.

'All of you must have been too ugly,' continues the woman, unabashed. 'You'll see.'

Gretel can't take her eyes off the two women, off the glass in their eyes. It's as if they're reflecting something onto Gretel – something terrible. Her village, the farmhouse, sinking under the mud. The debris of death, washing past her like a tide, and she's unable to do anything to stop it, she's so small, so worthless. She's the wrong twin.

'Leave us be,' begins Snow, but her resolve seems to waver. 'Take your hands off Hex. We're getting out of here, and then…'

'And then what?' The women limp closer to Snow, still holding Hex. As they approach, Snow allows her axe to drop by her side.

'Are you going to do something terrible?' asks one of the women.

'We did something terrible,' says the other. 'It's why we're being punished.'

'Poor little Ella,' breathes one woman, tears gathering around the bottom of the glass shards.

'Our poor sister,' sighs the other. 'Torturing her so, driven mad, we were, mad with envy; we never understood our own ugliness, never found peace with it. But now we understand. Her punishment is just, and fair.'

These are the Glass Witch's sisters, realises Gretel. If she did this to her own sisters, what hope is there for the rest of them?

She is nothing. She can't get rid of the sensation of smallness, of worthlessness. It's worse now than it was in the dream, or in the Glass Palace. It squeezes at her heart and makes her whole body want to shrink.

'*My* sister never hurt anyone,' blurts Hex. 'Queen Ella punished her anyway.'

'Perhaps her crimes were in the future,' says one of the eyeless sisters.

'Little Ella sees all,' adds the other. 'She had beautiful reasons for making you such an ugly thing.'

Hex ducks his head down miserably.

'Hey,' attempts Jack, but he stumbles backwards when they turn their gaze onto him. 'Your eyes… there are Giants in your eyes…'

The sisters turn their attention back to Snow.

'She had good reasons for bringing you here to be punished,' says one.

'Who are you going to hurt?' asks another. 'Who are you going to get killed? Better to just stay here, and accept a new fate.'

Snow stares at them, her axe still hanging by her side. 'I can't stay. I need to get back to her,' she says quietly. 'I'm going to win this, and make the world safe for her. And I'm going to ask her to marry me.'

'Ask away,' replies one sister.

'But you know,' says the other, 'you're no good for her.'

Snow drops her axe with a clatter.

'The way you treat her,' continues the sister. 'Keeping her away, having her cook and clean and fret…'

'Locking her in the kitchen, with your words,' says the other.

'To keep her safe!'

The sisters shake their heads. 'Ugly,' they chorus.

'But I have to…' mutters Snow.

'Stay,' chorus the sisters. 'Forever.'

Gretel should say something, should do something, but she's too small and useless. The wrong twin. She shouldn't even be here.

She wants to curl up here in the wilderness and keep on curling into herself until she's as small as she feels.

It's hopeless. They're no better than Ella's sisters – they're all horrible, hideous little things that have angered the great Glass Witch so. They'll be stuck out here forever, finally seeing their own ugliness, their own worthlessness, and yes, it's no better than they deserve. She slumps to the ground, feeling the mud sucking at her, the way she did in the dream, only maybe it wasn't a dream after all, maybe she was finally seeing things clearly. There's no fighting it. There's no reason to fight at all. Witches and humans cannot live together. Snow has known it all along, so have the huntsmen. All of this, this whole endeavour that she foolishly started by stupidly going into the Darkwood in the first place, it was all a terrible mistake. She's the wrong twin, she always has been, and the only way to rectify the issue is for her to be punished out here in the badlands, where she belongs, and for Hansel to…

She remembers the vision of Hansel from the dream, no longer a boy at all, everything about her brother consumed by a tower of crackling energy and thrashing shadow that churns the earth and strangles the sun. Perhaps that's his true form – a mighty fountain of pure power, his mortal body no more important than hers. Perhaps he is a weapon, to be owned and wielded by somebody with a magnificence that Gretel cannot fathom.

The thought fills her with a heavy, liquid sadness that sinks her even further into the mud. She tries to cry out to Hansel, to reach across to him with her mind, and is aware of something else – some*body* else – in the thought with her. An interloper, unseen. The prickle on the back of the neck when one is being watched.

Hansel? Gretel calls with her mind, helplessly.

Hansel? Another mind mirrors, in light, mocking tones. *Haaaaanselll?*

Miles away, Hansel is already running towards the farmhouse even as Daisy and Scarlett dash out to find him.

'Hansel!' calls Daisy.

'Something's up,' pants Hansel, 'I know. I just felt it.'

'I was watching the Citadel,' explains a particularly hairy Scarlett, 'and then the Mirror just went to static and started shouting for you.'

Hansel tries to get his breath as he skids into the kitchen. It's something to do with Gretel – his mind is suddenly full of her fear and sadness. His heart is hammering and he's positive it's not just from the running.

'Hansel!' calls the Mirror. It doesn't sound in the least bit perturbed, which is something, at least.

'What's wrong?' Hansel gasps.

'Nothing,' the Mirror tells him, in excited tones. 'I just had a breakthrough on Ashtrie. Look!'

The static fades to show a strange, silver forest. Stunning crystal spires sparkle above the treetops.

'It must be because Snow's there,' continues the Mirror. 'Our link must have finally allowed me to see the kingdom of Ashtrie. Isn't it beautiful?'

The image in the mirror changes. Now it's a grand hall made of exquisitely cut glass. Through it moves quite the loveliest woman that Hansel has ever seen. He has no words to describe her other than 'lovely'. Her hair is… lovely. Her eyes are… lovely. Her dress is the colour of the sky. That's all he can tell.

'That's the Glass Witch?' asks Daisy, breathless. 'Oh, she's…'

'She's lovely.' Scarlett cringes like a dog being admonished.

Hansel can't take his eyes off her. He still feels Gretel calling out to him in his mind, but there are two voices now, somehow – his sister and a strange, tinkling, melodious echo. As he watches the woman in the Mirror, the lovely echo grows louder, swallowing up Gretel's voice until he can't hear his sister at all, only this delightful, enchanting voice calling his name over and over, beckoning him.

'We should leave,' murmurs Daisy quietly. 'I shouldn't be looking at her. I'm just a stupid little yokel brat.'

'I'm a beast,' whines Scarlett. 'Nobody wants me. I should run into the middle of the forest and eat stones...'

A part of Hansel knows that this is wrong. A part of him still wants to reach out to Gretel and ask her what's the matter. A part of him knows that Daisy and Scarlett shouldn't talk about themselves that way. A part of him wants to hug them and smile, and remind them that they're loved. But that part is trapped and tiny somehow. It can't make his body actually do anything. Too much of him is entranced by the woman in the Mirror, with her dress made of sky. As if reacting to a natural pull, he reaches out and touches the crackling, cold surface of the Mirror. In the image, the Glass Witch raises her own hand up against his, moving like a reflection.

He looks into her eyes. She looks into his. He smiles. She smiles. Perhaps she *is* his reflection. Perhaps there's a deep magical connection between them. Perhaps they are one and the s...

Her long, lovely fingers push through the glass and interlace with his.

'Wait,' says the Mirror in a curiously distant voice, 'this shouldn't...'

Hansel can't look away from those lovely eyes, every colour and no colour, dancing with light.

'A perfect fit,' she says in her perfect voice, musical like wedding bells.

She grasps his hand tight, and pulls, and he is surrounded by nothing but eternal cold, bright beauty.

17

Diamonds and Dogs

'Hansel!' The sensations of despair and self-loathing that consumed Daisy only moments ago quickly disperse at the sight of Hansel being pulled into the Mirror. It's like waking out of a nightmare, only to realise that the house is on fire.

She lunges towards the Mirror, as he helplessly disappears into its smooth surface. For a moment she can see him on the other side, the Glass Witch curling her long, tight fingers around his shoulders, and how has Daisy only just noticed how *old* the Glass Witch is? She tries to call to Hansel, to reach out into whatever magical void he was just pulled into, but her hand just hits the unyielding glass of the Mirror, which now shows only the normal reflection of the farmhouse's kitchen.

'Hansel,' she calls again, smacking the Mirror with her flattened palm, wildly looking around the reflection and the kitchen, in case all of this has somehow just been in her imagination.

'Oh no,' quavers the Mirror's voice. 'Oh no, no, no, I'm so sorry, how could I have let this happen?'

'He's just… gone.' Half wolf in her panic, Scarlett sniffs desperately for Hansel's scent. 'He's nowhere!'

'She took him,' wails the Mirror. 'She was controlling me, and I didn't even know!'

'How did she take him?' Daisy demands. 'Where?'

'Her palace,' says the Mirror. 'She controls glass, images, minds… Glass and image and mind is all I am! She's been using me for who knows how long. Watching all of you through me while blocking me from seeing her… her rage, her hatred, her avarice… this is all my fault.'

'What is she going to do with Hansel?' Daisy asks.

'She wants his power,' the Mirror tells her miserably. 'I don't know for certain how she intends to take it, but often with young men, she… well, she marries them.'

'Urgh, what? He's thirteen!'

'I know.'

'She's got to be older than his stepmum – that's *horrible*.'

'All of this is horrible,' moans the Mirror.

Daisy takes a deep breath, trying to stop herself from trembling. 'I'm going to get him back. As quickly as possible.' She addresses the Mirror. 'Can you send me to the Glass Witch's palace as well?'

'No,' the Mirror tells her, 'it was her magic that let her drag him through, not mine, and she's closed it now.'

'Then I need to find the fastest way to travel to Ashtrie.' Daisy ponders her options. She doesn't have many, right now. 'Scarlett,' she says, 'how fast are you Werewolves?'

'Fast,' admits Scarlett. 'Much faster through woodland than a human.'

Daisy rolls up a sleeve. 'Then scratch me.'

'Um…'

'Or bite me, or whatever it takes to make me like you. I have to get to Hansel right now, and I'll need to be stronger than this if I'm going to fight that old witch.'

'That's not how it works.' Scarlett cringes. 'It's genetic; I can't turn you – that was just huntsman propaganda.'

'Oh.' Daisy's hopes are running out, fast. Turning into a Werewolf wasn't a great idea, but with all the other witches gone and all the new weaponry still in development and construction, it was the only one she had.

'But,' adds Scarlett, 'I can carry you.'

'What?'

'You're a slip of a lass; I can still run full pelt with you on my back,' Scarlett tells her. 'And I have a pack to call on. Please?' The Werewolf fidgets with her cape. 'I just want to be useful.'

Daisy hugs her. 'Thank you,' she whispers.

'Thank *you* in advance,' replies the huge woman, leaning into the hug. 'I'm afraid you're going to have to carry my britches and boots the whole way.'

And that's how Charles the Magnificent Unicorn, busy as he is, majestic as he is, finds himself hurriedly grabbed outside the farmhouse, and tasked with minding a very upset magic Mirror in the kitchen, while Daisy Wicker rides off towards the forest on the back of a great red Werewolf, with the wolves of the woods following, along with the village's dogs, growling and barking and yapping together.

'Poppet?' cries one village woman, chasing after the disappearing mega-pack. 'Where's she going? Poppet!'

'I think,' Charles tells her, through the kitchen window, 'your Poppet is going to war.'

'Oh,' frets the woman, clutching a tiny lead and collar. 'But she hasn't had her din-dins yet.'

Poppet, bred down from wolves over the millennia to be no bigger than a guinea pig, has never felt so alive. Poppet, who has spent her life being bullied by cats and hedgehogs, has *not* had her din-dins yet, and will likely dine on whatever fresh kill the wolves running with her manage to bring down. Poppet has heard the big alpha wolf's howl, and she will follow, part of a mighty storm of teeth and claws. Poppet is seven inches of freedom, fear and fury right now, and she feels *amazing*.

In the badlands of Ashtrie, deep in her chasm of despair, Gretel feels the fingers around Hansel. She feels the cold; she feels the terror.

'Hansel,' she breathes, rooted to the ground, too useless, too small to do anything to help him.

'Hansel,' she whispers, and *why* exactly can't she help him, this time? Because she isn't magical at all, another part of her brain reminds her, because she's just a silly little girl with a hammer and a wrench and a dull ache in her pitiful human belly.

'Hansel,' she says out loud, horrible memories of the last time her dear brother was taken prisoner swimming to the surface of her miserable mind. That cage the huntsmen put him in, when they took Nearby. Look what happened that time, Gretel. It's happening again.

Look what happened that time.

You came for him, that time. You and your friends from the Darkwood. You made half a village disappear. You and Daisy escaped a burning rack. You helped to set him free.

(You're just a silly little unmagical girl with a half-baked idea and a bag of doodads.)

But sometimes, that's enough.

(You're the wrong twin.)

Yes. But sometimes, the *wrong* twin is the *right* twin.

(That doesn't even make any sense.)

Shut up, brain. Shut up and get up. Hansel needs help.

She gets to her feet. 'Hansel,' she says again. 'She got Hansel.'

She looks around at the gathered group. All of them are slumped on the dry, lumpy ground. The two sisters sit propped against one another like rag dolls losing their stuffing. Jack and Hex lie together, fingertips touching but both isolated inside the unhappiness of their own heads. Only Snow manages a slight eye twitch in Gretel's direction. Gretel takes Snow's face in her hands, and stares straight into the reluctant princess's dark eyes.

'Snow. I get it. You were born a certain way and you didn't ask for it, or the powers that came with it. That's how Hansel always felt about his magic. You get to choose what to do with it. You don't want to be princess, or queen? Be the White Knight, be the warrior who swore a vow to protect all of the Darkwood...'

'And your village,' mutters Snow.

Gretel nods. 'And my village. Including Hansel.'

Snow's expression takes on a familiar, grumpy shade. 'After you tricked us.'

Gretel smiles. 'Yep. But you still swore a vow to be a protector.'

Snow sits up, her gauntlets worrying noisily. 'What if the sisters are right? About Buttercup? What if I've been going over the top trying to protect her, ended up making her miserable?'

'Then,' Gretel tells her, 'you get up, face down the Glass Witch, get back to Buttercup in one piece and apologise to her.'

'Oh,' sighs Snow. 'I was sort of hoping you'd just tell me that the sisters are completely wrong and everything I do is fine.'

'No, they've sort of got a point there, I'm afraid,' Gretel tells her.

'Ugh.' Snow gets up, and nudges Jack with her sabaton. 'Up you get, Trott, stop lounging about.'

'The Giants,' mutters Jack.

'Giants can't be helped right now, but Hansel Mudd can. He's in trouble, and *you* swore a vow to protect everybody from Nearby Village.'

'Can't,' groans Jack.

'Can,' snaps Snow, 'because I'm telling you to and you're scared of me.'

Jack blinks, and becomes more like the usual, cocky Jack. 'Am not.'

'Are.' Snow shakes Hex. 'Rise and shine, birdie, your boyfriend's coming with us to rescue a kid; I assume that means you want to come with, to be all loyal and possibly fit in some snogging.'

'We have *not* been snogging!'

'You have been, Jack,' Gretel tells him as Hex blearily tries to focus, 'we've all seen you. Nobody blames you. You've got a handsome new boyfriend, it must be exciting for you.'

'"Handsome"?' manages Hex.

'Gorgeous,' confirms Jack.

'Yes, Hex,' snaps Snow, 'you're very pretty, if one is into that sort of thing. Not ugly.' She points at Jack. 'And not a Giant killer.' She points at Gretel. 'And what was the thing that was making you go all sad, New Girl?'

'Um,' says Gretel, frowning at the slumped sisters, 'that I'm all tiny and useless because I can't do magic?'

Snow snorts. 'Tiny? Yes. Useless? Don't be ridiculous.'

Gretel smiles gratefully, and gives one of the sisters a little shake.

'What are you doing?' asks Hex.

'We shouldn't leave them out here.'

'What? But they're the ones who…'

'Oh come on, they're obviously under the Glass Witch's spell, too.'

'They'll slow us down,' Snow argues. 'They just almost made us give up all together.'

'And we were able to overcome it,' Gretel argues. 'They know the Glass Witch – they're her sisters. They could have useful information. And besides, your vow was to protect *all* the creatures of the Darkwood.'

Snow huffs. 'Technically, this isn't the Darkwood.'

Gretel already knows from Snow's expression that Gretel's won this argument. 'Still, though.' She shakes both of the sisters by the shoulders again. They turn their glassy stares to her. 'Hey,' she says softly. 'We're going to talk with Ella. We think you should come with us.'

'Poor little Ella?' gasps one. 'No!'

'We can't show our faces,' moans the other, 'not after what we did.'

'Did either of you actually ever apologise to her for what you did?' Gretel asks. 'To her face?'

The sisters look confused. 'No.'

'Do you think maybe that might be a nice first step?' Gretel adds.

'She already knows we're sorry,' mutters one of the sisters. 'You don't understand – she's so mighty, so powerful…'

'Er, I do understand what it's like to have a powerful witch in the family, thank you very much.'

'Yes,' says the other sister, her face creased with concentration. 'Yes, the Mudd Witch. Her new Prince Charming.'

Gretel gets to her feet. 'OK, I don't like the sound of that. This Glass Witch does know Hansel's just a kid, right?'

'It's... wrong,' says one of the sisters. She seems scandalised even to hear herself say it. She shakes her head violently as if trying to shake away the thought. 'No. No. *We're* wrong.'

'Doesn't mean she's right,' retorts Snow.

'Yeah,' adds Jack. 'Forced child marriage is a bit of a red line, isn't it? Which way is it you said we should go, Gretel?'

Gretel checks her astrolabe again quickly, and points out the right direction.

Jack nods. 'Hex, could you fly me? We might be able to see the Glass Palace from up high; I can clear you a path.'

'The Glass Witch said your powers won't work here any more,' Hex reminds him.

Jack tries to beckon to a bit of dry scrub. Nothing happens. 'Trousers.'

'What about...' Gretel can feel herself thinking clearer and clearer all the time. She notices something on the ground that has been there all along. The lumpy, dry ground of the badlands is strewn with glittering, transparent stones. She picks one up. It's the size of a crab apple.

Jack stares at it. Gretel can practically see money signs in his eyes. 'Are those diamonds?'

'The diamond desert,' says Hex, nodding. 'It's the worst place in the world.'

'Yes, but it's full of diamonds! These are your "badlands"? Look at that one, it's the size of a woman's fist!'

'We changed its name to the badlands, because treasure hunters kept dying out here,' Hex explains.

Jack shakes his head. 'Ashtrie is really weird, no offence.'

'Little more urgency, Jack?' asks Gretel. 'My brother's been witchnapped.'

'Yep!' Jack replies brightly.

'Help me collect a load, then – if you find the Glass Palace from the air, you can drop us a trail of them to show us the right way.'

Jack screws up a face, as if pained. 'You want me to throw the diamonds away?'

'Jack!'

'Fine! Yes, fine!'

They hurriedly scoop up as many diamonds as possible. After a few minutes, Jack has a whole knapsack full of them.

Gretel is surprised when the final handful of diamonds poured into Jack's bag comes from the two sisters.

'We'll come,' one sister tells her.

'We should apologise,' says the other.

'And like you say,' says the first, uncomfortably. 'Kidnapping young boys to marry... that's not right.' She awkwardly pats Gretel on the shoulder. 'You will be able to follow a trail of these stones even after sundown – they glow at night.'

'Oh, well, of course the massive diamonds just lying around in the badlands also glow in the dark,' says Jack, helping Hex out of his tunic. 'Ashtrie is *so* weird.'

'Is it me,' says Snow, as they watch Hex take off with Jack, 'or are things starting to seem clearer?'

'Little Ella isn't concentrating her magic on us so much, right now,' says one of the sisters.

'She has her hands full,' says the other, 'magically speaking.'

'Trying to hurt my brother, you mean,' mutters Gretel, setting off in her best approximation of the right direction.

'Not necessarily "hurting",' replies one sister. 'She may simply be... controlling his mind.'

'Right,' sighs Gretel. 'Great.'

18
What Happened in Ashtrie

Buttercup turns out to be the first one to use her magic in public. It ends up being such a little thing – a thin woman in faded clothes, dragging a hungry-looking child in one hand and holding a sign offering to do odd jobs in return for three silvers or a day's food in the other. Everybody else in the square is carefully ignoring the woman and her child, so Buttercup doesn't receive much attention when she picks up a decorative stone urn full of decorative stone fruit and turns it into a colossal vegetable pasty for them.

'It's OK,' she murmurs, watching their wary faces. 'It's safe to eat.' She plucks a pastry grape from the top, puts it in her mouth, chews, swallows and shows the woman her now empty mouth.

The woman takes it from her, her eyes still wary. 'You one of them?'

Buttercup nods, smiling. 'We're friendly. Enjoy dinner, on us.'

The child takes a moment away from smelling the heady scent of the piping hot pastry, to regard Buttercup curiously. '"Us"?'

'I know I might not look it at first glance,' Trevor tells them, emerging from Buttercup's hair and removing a tiny little fake beard, 'but I'm actually "one of them", too.'

The woman and child watch him, eyes wide.

'Plenty more food at Buttercup's Basement Bakery, under the Hogshead Inn,' Trevor announces. 'Tell a friend!'

The woman looks from the pasty to her child, to Buttercup and Trevor. 'Thank you,' she tells them, in a genuine tone. 'Think I will.'

Buttercup surprises herself by running all the way back. She doesn't know whether she's powered by anxiety at getting caught by huntsmen, or an energising giddy thrill. She magicked pastry! For normal humans! In public! In the Citadel! And they *thanked* her! And they said they'd spread the word to friends! Buttercup passes under one of the many posters of Morning Quarry. This particular one depicts Morning with her usual sunny, lopsided grin, both thumbs held aloft and the slogan 'We Can Kill Them All!' The fear briefly rises in Buttercup that those 'friends' of the woman she just fed could include huntsmen or assorted witch-haters who could come for them at the bakery, but she makes herself compartmentalise it away. She ducks out of the way of a well-heeled man, holding her hands away from the particularly fancy coat he's carrying from the laundrette, so as not to accidentally cakeify it. She doesn't stop to see that his alarm over her sudden movement causes him to yank the precious coat too far in the other direction, fumble it and drop it into a puddle.

'Not again,' he cries, but Buttercup is too far down the street to hear.

When she gets back to the bakery, she finds it empty with the exception of Odette, who has artfully draped herself – and the entire tin bath full of lake water keeping her human-shaped – in a large smock. It creates a very strange shape for her indeed, made all the stranger by the fact that poking below the smock is a wheeled chassis that's been riveted to the tub so Odette can move about while in human form. It had actually been Patience's idea, and Rumpel was able to quickly knock something up. Patience swore that it looked not dissimilar to the wheelie-chairs used by some humans and they could just pass Odette off as having bad legs. While technically that's true, the smock makes the whole thing look like Odette has gone to a fancy-dress party as a sailing boat.

The constant sloshing noise and stench of lake water from the hidden tub only serves to add to the nautical impression.

Still, it could be worse. The bakery could currently be staffed by a single mute swan.

'The others went out,' Odette tells them, wheeling over with a series of wet noises. 'Rumpel's collecting shoes to fix, Salad's gone to the infirmary, to see if any patients might have lost their hair to sickness or injury... Patience went looking for places the others can do good, but for now I think the rest are just spreading general cheer; Old Nikolas grabbed them, and you've seen what he's like in full swing. I offered to keep shop since I kind of stick out no matter which form I'm in.' She looks horribly sad for a moment before forcing a little smile. 'I sold five buns! How did you guys do?'

Trevor breathlessly tells her about the pasty incident.

'That sounds great!' Odette's smile freezes a little. 'And you're sure they won't just send an angry mob here? And that people's minds can actually be changed about witches, just generally, you know? After everything? Whole lot of refugees from Ashtrie in Myrsina, you know.'

'Aren't most of the Ashtrian refugees magic too, though?' Trevor asks.

'Oh yes,' Odette tells them. 'Queen Ella treated other witches the worst.' She indicates to the bathtub. 'All of this was because my boyfriend Siegfried had powers. She promised to reverse the spell if he married her instead of me.'

'I take it he refused?' interjects Trevor.

'Oh no, he gave himself up to her. That's the last I heard of him. Fifteen years ago, now. He was only eighteen. I think she must have killed him, or turned him into something. He wasn't the last witch boy she took.'

Buttercup nods sympathetically, and tries not to worry too much about young Jack and Hex, heading straight into this horrible queen's lair.

'It was too much power,' sighs Odette. 'There was a time, she controlled *everything*. It's hard to describe the human toll it took to overthrow her. I'd say about a tenth of the population. And the western half of Ashtrie is still hers. The forest and the diamond desert...'

'You have a diamond desert?'

'Yeah, it's much worse than it sounds. She gets people lost out there for years. Decades. Turns them around, turns them against each other, makes them see things, makes them feel things...'

'Makes them feel things?' asks Trevor brightly. 'So, in theory, she could make people, say, feel like witches are fine again?'

Odette stares at Trevor. 'You know, I was wondering whether you might be like me – a human who's been turned into a creature, but you're not, are you?'

'Nope,' replies Trevor proudly. 'I'm just a common household hyper-intelligent talking spider.'

Odette nods. 'Figures.'

'How could you tell?'

'Because nobody who's been transformed would ever suggest the Glass Witch's powers could be used for our cause.' She makes herself look as dignified as she possibly can, in her wheeled tub of stagnant lake water. 'Nobody in a position such as mine would ever say something quite so stupid.'

Stupid.

How could he have been so stupid? Of course the Glass Witch was using the Mirror to her own end. He should have seen the trouble coming. He should have seen the complete absence of any sort of warning visions as a sign that something was wrong, that his magical foresight for danger was being blocked, somehow.

And now, he's... where? He doesn't know, he doesn't dare open his eyes to look, but he knows it's bad. He knows he's trapped. Another cell, another cage like in Nearby when he nearly lost it. He takes deep breaths, and brings the thrashing magical anxiety under control. He opens his eyes, and looks at this new cell he's been thrown into.

It is the most beautiful palace he has ever seen, even in dreams. A poor farm boy like him could never even imagine such absolute majesty. The exquisite décor is at once every colour on the spectrum and no colour at all. Is this why he had no warning – that even his magical sense for danger could never conjure up something as wonderful as Queen Ella's palace?

Enchanting music swells from somewhere – Hansel can't tell where; maybe it's playing directly into his mind. A woman steps towards him, forming herself out of shards of light. She is utterly, utterly lovely. She shines like a low winter sun, cold and dazzling to the point that she's painful to look at.

'Hello, dear,' she says, her voice melodious, harmonised by music already playing from who-knows-where. 'I'm sure you know all about me already.'

Hansel tries to concentrate, tries to see the woman behind the blindingly bright glamour. 'Ella Hardup,' he manages.

'Oh nobody's known me by *that* name for many years, my Prince,' she twinkles, and the beauty of her hurts his eyes with a pain that burns all the way into his brain. 'Try again.'

'Queen Ella,' he gasps. 'The Glass Witch.'

Ella nods gracefully. 'And a queen needs her palace...' She gestures around at the lovely hall. 'And her servants...' She indicates to a number of odd creatures milling about the place. Hansel hadn't noticed them before Ella pointed them out. Most of them are frogs, lizards and mice, but they look at him with eyes that... they remind him of Hex, in full raven form. Animals, but not quite.

Ella takes his hands, with a smile. 'And a queen needs her Prince Charming, of course.'

Wait, does she mean him?

'Me?' he asks.

'So modest,' sighs Ella

'But I'm…' he falters.

Not good enough, his thoughts add, automatically. *Magically unfocused and chaotic; a failure; a grubby simpleton; a barely literate farm boy…*

'I'm… already sort of seeing someone,' he tells her out loud.

Ella raises an eyebrow. 'Well, that's easily fixed…'

'And,' he adds, 'I'm thirteen.' He tells himself hurriedly that it's an easy mistake for her to make. He is big for his age. He wishes, not for the first time, that he wasn't. Being a hulking farmhand at thirteen is handy for lugging tills and wrestling uncooperative livestock, but it can make a boy self-conscious and clumsy, whether talking to a pretty basket weaver, or trying to blend in in the Citadel, or being aggressively proposed to by a terrifying, beautiful witch queen. 'It'd be inappropriate, ma'am. Also illegal.'

Ella cocks her head at him, her smile a little more brittle than before. 'Oh, I hope you don't turn out to be another false prince, another heartbreaker. My last husbands were heartbreakers, so cold. I had to show them how cold they were being.' She indicates to a half dozen or so frogs, sitting miserably in her shadow. 'Oh, do tell me you won't be so cold,' she sighs.

Hansel gazes at the frogs, aghast.

'They were weak, cold boys,' adds Ella, noting his horrified expression with a touch of satisfaction. 'But you're strong. You have so much to offer. I can feel the magic radiating off you. Why, it's as if you have the whole of the earth channelled through you.'

Hansel feels the magic try to spill out again, try to spread into the sky and burrow into the ground.

'Imagine if we were to join forces,' continues Ella. 'Our powers, combined. We'd be unmatchable. Unstoppable.'

Hansel sees it – he sees the two of them overwhelming the whole huntsman army, burying them all.

'You just need someone more experienced to have your back, help you focus. Someone who understands a power as mighty as yours.' Ella graces him with a lovely smile. It burrows painfully beyond his eyes. 'Because without focus, dear boy… well.' Her smile disappears.

Mud, everywhere. Rising like a thick, filthy tide, swallowing buildings, swallowing towns, swallowing everything. His own village, his own home, drowned to the rooftops in it. Bodies. Humans, magical beings, animals, all gone, all just meat now, bobbing through the sludge. His friends. His family. Daisy. Gretel.

No.

And him, what's left of him. Just magic. Just a plume of thrumming, crackling power, churning the ground, eating the sunlight. Destroying everything. Everything.

'Why are you showing me this?' he manages.

'It's just what's already within you,' Ella tells him gently. 'I know you've felt it, when you've lost control before. The sensation that you could lose everything to it, even yourself.'

It's true. That time during the liberation of Nearby, when he became so scared that he passed out, and the magic took over. He was lucky that time that the magic burnt itself out quickly without doing too much damage.

Ella takes his hands in hers. They're so small, and so cold. Like a porcelain doll's.

'It's all right. I understand what it's like to be as powerful as you. To spend your childhood having to hide it away as you toil away in squalor and poverty.'

Hansel looks into her eyes, and deep inside of him, his magic does want to reach out to her, even while the rest of him wants to run and hide. The part of his mind that sends him magical warning visions is going haywire. It wants to pull at the Glass Witch's vision of death and destruction, to tug and tug at the illusion Ella has planted in Hansel's head, to follow the threads of it and see what's on the other end.

Her face lights up at the sense of magical connection.

'Yes,' she breathes. 'Together, we can rule everything, everyone. We deserve to be magnificent.'

He pulls at the threads of the vision. She realises, a moment too late, what it is he's trying to do. Her breathtaking beauty changes suddenly, and becomes something so twisted up with fury that it's practically unrecognisable.

But Hansel has already seen what's at the other end of Ella's magic. A different vision. Not a monster, not a magnificent, glittering queen, not a blinding flash of cold sunlight. A sad, scared little girl, hurting and hungry and abused, filthy from toiling amongst the ashes of the kitchen fire. Years and years of this misery. Cruelty. Insults. Impossible tasks meted out in the knowledge they were impossible, just for the vicious pleasure of watching her try, and fail. Changing rules without telling her, so that they could punish her. Lies upon lies upon lies until she thought she was losing her mind. Treating her as if she wasn't a person, until she decided that maybe she shouldn't even be a person any more. Turning herself into a mouse, a lizard, a frog just so that she could escape for a while, but finding that her magic would always reset at midnight, and she'd always be caught. Whispering to the plants in the vegetable patch for company and feeling them whisper back. Changing them into pretty things, just for a while at first, just so that she could have something pretty in her life. Finding herself doing it more and more. Casting glamours over her ragged dress to make it sparkle when she spun, when nobody was looking. Yearning desperately for a bit of beauty in a life made ugly out of spite.

Never yearning for love – never daring to do that. Her father had told her that he loved her, and he'd disappointed her. Her stepmother and sisters told her that they loved her, and they were so cruel. Love was not something little Ella wanted any more of, thank you. It just hurt.

Hansel sees an invitation to a party shredded, in the knowledge that all Ella wanted was to go to a fine party in a nice dress like one of the beautiful people, just one time. The final straw. He sees how Ella snuck out as a newt, turned a pumpkin into a coach, turned mice into horses and frogs into footmen, and cast glamour upon glamour on herself, layering the magic until one could barely see Ella under it all. Of course, the prince was enchanted. It was an enchantment, that's what it was supposed to do, but Ella overstretched herself. She allowed herself to have fun that night. She allowed herself to simply enjoy dancing in a beautiful ballroom, and being a beautiful thing. She almost missed midnight, when her magical glamours would reset.

Never again. She would never make that mistake again. She would shun simple joy and fun for the rest of her life.

Hansel sees how, after that night, Ella understood the power of her pent-up magic, and found a window of opportunity. Planted a magical vision of a glass shoe – the one element of her various glamours that the prince had obsessed the most over that night – and ensured that it could never fit anybody else. The hope, the anxiety, as she waited for the search to finally come to her home. The sudden burst of emotion when the carriage drew up and the page rapped on the door. Not relief, not elation – rage.

Rage, that this is what she'd come to, a witch so gifted and clever that she could enchant a prince not once but twice. She knew, when the prince stepped through the door, that her years of penury and abuse at the hands of her sisters were at an end, and she was furious with them. Her revenge started straightaway as she waited in the kitchen watching them through a crack in the door. She filled their heads with a desperate need to be the one the shoe fit. Watching quietly, unseen, as they, in turn, snuck into the kitchen to grab a knife and hack at their own feet in a desperate attempt to fit their bodies to the shoe instead of the other way around. Watching breathlessly as each tried, wailing, to jam the injured foot into the shoe, in front of the horrified onlookers.

The shoe, of course, still didn't fit. Impossible tasks meted out knowing they were impossible, just for the vicious thrill of watching them try, and fail.

Stepping out demurely from the kitchen, amid the blood and horror. A poor girl dressed in scraps, in the middle of this madhouse, but oh so pretty, under more subtle glamours. The prince, enchanted again. The shoe, suddenly a perfect fit. She didn't mind the blood. In fact, she liked it.

And now, Hansel sees a princess. Still lonely. Still cold. Still hungry for... for something. It wasn't enough. All of this wasn't enough. She was still so empty. She needed more. More beauty. More power. More vengeance.

No love. No joy. Too dangerous.

Under all of that glamour, all of the layers, the bright beauty, Hansel sees her, at long last. Ella, still bruised. Still so sad.

He reaches out to the real Ella, still shrouded in dirty scraps after all these years.

'Ella?' he breathes. 'It's OK. You don't need any of that stuff. You can allow yourself to heal, put your past behind you...'

'Put it behind me?' The real Ella disappears again, under layer upon layer upon layer of glass, until she's little more than a smudge. '*Heal?*'

'I know it seems impossible, but...'

'How can one "heal" from perfection?' seethes the Glass Witch.

The part of Hansel that issues magical warnings is very suddenly ringing an extremely loud siren at him. Hansel dives from his spot and rolls away just in time to see the floor where he was standing explode into six-foot, ready-to-impale spikes of glass.

19

People in Glass Houses Shouldn't Throw Curses

New shards of glass follow Hansel as he tries to roll away, some of them missing his skin by fractions of an inch. Two of them erupt so close to his retreating body that they tear gashes in his clothes. He pulls himself to his feet, panting, as Ella approaches him, the dazzling beauty of her glamour fractured with rage.

'Ella,' he gasps in an approximation of a warning tone, 'you don't want to kill me.'

He hopes that that's true – after all, she was only just talking about teaming up.

Well. She was talking about marriage, but Hansel mentally sidesteps that for now and hopes that she means more of a magical union. Either way, it won't be possible if she kills him, or… are all those frogs really former paramours? Yeah, he's not going to be much use to her dead or amphibian. Still, though, he's just made a very powerful witch very angry, and should probably do something about that before she responds in a way that they both regret.

'I understand…' he attempts.

'No you don't!'

Hansel's sense of magical warning flares again. He doesn't even have to think about it this time. A wave of his magic crashes out of him as instinctively as he would snatch his hand away from a hot iron. It's a surprise for him, but not as surprising as the ease with which his own magic pushes back the transformation spell Ella is trying to use on him.

'Ella, stop!'

Glass shards erupt again from the floor and the walls. His magic pushes him away from it, snapping the spikes. Ella tries another transformation spell on him, but again his magic blocks it as an automatic reaction.

'But I can *make* you understand,' Ella tells him. A cage of glass clatters down over him. She hits him with the transformation spell again, much more powerful this time. His magic, its focus thrown by the cage of glass spikes, can't knock back the spell as instantly or easily as before, and it buries into him.

He's overpowered by the sensation. He realises now how it is that transformation spells work. They tell the mind of their target that they *should* be the shape the spell wants them to be, that they *deserve* to be a frog or a mouse or a bird. They do it so convincingly that the mind agrees, and changes the body to fit. He is filled with the belief that he should be a frog, that he needs to become small and cold and slimy on the outside to match how he feels on the inside. He can feel himself starting to change, when his magic comes roaring back, with a fresh intensity. Hansel's magic fills him and continues to swell, pushing outside of his body the way it sometimes does in moments of panic. It forces out the transformation spell and keeps on going, sucking away the light for a hit of power, lengthening the shadows and turning them solid, burrowing into the ground, pluming into the air, smashing the glass of the cage and still not stopping. Hansel hears more distant smashing, feels the columns and banisters of the crystal hall beyond breaking against the tendrils of his magic. He tries to pull it back in, but it doesn't work.

'Sorry,' he wheezes as glass smashes all around him and Ella grunts in surprise.

When his magic eventually calms down a bit and the sunlight comes back, he sees the Glass Palace anew – a hall of shards. Bits of wall and ceiling are still tumbling and smashing, but it sounds more pathetic than the ear-splitting crashes that were going on only a moment ago. Ella still stands in a protective dome of magic along with her frogs, looking around her surroundings with the horrified expression of someone who may only just have realised that glass might not be the most practical of materials to build a home out of, let alone have a fight in. She looks smaller, older, sadder than before. The fight must have drained her of her glamour. It's no way for anyone to live, thinks Hansel.

He mentally promises her that, should they somehow all prevail in overthrowing the huntsmen, he will come back to Ella's castle with some proper, grown-up witches who actually know what they're doing – Snow and Gilde and people like that – to help Ella. But right now, he can see that she isn't going to join in their fight against the huntsmen, and approaching her over it will only make things worse. He needs to get out of there and send word to Gretel's party to head back to Myrsina as soon as possible. They'll just have to avoid using the magic Mirror until all of this is fixed.

'Well,' he says, as nicely as he can amidst the shattered reminders of his magic's destructive power, 'I'll be off, then.'

'No,' replies Ella. It isn't a threat or a demand – it's a plea.

Hansel stalls for a moment, looking with pity into Ella's sad eyes, and doesn't see the ball of molten glass gathering above his head until it's too late.

Ella's expression doesn't change as the glass drops onto him, enveloping him with thick, oozing, burning heat. All of his magic automatically turns itself inwards to protect him from the impossibly high temperature suddenly plastered all over his skin, and as the glass swiftly cools and solidifies, the magical tendrils aren't able to claw into the air to draw power from the rapidly setting sun, nor to root him in the earth. All of his magic is trapped inside him, swirling, crackling, blotting out his thoughts, desperately keeping him alive, caught like an insect in amber.

'Got you,' mutters Ella, looking around at the ruins of her palace, but Hansel doesn't hear.

Night falls. Up in the air, a thief clings happily to his boyfriend's clothes and feathers and, not quite so happily, takes a glowing diamond the size of a peach out of a bag and lets it fall to the forest floor below.

'It physically pains me to let go of something this pretty and shiny; I hope you know that,' he tells the huge black bird on which he rides.

The raven cannot smile, but it gives the thief a fond sideways glance.

The thief leans in a little closer to the bird's sleek black head. 'Obviously, I'm not intending to let go of the prettiest, shiniest thing of all.'

The raven rolls its eyes.

The thief frowns, his eye caught by something ahead in the trees, picked out in the cold moonlight. 'What's that?'

Behind them, a line of glowing jewels glimmers in their wake, lighting up a pathway through the trees. A dark woman in bright armour follows it at a surprisingly fast pace, considering how she's supporting not one but two blind women with a hobbled foot apiece. She's followed by a very worried-looking teenage girl.

'Something's really wrong,' calls Gretel to Snow. 'Wronger than usual.' She overtakes Snow. 'Could we maybe pick up the pace a bit?'

Snow grunts. 'Good job I'm not wearing full armour and carrying two adult women, or that might be a bit of a difficult ask.'

Gretel goes from a fast walk to a run, scrabbling through the quiet, silver trees to follow the glowing line of stones as fast as she can. She's concentrating so hard on hurrying and following the path that she doesn't notice the noises up ahead until the shimmering track comes to an abrupt stop.

She scours the ground for another diamond, but can find none. Snow is still struggling with the sisters through the trees behind her; she can't see Jack and Hex above the trees. For a horrible moment she's completely alone, lost in the silver woods of Ashtrie, with nothing but the sounds of the silver forest…

Wait a minute. Sounds? The forest was silent before, and now…

She tries to control her ragged breaths. She can hear Snow clanking and cursing some way behind her, but ahead of her there's… there's something else. It sounds like… barking? Like lots and lots of barking, getting closer. There's a loud rustling from up ahead, and Hex lands clumsily, letting Jack off his back.

'Dogs?' Gretel asks Jack, bewildered.

Jack throws the newly human-shaped Hex his clothes. 'A huge pack of them, coming this way.'

A howl starts up – wild and joyful and surprisingly close. Gretel can hear many different breeds in the howl, not all of them domestic.

Snow crashes into view, panting under the weight of the sisters. 'Wolves,' she manages. The sisters look terrified. 'Don't worry,' Snow adds, 'the wolves are on our side. Probably.'

'I don't know.' Hex looks fretful. 'Those can't be our wolves; you guys sent Scarlett off to the village – she wouldn't be all the way out—'

'Hexy!'

A huge ginger wolf leaps out of the trees, mid transformation, and is just about the shape of a tall woman in a red cape by the time she lands, arms first, onto Hex, attacking him with a warm hug. 'You're OK!'

'What are you doing here?' Snow demands as they're surrounded by excitable dogs and wolves.

Daisy fights her way through two wolves, a leaping spaniel and the painfully whipping tail of an ecstatic mastiff.

'Hansel was taken. We're the rescue party.'

'Oh,' replies Gretel, fending off a multitude of noses attempting to sniff out an embarrassing greeting, 'us too.'

'Yes' – Jack grins – 'the gang's teaming up again!' He glances at Snow. 'I mean, I assume we're teaming up and you don't want to try to go off alone for mysterious reasons yet again, Snow?'

'Where's the rest?' asks Snow.

'Oh, they couldn't come,' replies Daisy.

Snow looks relieved.

'They went off to the Citadel days ago.'

Snow looks aghast. 'What? What did Buttercup say about that?'

'That… she was going to the Citadel?' replies Daisy, unsure.

'It was sort of her idea,' Scarlett adds.

'*What?*'

Jack pats her on the shoulder. 'We don't really have time for your love life right now, Snow.'

Snow opens her mouth and closes it again.

'We'd just spotted glass spires through the trees when we noticed the pack,' Hex tells them. 'If the bigger wolves can give you guys a ride, we can lead you there in good time.'

'In good time for what, though?' asks Daisy quietly.

Gretel doesn't reply. She has a horrible feeling that, whatever it is, it might be too late.

'Midnight,' mutters a voice. Gretel turns. It's one of the sisters. She lifts her sightless eyes. 'If we're to stand a chance, we need to get there by midnight.'

Hansel has no idea how long has passed. There is no time, inside the glass. He's somehow alive and conscious without movement, without air. He can't even be sure that his heart is beating. The only thing he's aware of moving inside him is his magic, swirling, trapped in him, within the enchanted glass. Ella is speaking, but he can hear nothing beyond the roar of his own magic, turned inwards. Something has to give. He feels as if he's about to explode, to turn himself inside out and take what's left of the Glass Palace with him – Ella, those poor frogs. He doesn't want to explode the frogs; they've been through enough already. He tries to quell the thrashing, panicking, pent-up magic, but he knows that it can't last long. He thinks about the image of himself as just a mindless pillar of dark magic, destroying everything in its wake. It's hopeless. Everything's hopeless.

Amongst the smashed glass is the remains of a glass clock. It stopped working when its intricate glass gears and cogs were shattered during the magical fight. If it were still functioning, its delicate glass hands would both be pointing upwards and its little glass hammers would be preparing to hit its glass chime twelve times.

Ella has lost track of time.

Her magic resets every midnight.

The reset comes without warning. The power holding the Mudd Witch just... clicks off. Usually these days, with enough concentration, she'd be able to maintain her spells and glamours over midnight with little more than a flicker of interruption, but the fight has weakened her, and this boy is so powerful, so difficult to contain, and also there's the small matter of the massive pack of wolves and dogs suddenly breaking through the smashed walls of the palace and running full pelt towards her, bringing a Werewolf, her raven boy, the Myrsina witches and her own sisters with them, which is a tad distracting.

For a moment – just a moment – everything's stretched too thin. She doesn't know which front to fight on first. Something punctures her magic, and cracks, and the crack spreads across a surface that is suddenly too fragile to maintain its form, and everything collapses into glittering shards and noise.

20
The Crystal Maze

'Chaos' is a word that gets used in hyperbole a lot. Shop's got slightly more people in it than usual, including a number of children who, for reasons known only to some ancient sprite of mischief, have had their shoes fitted with wheels? Chaos. The cat chooses the moment you're already running five minutes late leaving the house to throw up inside your child's wheeled shoe? Chaos. Gretel understands that those things aren't true chaos. When you've had to flee for your life, lived through the invasion, occupation and liberation of your village, been taken prisoner by bears, survived the firebombing of a forest and had your house blown up, you tend to avoid such exaggerations.

Nevertheless, what happens when she and the pack leap over the shattered walls of the Glass Witch's palace can only be described as chaos, and a whole new level of chaotic chaos, at that. Several things happen at once. Gretel sees, in the middle of the smashed hall, her brother, encased in glass like a bubble in a vase, but before she can do or say anything, the tendrils of his magic burst forth, sending glass flying in all directions. This causes the dogs and wolves to scatter in alarm, fleeing the glass in a noisy chorus of yelps and barks. Gretel tumbles from a frightened wolf's back towards the treacherously sharp floor, shielding her face with her arms, but Hex's beak swiftly pulls her upright as he lands, leaving her on her feet and blinking with bewilderment.

Hansel is screaming, desperate to control the thrashing magic. The Glass Witch is screaming, her painful beauty flickering and fading into something dirty-looking and ragged.

Somebody else is screaming. Gretel frowns in the direction of the voice. It's a man, completely naked and surrounded by several very upset-looking frogs. Hex, human-shaped and also naked, screams at the frog-covered man, pointing his wing at him. As Gretel watches, a frog, mid-leap, turns into another naked man, with a horrible wet noise, and lands on the first screaming stranger. That makes three naked screaming men, which is too many naked screaming men for Gretel, to the tune of three.

Scarlett isn't *quite* naked in human form because she has her cape, but she *is* naked-adjacent, so of course she starts screaming and pointing at the frog-men too, because all the other people without any drawers on are screaming – may as well.

Snow approaches the Glass Witch, still supporting a sister on each shoulder, a small axe drawn.

'Ella?' says one sister.

'Don't you come near me,' seethes the Glass Witch. Gretel can see that her face is streaked with tears.

'We wanted to say we're sorry,' says the other sister.

'Of course you're sorry, now that you're being punished.' The Glass Witch – Ella – seems to grow a crown of glimmering, angry spikes. 'And yet you dare to come to my palace, to speak to me. I'll punish you more. I'll punish you all!'

Snow nods at the screaming men. 'Your frogs are changing back.'

Ella snarls at the men. 'Oh no you don't.'

'Please,' manages the first man, 'where's my Odette, what did you do to h...'

His entreaty turns into a low groan, which turns into a croak. He and the second man are frogs once more.

'Her spells can be broken,' cries Hex. 'how did he do that? Could I do that?'

Ella glares at the group, haughty and hateful and… maybe a little bit scared.

'A temporary blip. Midnight holds no concern for me, any more.'

'Are you sure?' Snow cocks her head. 'Looks to me like your power might be starting to unravel.'

Ella draws herself up… and up… grows to twice, three times the size she should be, her glamour shimmering in overdrive so that it hurts Gretel's eyes.

'I'll show you how much power is in me, vermin witch!'

The shards of glass on the floor shoot upwards – they manage not to hit or cut anybody, but they fast form a wall in front of Ella and the still struggling Hansel. Before anybody can do a thing, a second wall manifests behind the group, with a ceiling overhead so that Hex and Scarlett won't be able to fly or jump over.

Snow sighs, shrugs off the sisters for a moment and pushes at the wall of shattered glass. It doesn't give. She punches it with her metal gauntlet. Still nothing. She smacks it with her axe. The only thing that happens is that it makes a thoroughly unpleasant high-pitched sound.

'Well, that'll teach me to tease a witch about their powers, won't it?' she mutters.

Gretel can't see Hansel through the confusing kaleidoscope of broken glass, nor can she hear him any more, but she knows that he's still close by. Each end of the glass tunnel they've all been encased in leads off into darkness.

'She's toying with us again,' says Hex, miserable but thankfully back in clothes.

'This doesn't feel like she's playing,' notes Daisy.

'She's upset,' breathes one sister.

'Who knows what she'll do to us this time?' adds the other.

'If she's upset, then she's losing control,' says Gretel, peering into the gloom of each side of the tunnel. 'Scarlett, can you track Hansel's scent through this thing?'

Scarlett sniffs the air, then grabs her hood. 'Follow me,' she says, and pushes the hood up. She turns full wolf again with a gristly crunch and takes the lead through the glass tunnel, sniffing warily.

Hansel stops screaming. He's finally got the magical outburst under control again. His sister was here – and Daisy and a load of dogs, which was weird. It wasn't an illusion; he still feels them close. Ella, too. He feels her as well, close by. She's *furious*. He tries to look around himself, but everywhere, all he can see is his own cracked, twisted reflection, gazing back at him.

So, Ella's still fighting, still trying to grind him down.

He turns a full circle, finding only his warped face in every direction. He tries to stay calm, and imagines what his sister would say in this situation.

She would tell him that it's good they've got the Glass Witch angry, that it could be the weak spot where they should apply pressure. She would tell him that it's good Ella made this cage of grotesque reflections out of such strong magic, because it means she's overcompensating. She would tell him that everything's going to be all right.

'It's good that we've got her angry,' mutters Gretel to herself, unsure, as she jogs after the Werewolf through the glass tunnel. 'It's her weak spot. She's overcompensating, now. Everything's going to be all right.'

She glances over her shoulder for reassurance from the others. Hex and the sisters, for all of their joint experience at the mercy of Ella's wrath, are not wearing expressions that suggest agreement with her whole 'the angrier we make her the better, it'll be all right' argument.

'Wish the rest of the pack hadn't run off,' mutters Daisy.

'Really?' replies Jack, his tone deliberately light. 'A hundred dogs and wolves? Trapped in here with us?'

'Those frogs were able to change back,' says Hex quietly to himself. 'Are her curses slipping? Why didn't my wing change…?'

Scarlett stops abruptly, her ears pricking.

'I hear it too,' says Hex, pushing forward.

Gretel can just about make it out, now. The sound of a woman crying, but trying to make no sound.

'It can't be…' mutters Hex, running ahead, still hand in hand with Jack.

Gretel tries to follow, but Scarlett stops her, pushing her hood back until her face is human enough to form words.

'Smells like… nothing,' Scarlett growls.

'Oh,' breathes Gretel. She runs to Hex and Jack.

'Hex?' says Jack.

Hex is squinting off into the shadows that envelop the source of the stifled weeping.

'Septa?' he asks.

A young woman stumbles forth. She has Hex's dark hair and soft eyes. Her hands are covered with scabs and bloodied sores.

'Septa!' Hex tries to go to her, but Gretel and Jack hold him back.

'I'm sorry, Hex,' Gretel tells him. 'She's not real.'

'Septa died,' adds Jack gently. 'Remember, love?'

'But she's there.' Hex begins to cry. 'She saved me! Saved us all! Why can't I save her in return?'

'That's not how it works,' Gretel tells him. 'Siblings are there for each other because they want to be, not for anything in return.'

'But it's not fair…'

'I know.'

The weeping image of Septa reaches out a mangled hand to Hex's wing. Her face is full of regret.

'It's because she couldn't completely lift the curse,' sobs Hex. 'If it weren't for this stupid wing, we'd have all been free. It's my fault; I wasn't strong enough to become whole again.'

'It is *not* your fault,' replies Jack firmly.

In the gloom behind Septa comes a great flapping of mighty wings.

'It's not real,' cries Gretel to the group in general, and a little to herself, as out of the shadows comes a raven, even bigger than Hex, filling the tunnel impossibly with its furious wings, anger and disappointment in its eyes. From beyond it comes another, and another, and another and another. Hex's five older brothers.

'Primo,' wails Hex, 'Dyo, Tripta, Quant and Quinn, I'm so sorry.'

'It isn't real,' Jack shouts to him above the cacophony of flapping feathers and throaty caws. 'Also, no offence, but your family are terrible at naming kids; if we end up getting nippers, I'm doing the naming.'

'Trott,' shouts Snow, 'you've been courting all of three days, we're stuck in a death tunnel and he's being haunted by his dead sister – now's not the time to talk long-term plans.'

'Yeah, I don't take relationship advice from you, Snow, sorry.'

'The ravens have gone,' notes Daisy.

So they have.

'See?' Gretel adds. 'Not real. They disappeared when we started paying more attention to Jack than to them.'

'Yeah.' Jack beams. 'Everybody pay attention to me!'

There is a rumble from somewhere in the dark tunnel, like a growl of approaching thunder.

'Wait, no,' adds Jack, his grin freezing into a frightened grimace, 'nobody pay attention to me, especially not…'

The Giant bursts from the gloom, pounding down the hall of glass towards them. Jack scrabbles and runs from it, with the rest following even as they call to him that it's an illusion.

'Obviously that's not real,' shouts Gretel. 'How would it even fit? The ratio's all wrong.'

Indeed, the Giant is somehow able to both be an impossibly huge leviathan bearing down on them, and also to fit inside a claustrophobic tunnel of smashed glass. It makes no sense, and yet the rumbling of the ground behind Gretel and the swipes of its mighty arms are making her want to run away from it, real or not.

'YOUR FAULT,' bellows the Giant. 'YOUR FAULT!'

The tunnel leads them through a forest – the green twisted trees of the Myrsinan area of Darkwood rather than the silver perfection of Ella's territory. They pass a woodcutter who looks a lot like Scarlett's human form, but with close-cropped hair and the miserable, hunched demeanour of somebody utterly uncomfortable in their own skin. The Werewolf stops and stares at the figure for a moment, before shaking her head and getting back on to the scent. Clearly, whatever illusions Ella's throwing at them, if she can't get the smells right then it isn't going to work on Scarlett.

The forest quickly changes to the Citadel streets. The Giant, Gretel notices, is no longer chasing them. Ella's trying to keep up too many illusions at once, trying to reach into all of their minds and reflect back all of their regrets and fears – the result is fast becoming an unstable mish-mash, a too-large patchwork piece sewn together too hastily, unravelling the moment you pick at a single thread. There is screaming, ahead.

Not real, not real.

They round a corner. The screaming is coming from a great scaffold built in front of the castle's main gate. A woman is tied to a rack. Huntsmen, everywhere. They're burning her.

Not real! Not real.

'Mum…?' mutters Snow.

'It isn't real!'

'The memory's real,' breathes Snow. 'The hatred that caused it is real. The threat of it happening again…' She squints at the woman on the platform, and breaks into a sprint, throwing the two sisters from her shoulders.

The woman on the scaffolding is no longer Snow's mother. It's Buttercup.

'It isn't real,' shouts Gretel after her again. 'Ignore it and it'll go away, like all the others!'

Snow barges through the crowd watching the grisly execution, pushing huntsmen and civilians alike aside with rough shoves. 'You don't get it,' she bellows back. 'This *is* real! She went to the Citadel! I'm not there to protect her! They'll kill her!'

Gretel runs to Snow. 'She'll be fine, she has back-up, we made sure she'd be safe…'

'We *can't* make sure she's safe, New Girl, because she is a *witch*, and they are going to kill us all if they get the chance, do you understand that? No exceptions. They want to *erase* us. Scorch us from the land…'

'I understand that some of them do—'

'No, you don't get it!' The crowd between Snow and the screaming image of Buttercup becomes a thick wall of bodies. They don't move when Snow shoves them with her hands or their shoulders. 'And I keep letting myself forget, and buy into your beautiful dream.' She pulls out two axes.

'Woah, hey!' Gretel forgets for a moment that the crowd of unarmed civilians Snow has drawn weapons on are illusions.

'This pretty little nonsense-tale that they'll let us live together in peace!' She swings her axes, and a group of men and women standing between Snow and the scaffold fall. 'They will kill us, Gretel! They will kill *her*, unless I stop them! It's us versus them!'

'Snow, stop!'

'Witches versus humans!' She swings her axe again; more people fall.

'No, it isn't!'

Snow spins on her heel, one bloodied axe a fraction of an inch from Gretel's face. 'Name one good human!'

'Er… me?'

Snow's expression changes. She looks like she's been slapped, but with something soft.

'Daisy?' continues Gretel. 'Her mum? My stepparents still looking after the Dwarves? My village in general, even Carpenter Fred – although he's a little bit of a turnip, he's got a good heart, if you can find it. Hex? These guys?' She waves a hand in the direction of the sisters. 'Sorry, I never did catch your names.'

'S'all right,' calls one of the sisters.

'I'm Mopsa; that's Dorcas,' adds the other.

'Course we can live together peacefully,' Gretel continues. 'We already do.' The screaming has stopped. The scaffold, the crowd, the whole Citadel, in fact, are all gone. Snow allows the axe to fall by her side, which is a relief to Gretel, and then bursts into tears, which comes as the opposite of a relief.

Gretel has never seen so much as a glisten in Snow's eyes before. Up until this point, she wasn't certain that Snow was physically capable of crying, but here are the tears now, fat and full and disconcertingly loud. Gretel has no idea what to do about it. She looks over her shoulder to Jack for advice, but this development seems as new to him as it does to her. Perhaps princesses only cry once every thirteen years or something. This definitely feels like over a decade of pent-up tears all coming out in a single, unmanageable deluge.

'I'm just so scared,' wails Snow. 'I'm so scared all the time; they took everything away, everything, they can take it away again. I can't lose her, not her, you don't understand, nobody understands…'

Gretel lays a gentle hand on her shoulder. The action would have made her feel a lot more mature had she not had to stand on tippy-toe to reach.

'You really think you're the only person to love someone?' Gretel asks softly. 'And be terrified of losing them? Come off it, Snow. Get over yourself.'

Snow blinks at her, incredulously, then at Jack and Hex, then Daisy, looking worried and awkwardly patting a Werewolf, then at the two sisters in a heap on the floor.

She sniffs, and wipes a globule of snot from her nose with the back of her gauntlet. 'Stupid Glass Witch, made me look like I was crying,' she mutters.

'Nothing wrong with crying,' Hex reminds her.

Snow doesn't even acknowledge him. She nods at the Werewolf. 'Keep tracking Hansel then, Wolfie. The Glass Witch is throwing all she's got at keeping us here but it won't stop us now.'

She hefts both sisters up. Gretel just about notices that one of them – Mopsa, she thinks – has been distracted by something in her hands, which she slips into a ragged pocket as she's hauled up to stand.

Gretel takes a breath to mention it, but before she can, Scarlett catches scent of Hansel again, runs full pelt at a large shard of glass wall, and vanishes. Gretel gives chase, following the Werewolf into the shard of glass, which melts away around her, nothing but shining air. She finds herself back in the smashed remains of the Glass Palace's grand hall, where she sees the Glass Witch in the process of turning her brother into a spider.

21
She Just Liked the Tutu

'Something's afoot,' mutters Trevor. 'I can feel it in my knees.'

'You're always saying that,' replies Patience.

'Yes, well there's usually something afoot, isn't there? 'Specially these days.'

It's the middle of the night, but Trevor can't sleep. Firstly, he's too excited to sleep and secondly, he's a spider and therefore doesn't 'sleep' in the same sense as we'd understand it; he just sometimes lowers his metabolic rate to conserve energy. He is not, however, currently lowering his metabolic rate because, as was just mentioned, he's far too excited.

The plan has been going well. Several infirmary patients are now grateful recipients of witch-hair wigs. Several more people based at a few different locations around the Citadel now have shoes fixed good as new by a curious cobbler shop that appeared and disappeared mysteriously throughout the day. Admittedly, fixing shoes good as new is the basic premise of a cobbler's shop, but there was something magical about the way these shoes were fixed. Rumpel took pains to visit the poorer communities – places where it was likely that the shoes would all be second-hand at least, and fixed them so that they were almost exactly the same quality that the shoes' original owners had bought them in. The 'almost' caveat was that Rumpel was careful to maintain the softness of the well-worn leather. It's no use having shoes 'as good as new' if you're on your feet all day and new shoes give you blisters.

Bellina has barely been seen since Old Nikolas snatched her up as his 'Special Midwinter Fairy Helper, yes?' and took her, complaining, out to spread cheer. They dropped in to the underground bakery in the evening for hot tea and pie before heading out again, Bellina's tiny face ruddy with cold and twinkling with glee, in spite of her loud protestations. Wrapped in a scrap of thick green felt, the Thumbling looked like one of the sprigs of holly that gravitated towards Old Nikolas's coat and hair. It seems that they are doing this at exactly the right time of year for Old Nikolas, whose powers and general welcomeness amongst non-huntsmen are strongest in the weeks running up to midwinter. A magical being that people actually want to see – even in the Citadel. The thought made Trevor's abdomen swell with pride.

Trevor and Patience have spread what whispers they could amongst those inclined to listen, but the real impact today was made by Buttercup and her stealth pasty. A trickle of ragged children came to the bakery in the afternoon after Buttercup had magicked the first pasty for the starving kids. All were polite, and hungry, and thankful for the loaves and cakes 'Miss Witch' had made for them out of a pile of bricks and damp firewood. By evening, the trickle became a stream. Not just kids now, but thin-faced women clutching babies and men who looked too old to be muddied from a day of manual labour. Buttercup mentioned something about quite how many hungry people there were. Patience replied yes, and wasn't it wonderful, they would be able to change public opinion on witches in no time at this rate, and Buttercup fell into a strange, sad quiet for the rest of the night.

Buttercup sleeps in front of the hearth now, along with Odette and Gilde. Gilde, it transpired, had a very different take on how she should go about 'using her powers to help the community'. When word got to the bakery in the late afternoon that the market district of the Citadel was being terrorised by a runaway dancing bear in a tutu, Trevor assumed that this would be exactly within Gilde's magical remit to save the day. On further thought, however, he wondered whether Gilde's idea of 'saving the day' might have actually been to free a poor tormented dancing bear and allow it to roam the butchers' stalls unfettered. Gilde came into the bakery at dinner time, very pleased with her good deed. The bear, to Trevor's knowledge, was still out there somewhere and apparently still wearing a tutu.

All in all, a mostly good day, rampaging tutu bear notwithstanding. And yet, Trevor just can't shake the feeling in his knees. Something's up.

Maybe it's the turning of the tide.

There is a knock at the door.

'Shop,' calls Patience in bored tones as she drifts listlessly across the ceiling. They have dispensed of a closed sign, since it was getting ignored by the largely illiterate clientele anyway, and it kept getting turned into stollen. The hungry of the Citadel, it seems, never sleep. The stream of people has thinned back down to a trickle overnight, but it has remained a consistent trickle nonetheless. Road sweepers, nightsoilmen and the like still need food and, despite having jobs, they seemingly can't always afford it. It's been a couple of hours since the last 'customer', but as Odette murmured as they were settling back down to sleep earlier, soon the night workers in need of supper will be replaced by knocker-uppers, delivery men, dairy hands and other early-morning workers in need of breakfast.

Buttercup gets up wearily, wraps a cloth around her hand and goes to the door.

'One second,' mutters Patience. She disappears momentarily, then reappears in the same spot on the ceiling. 'It's fine, they're civilians.'

Buttercup opens up. Behind the door are three men and a woman.

'Are you the lady who does the...' The woman thinks about how to put it. 'The special breads and whatnot?'

'Hang on,' mutters Trevor, really not liking the feeling in his knees.

'Yeah, hang on,' adds Patience quietly, a mere wisp on the ceiling. Trevor can see that she's now unsure about the expressions on the men's faces.

In spite of their 'hang ons', Buttercup nods with a yawn. 'What do you need?'

'We need you,' replies the woman, with sharpness sliding from her soft tones like a sweet little pussycat's murder-claws, 'to stop poisoning the children.'

'What?' Buttercup gasps. 'My food is safe; it always has been. Has... has somebody got sick? How...?'

'Poisoning them by shoving *magic* down their throats!'

Buttercup backs away, but the newcomers follow her into the bakery.

'Get help,' whispers Trevor to Patience, who nods and vanishes.

'It wasn't magic, it was just pasties,' Buttercup protests.

'*Magic* pasties,' snaps the woman.

'They were hungry! I was helping!'

'Nobody's *that* hungry!'

'Yes, they were, lady,' retorts Gilde, awake and twinkling with passive-aggressive menace. 'I'm sure you know all about the poor in this fine, rich citadel o' yours; you seem the type to always be lookin' ter how you can make other people's lives your business.'

One of the men frowns at the others. 'Why is she talking like she's out of the olden days?'

'Is that a swan?' asks another of the men.

'A den of magical disrepute, is it?' The woman glowers. 'We'll see what the huntsmen have to say about this.' She turns to the men. 'Get them!'

'Bagsy not the swan,' say all three men at the same time.

'What?' asks the woman.

'They can break a man's arm,' says one of the men while another protests, 'I don't like their beaks.'

Trevor lands on Buttercup's head. 'Run!' he advises.

Buttercup runs, shoving past the intruders.

'Oi,' shouts one of the men. 'She's turned the sleeve of my best coat into pastry! That was *new*! And I just got it cleaned!'

Gilde and Odette are close behind, Odette sheltering Gilde's elderly, fragile frame with outstretched wings, an open beak and a glint in her eye that says 'I absolutely could break your arm if I wanted to'.

'Stop them,' screams the woman after them. 'They're witches! I found them!'

Their path is blocked by two large figures. They're not masked, but they wear the unmistakable cowls that mark them out as huntsmen.

'Witches, eh?' One grins. 'And in the heart of the Citadel as well, no less. The nerve.'

'And I found them,' shouts the woman.

'Shut up,' shouts somebody else from one of the upper windows lining the streets.

'Don't tell my mum to shut up,' shouts one of the men, 'we're cleansing the world of witchcraft!'

'Not at half past four in the morning, you're not!'

'Oh, where *is* she?' mutters Gilde, hurrying up to Buttercup and Trevor.

'Who?' asks Trevor.

'Swee'pea.'

'"Sweepy"?'

'Guys?' squeaks Buttercup as the huntsmen take a menacing step towards her.

'Swee'pea!'

'And who is Sweepy when she's at home?'

A new figure crashes out of a shadowy alley, lumbering at speed towards the group. It's a little larger than a tall man, covered in bloodstained fur, and roars from a mouth filled with huge, sharp teeth and the smell of slightly off raw meat. It is wearing a tutu.

'Swee'pea!' cries Gilde, happily. 'You get 'em, girl!'

'Shut! *Up!*' pleads the voice from the window again.

The bear sends the huntsmen and the gang of witchfinders scattering. Buttercup runs on.

'What do we do?' she pants.

'Go into hiding?' Trevor suggests. 'I sent Patience to find Rumpel; if we can get into his shop, we can disappear.'

'Fer how long?' calls Gilde. 'Cover's blown now.'

They come to the end of the alleyway. Beyond is an open plaza. Buttercup and the others stop in the gloom and wait silently for the coast to clear. Swee'pea is surprisingly good at waiting quietly in the shadows with them, for a bear in a tutu.

A different couple of huntsmen hurry through the plaza.

'A bear?' puffs one.

'Yep,' replies the other. 'You can get bear witches; there was one up near Slate.'

'Yeah, but... if they've got a *bear*...'

'If they get away this time, we'll find them again. Woman who said she was bringing them in had a list of the people she saw eating the witch's cursed foods. Gutter-folk, mostly.'

The other huntsman tuts.

'We'll just start hauling them in. Either they'll help us or at least we'll have a decent catch of collaborators; Head Huntsman'll be happy with that...'

They pass into a different alley, out of hearing range. Buttercup steps out of the shadows. She's carrying herself differently, and Trevor doesn't like it one bit. She turns to Odette.

'How far can you fly? As far as Ashtrie?'

'Buttercup,' warns Trevor.

The swan nods.

'Would you?' she asks. 'For me? For a message? Fly to the Darkwood and you should find my Snow; she's attuned to birds. Tell her I'm sorry but she'll have to do this without me.'

'Buttercup!'

'And tell her I love her. I mean, she should already know that, but better safe than sorry, right? It bears repeating, at least…'

'Buttercup, you can't!'

'Trevor, I must.' She takes him off her shoulder and gently places him on Gilde's sleeve: 'I can't have all those poor people arrested because I gave them magic bread and then ran away. You lot, find Rumpel's shop and lie low for a while, OK?'

'No!' Trevor shouts at the top of his little spidery lungs.

'Quiet!' shouts another voice from the surrounding buildings.

Odette ducks her head briefly in a sad goodbye, and takes off, rather ungainly, but then she is a large waterfowl trying to get fully airborne in a cobbled city square.

Gilde pats Swee'pea's flank gently. 'You best scat too, Swee'pea; ye'll only draw attention in yer fine froofs.'

The bear diligently lumbers away, a vanishing vision of lumbering fur and pink tulle.

'I'll take care of Trevor, sugarwitch,' Gilde tells Buttercup.

'No!' shouts Trevor again. He tries to hop back on to Buttercup, but Gilde grabs one of his legs and Buttercup is already striding away.

'We'll come for you,' Trevor calls. 'We'll rescue you! No witch left behind except possibly the ones we leave behind for their own good and this isn't one of those situations!'

'Shut up!' screams the voice from above, followed by the furiously flung contents of a chamber pot. The fact that the slop misses everybody below is the only upside to the whole miserable situation.

Gilde darts back into a shadowy alleyway. Trevor climbs up the wall to yell at Buttercup some more, but when he sees her again she's at the other side of the plaza, talking to a black-robed huntsman. He sees her allow the huntsman to grab her arm and lead her away. He wants to scream and shout, but he senses a magical shift to the wall, and it's no longer just the corner of an alley any more, it's a shoemaker's shop. Patience manifests in the alley at the same moment that the door opens and Rumpel and Salad hurry out of it, sleep-lined and breathless.

'We came as fast as we could,' pants Rumpel.

'Wasn't enough,' replies Trevor sadly.

Spiders can't cry.

Trevor wishes that they could.

22
The Boy Who
Wasn't a Spider

By the time Gretel and the others arrive, Hansel has been trying not to become a spider for a couple of minutes. He has already succeeded in not becoming a frog or a mouse, but Ella's latest attempt at a transformation spell seems to be working rather better than the previous ones. He's become accustomed to Ella's attack strategy – skulking around this cell of mirrors, hiding behind his reflections, magnifying everything he doesn't like about himself until it makes his body want to shrink and change. Up until a couple of minutes ago, he was coping pretty well with it, learning to anticipate her next moves, but this latest spell is a spanner in the works. Somehow, Ella has managed to reflect the shape of his magic back to him – that thrashing mess of dark tendrils inside him, sprouting out of him like tentacles... like legs...

Had Hansel known what an octopus looks like, his body might have attempted to take that form, but to Hansel, who before this autumn had spent his whole life within the same ten-mile radius, the sea is something that happens to foolhardy strangers, and the weird creatures lurking beneath its surface can stay right there, frankly. He knows the basics of how the sea works; he has seen three pictures of it and that was quite enough, thank you. Spiders, on the other hand, he has seen plenty of times, not least because his sister is now best friends with one. The image roots itself into him as he thinks about his tendrils of shadowy magic, and he is overwhelmed with the firm belief that his skeleton is the wrong way round, he has too few limbs and nowhere near enough eyes.

When the Werewolf bursts into the impossible chamber of mirrors, followed by his sister close after, Hansel is filled with shame that they can see him with his body in the wrong shape.

'Hansel,' cries his sister, and he wants to hear her through his knees instead of his ears, 'what is she doing to you?'

Others arrive, but Hansel barely registers them.

The Glass Witch speaks. 'Give *up*, you've lost!'

'No way.'

'He's mine!'

'He's thirteen, creep-o.'

'I just want his power. We will survive – one needs power to survive in this ugly world…'

'You're right,' says Gretel, 'we do. But we share our power, we don't take and we don't hoard.' She pauses. 'We're still willing to share with you. Pool together. Not just survive – thrive. Together.'

'Ella,' comes a voice that Hansel doesn't recognise, 'you've been alone too long. Please, sister…'

'I'm not alone!'

'Even your frogs have escaped.'

'And I will have new pets again, new insignificant little creatures, new insects beneath my heel…'

'Spiders aren't insects,' says Hansel.

'What?' asks the mighty Glass Witch.

'Spiders aren't insects,' he repeats. 'I spoke to one; he was very insistent on the matter. They're anorak… er…'

'Arachnids,' chorus Gretel, Snow and Jack.

'Yeah, that.'

'So what? They're small and nasty, just like you.'

The desire to become a spider grows even stronger, but it is now at odds with a new thought bothering Hansel's addled mind.

'Wait, is that why you're trying to turn me into a spider? Spiders aren't nasty or insignificant.'

He tries to order his thoughts. He thinks of the tendrils of magic – the power they represent, the fear they still hold over him. He thinks of a spider – cheerful and outgoing and utterly at ease with himself, at ease with being different – everything that Hansel wishes he could be. He thinks of a spider and feels warmth and comfort. He thinks of a spider and feels... better.

'Stop it,' shouts Ella. 'You're worthless! A crawling thing! Insect!'

'Then I can't be a spider.' He closes his eyes and smiles peacefully. No. He can't be a spider. He's not good enough to be a spider, and that's OK. 'Spiders are awesome. And, as I just mentioned, not insects.'

When he opens his eyes again, the mirrors are all gone. There's just the smashed remains of the palace. His sister is there, and her friends, and Daisy, who runs to his side. Ella is in the hall, surprisingly close, surprisingly small and grey, slumped amongst the glass.

Two women with injured eyes and feet hobble over to Ella, and kneel next to her.

'Just leave,' croaks Ella. She sounds exhausted. 'You people have a war to lose. I need to regain my strength so I can keep myself sheltered from whatever fate you bring upon yourselves.'

'You can't,' Snow tells her. 'They'll kill you, too.'

Ella sneers. She looks so old and thin. 'We'll see. Leave me alone.'

'Can't we stay?' asks one of the injured women at her side. 'Mopsa and me? We could look after you.'

'Keep you company,' adds Mopsa, the other woman. 'Start putting things right. We could be your maids.' She barks an odd laugh. 'Sweep the cinders for you.'

Ella shakes her head. 'Can't put this right. It's too old. You're still seeing things all wrong.'

'No, we see clearly now,' says Mopsa. 'We used to think we were better than you; now we see that we're beneath you.'

'You're neither,' replies Ella quietly. 'It's time you saw that.'

Hansel feels a new pulse of magic issue from Ella. It's weak – drawn from exhausted reserves – and directed only at the women by her side. The women look at each other – no longer with shards of glass in their eyes.

'You put their eyes back,' cries Hex.

'Their eyes were always there.' Ella's voice is low and rasping.

'Can you put us all back?' Hex asks. 'Those poor men…'

'I'm tired,' groans Ella.

'My arm,' persists Hex.

'It doesn't matter.'

'It matters to me!'

'It doesn't matter, because you're going to die.' Ella glares at them. 'All of you are going to die.' She looks up at the deep navy blue of the pre-dawn sky. 'Something's coming.'

Gretel turns, startled. 'A flying machine?'

There is no machine. There is something coming towards them, though.

'Is that…?' begins Hex.

'That's a swan,' says Snow.

23
We're Doing It Now

Gretel watches a large mute swan make an inelegant landing in front of them. It looks more self-conscious and sad than Gretel imagines a magnificent swan should be.

'She's like me,' gasps Hex. 'I can feel the curse on her. But she doesn't have a nettle shirt; she can't change back.'

The swan waddles towards Snow, gazing at her intently.

'Can you see her mind?' Jack asks.

'Ella blocked my powers,' mutters Snow with a frown. 'Here, Glass Witch, now that you're having your sulk about not being able to marry a child and keep him as a weird husband spider pet thing, d'you think you could see your way to uncursing your birds or unblocking my magic or... ah, fruit, where's she gone now?'

Gretel looks to the space between the two sisters where Ella was. She is nowhere to be seen.

'Fine,' growls Snow. 'Run away, see if we care. You. Swan.' Snow squats to the swan's eye level and takes the rather surprised-looking bird's head in both hands. 'Just think your message really hard. The block on my power must be weak as old knickers now; I bet I can get past it on my own.'

Princess and swan stare into each other's eyes. There is a long silence that grows more awkward with every moment of intense person-to-avian eye contact that passes.

'I was worried,' whispers Daisy to Hansel in the quiet. 'Was she really trying to marry you?'

'I did tell her I had a girlfriend,' whispers Hansel back.

'Awww,' whispers Daisy.

'If you two need any advice on romance or dating,' whispers Jack, 'I also have a boyfriend, so…'

'We know,' whisper Hansel and Daisy in chorus.

'We saw you snogging,' adds Daisy.

'We weren't snogging!'

'OK,' whispers Hex, 'people keep accusing me of "snogging", and I don't actually know what it means, is it a Myrsinan word for something disgusting? It sounds like it's something disgusting.'

Scarlett uncloaks. 'You know what you were doing by the well instead of fetching water that time, when you thought nobody was looking? That was snogging.'

'You were *watching* us?'

'I went to find out what had happened to the water you'd gone to fetch – people were thirsty!'

'No,' says Snow suddenly. 'No, that was an illusion sent to distract me. That wasn't real.'

The swan shakes its head and glares into Snow's eyes again.

'It wasn't real.' Snow looks away from the swan and meets eyes with Gretel, desperately. 'You said it wasn't real!'

'What is it?' Gretel asks, but the look on Snow's face tells her what it is. Gretel doesn't need any sort of psychic powers to recognise that expression. The realisation hits her in the stomach.

'Buttercup.'

'What?' The air of alarm spreads to Jack. 'What about Buttercup?'

'Is Buttercup OK?' Hex asks.

Hansel clutches at his head, the magical warning only just reaching him. 'Oh no, Buttercup!'

'Who's Buttercup?' asks Dorcas.

Mopsa nudges her sister and whispers something to her.

'Oh,' breathes Dorcas.

'We have to go,' Snow tells the group.

Scarlett nods, pulls up her cloak, and lets out a loud wolf howl, answered swiftly by the mega-pack nearby.

Snow turns to Mopsa and Dorcas. 'Our fight just became personal. You can stay here, if you want to.'

Mopsa and Dorcas look at one another again, their eyes finally clear.

'Our problem was personal, and you helped us anyway,' Mopsa tells Snow.

'We want to help you, if we can,' adds Dorcas.

'It's for love,' says Mopsa, 'isn't it?'

Snow nods, with a sniff.

'Then we'll definitely try to help.'

'It's a long way,' Snow tells them.

Dorcas looks a little sheepish. 'Can we have a lift?'

'You all can,' Hansel tells them. He holds up a hand to stop Hex, already halfway out of his nettle shirt.

'Oh,' mutters Hex. 'Oh, is he going to do the thing?'

'What "thing"?' asks Mopsa.

'It's really cool,' Daisy tells them.

'It's the fastest way,' Hansel tells them. 'Faster than flying, even.'

Odette looks offended, but doesn't take off. She allows Hex to gently place his wing over her body for support.

Hansel waits for the pack to gather around them – it takes a few moments for a small but determined troupe of terriers to catch up with the rest of the pack, letting out mighty yaps in joyful memory of the long-suppressed wolves inside their tiny trembling bodies.

'Hold on,' he says, and the ground beneath the Glass Palace gives way, leaving the glass behind, a glittering gravestone, a scattered remnant of Ella's magic. It is no longer a glass palace. It is no longer Ashtrie. It's just dirt, now. And dirt is the realm of the Mudd Witch.

The ground moves slowly at first, fast picking up pace once Jack discovers his own magic is unblocked, leaving him able to move trees and thickets out of the way. Before long, the forest changes from the ordered, frozen silver of Ashtrie to the twisted, half-burnt, gloomy mess of the Myrsinan side of Darkwood. Gretel notices a few of the remaining residents of the Darkwood have started running alongside the group on their magically moving patch of land. Gretel turns to Snow and shouts to be heard above the rumbling ground and the screams of Mopsa and Dorcas, who are still in the process of adjusting to the fact that one of their new party can make large bits of forest move around at stomach-churning speed.

'Are you doing that?' Gretel yells.

'What?' replies Snow.

Gretel nudges her head in the direction of the growing entourage of Fauns, Jackalopes, assorted critters and one rather dusty-looking Griffin.

'Are you doing that?' she repeats in an even louder voice.

'*What?*' repeats Snow. She glances behind her at the creatures. 'Oh,' she shouts. 'No. Maybe they're attracted to your brother's magic or something...'

A Centaur gallops up to draw level with them. If Gretel's memory serves her correctly, his name is Gary.

'What's wrong?' Gretel and Gary shout to one another at the same time.

'What do you mean?' calls Snow.

'Mudd Witch has you all on the move,' shouts Gary. 'Means something must be up. Another huntsman attack?'

Gretel shakes her head. 'They got Buttercup.'

Gary's face is a picture of indignation. 'They did *what?*'

'We're going to rescue her,' adds Daisy, clinging on to Hansel for dear life and also a little bit for fun.

'Too chuffing right we are,' calls Gary.

'No,' attempts Snow, 'you're not...'

'It's Buttercup,' shouts Gary to the following creatures. 'She needs our help!'

'You can't just follow us all the way to the Citadel,' shouts Snow.

'That's a good point,' replies Daisy. She turns to Hansel. 'We need to stop at Nearby.'

This seems to satisfy Snow, at least up until the point when Hansel pulls them all up to a grinding stop on the outskirts of Nearby and everybody tumbles off into the swollen refugee village.

Mrs Wicker is quick to welcome them, giving Daisy an embarrassing motherly squish and Snow an even more embarrassing deep curtsey.

'More homeless, is it?' asks Mrs Wicker, nodding at the sisters and various magical beings. 'Take them through to see Goggins; she'll find you tents and get you fed…'

'We're not stopping, Mum,' announces Daisy. 'We're picking up.' She whistles to catch Gregor Smithy's attention. 'Gregor! Get Bilberry, Farrier Ned and the others to open up the big barn. I'll be there shortly.'

'You're doing it now?' asks Mrs Wicker, her voice quiet and anxious.

'You're doing it now?' shouts Gregor, over her.

'They got Buttercup,' Daisy explains.

The whole atmosphere of the village suddenly shifts at the sound of those words. A disquieted murmur very quickly blooms into an indignant hubbub, and runs the risk of avalanching into an uproar of rage – perhaps even a ruckus. Villagers and refugees alike start to gather around the group.

Mrs Wicker nods at Daisy, Hansel and Gretel. Her expression is still one of apprehension, but she seems to understand something as yet unsaid.

'You're doing it now,' sighs Mrs Wicker.

And Gretel understands that, yes. They're doing it now. Whatever it is they've been building up to, they're doing it now. No more skulking, no more waiting for the right moment or drawing up plans, no more quietly gathering allies. That route has come to an abrupt stop. They can't leave Buttercup in the huntsmen's hands. They're doing it now.

'Absolutely not,' barks Snow. 'We can extract Buttercup quietly.'

'Not from the Citadel,' Gretel tells her. 'You know that.'

'We don't need an army; you can just come up with another sneaky plan,' Snow snaps, 'like when we liberated this village.'

'You mean when we used an army as a distraction to raise a second army?'

Snow looks around desperately at the crowd. Refugees, skinny and tired. Frazzled villagers: old men and women, weary workmen, widows, children. 'No,' she said. 'I won't do it. I won't lead you into battle.'

Daisy gazes at the princess. Pretty Daisy, who always fluttered and flapped around boys she liked, who pretended she didn't understand machinery or big words, rather than cause trouble or risk people not liking her. 'Then I will,' announces Daisy.

Gretel watches Snow blink at Daisy's statement. The thing about Snow is, it's really difficult to go against her wishes. There's something about a huge, posh woman covered in armour and skulls and axes and raised never to take no for an answer that does something to a person's resolve. Therefore, Gretel's pretty surprised with herself when she says, 'Me too.'

Snow glares down her nose at her. 'You're all going to get yourselves killed.'

'Possibly,' replies Gretel cheerfully, 'but all of us have been on this path for a while now. Started for me when I ran into the forest, and was taken in by the White Knight and her friends. Ever since then, there's been no turning back.'

Snow sneers. 'Are you trying to use *sentiment* on me, New Girl? It's not going to work.'

'Yeah, it is,' Jack tells Snow, with a clap to the back, 'because it's not about you. It's about Buttercup. And you're going to go even though you said no, and I'm going to go even though I'm a coward, and all these people are going to go – look at their faces. It's Buttercup. You've never been able to control the way Buttercup makes people feel. That's her magic.' Jack pauses. 'That, and buns.'

Snow gives them all a cold, hard glare, then storms off in the direction of the road towards the Citadel.

'I'm going to rescue my fiancée,' she announces. 'If any of you gooseberries decides to join me, on your own heads be it. If you can keep up.'

'"Fiancée"?' Mrs Wicker calls after her.

'Yep,' shouts Snow over her shoulder. 'You'll know her when you see her. Soft, bit wobbly, wears a lot of black, distinct bready smell.'

'Majesty?' cries Old Mother Goggins, her face a picture of awe. 'You're betrothed?'

'Technically not yet,' Snow shouts, 'but if I'm taking a whole army to the Citadel to rescue her, she's pretty much going to have to say "yes", isn't she?'

Old Mother Goggins puts her papery hands to her mouth, her eyes bright with tears. 'Lisbet Grief,' she says, 'fetch me a weapon.'

'Fetch it yourself,' shouts Lisbet Grief from the other side of the crowd.

Goggins snatches a crossbow from a complaining Faun. 'We're all fighting this 'un. And we're all living to tell the tale.'

'Mother Goggins,' Hansel reminds her gently, 'you're eighty-three.'

'And I'd storm the Citadel singlehanded,' Goggins replies, 'if it meant I'd get to see a royal wedding.'

24
Tanked Up

Snow clanks furiously down the road. It really is in horrible condition. Still. Not her problem. Not as if she'll ever be queen.

Not as if she's likely to so much as still be alive by tomorrow.

She'll get Buttercup out of there. She has to. She'll get the others to run away, maybe. Leave Myrsina altogether – take a ship, or something.

Otherwise, they're all going to get themselves killed. Likely that Mudd boy's already heaving up the earth and dragging hundreds of bedraggled homeless monsters and village yokels onwards, completely depleting all of his powers before the battle.

After a few minutes of angrily clanking she becomes aware of a great, deep rumbling behind her, drawing closer. She sighs testily, stops and turns.

'You know,' she shouts, 'you're going to completely knacker out the Mudd Witch doing th…' Despite herself, she trails off in astonishment, gaping at what trundles towards her and grinds to an awkward stop in front of her on the ruined road.

'What the fruit is that?'

It is not, as Snow expected, a magically driven slab of rock with four hundred people on it. It's even weirder than that. It is a huge metal container, on its side, with two dozen wheels fitted to the bottom and the top cut so that a roof of sorts currently hangs open on hinges. Some sort of machine at the back is puffing smoke like an asthmatic Wyvern. Among the fifty or so heads she can see popping out of the open roof are Jack, Hex and a particularly pleased-looking Gretel, holding on to a metal yoke that seems to be steering the thing.

'It's steam-powered,' Gretel shouts to her over the noise of the wheezing machine. 'D'you like it? Thought we'd probably need some sort of armoured land vehicle. Farrier Ned was able to make this out of the old water tank. I call it a, er...' Gretel flounders a little. She has always been just so bad at coming up with names for her inventions. 'A land water-tank.'

Snow sighs, and clambers in. She takes a seat on one of the wooden benches next to Hansel, whom she's glad to see is at least getting some rest after the small matter of defeating the Glass Witch of Ashtrie and magically dragging them all the way back to Nearby. Several of the faces she expected to see are missing, however, along with a large number of people who were, only an hour or so ago, itching to join the fight.

'Where are the others?' she asks.

She meets eyes with Gretel again, who gives her an impish little smile.

'Don't tell me,' she sighs, 'you've got some other badly named inventions you're planning to surprise me with.'

'Tee hee,' replies Gretel smugly.

Snow huffs, to hide a fond smile. The New Girl honestly has grown on her an awful lot, these past months. She really hopes she isn't going to have to watch the kid die today.

'Morning!' calls a voice. It's bright and friendly, the voice of a fun auntie. It would be a lot more appealing if it weren't speaking to Buttercup from the other side of a cell door.

Buttercup remembers that voice, from only a week or so ago. It was the cheerful voice that ordered the forest to be burnt down. She looks up and sees the amiably crooked, big-cream-cardigan grin of the woman who last week attempted to kill a child.

'Morning.'

It is indeed Morning – the Head Huntsman, and, for once, also morning-the-time-of-day.

'So sorry I haven't had a chance to pop by sooner, Buttercup,' continues Morning in pleasant tones. 'Busy busy – I'm sure you can imagine how it is. I suppose it's been a bit bewildering for you, kept out of the loop and everything since you got arrested, so I thought I should come down here and update you on how your case is progressing.'

'Thanks,' replies Buttercup out of sheer ingrained politeness, before she can stop herself.

Morning flaps her hands graciously, as if she were being praised for offering to pay for dinner. 'Least I could do. Um. So, the situation so far is, we're killing you. Tonight.'

'Right,' manages Buttercup.

'There was talk about doing it at dawn, as per tradition, but honestly, who wants to get up at that hour to see an execution? I don't; I'm sure you don't, right? You don't want to get rudely awakened at silly o'clock only to be marched to the scaffold and burnt alive before breakfast – come on. I thought we'd shake things up a bit, start a new tradition. So we're doing it at midnight. It'll be more dramatic; we can get a sort of a carnival atmosphere going for you. So, yep. That's it, really. Any requests for a last meal? You know, since you can't make any of your own food right now.' Morning nods to Buttercup's shackles, keeping her hands raised up above her head, unable to touch even her own chains and manacles.

Buttercup doesn't know what to say. She's going to die, and that's the best-case scenario. More likely is that Trevor and the others are going to try to rescue her, and they're all going to get themselves killed, and *then* she's going to die.

'I'll have Chef whip you up something nice,' continues Morning merrily. 'Honestly, I can't thank you enough for turning yourself in; I take it you're not alone. We should be able to kill quite a few of your friends when they try to rescue you.' Morning bites her lip excitedly. 'Think your princess'll come? Or the Mudd Witch?'

No. No, Snow will still be in Ashtrie. And if Hansel has any sense, he'll have seen all about this problem through the Mirror and brought the rest of the group back to the relative safety of Nearby. She doesn't hope for anything else. It would end horribly. People would get hurt. For her. She wouldn't be able to bear it.

Buttercup shakes her head.

'We'll see,' says Morning brightly. She raps at the bars lightly – the universal signal for 'well, I'd best be going'. 'Well,' she adds, 'I'd best be going. Loads to do. It was so nice catching up, and I'll see you later!'

She leaves. Buttercup waits a while as the footsteps fade away. Nobody's coming. Nobody's coming to rescue her.

She really, really hopes nobody's coming to rescue her.

Somebody's probably going to try to come and rescue her. She leans her head back and for once says a proper swear word – loud and clear and filthy.

What are they going to do – arrest her for it?

In a shady alleyway of the Citadel, a middle-aged couple are destroying a shoe. This seems to make no sense. They're clearly poor; their clothes are patched. They need those shoes. They knock, and all of a sudden the alleyway isn't an alleyway after all, but a backstreet cobbler's.

'Hiya,' says a voice from somewhere near the door.

The couple squint in the vague direction that the voice has come from, but seem confused.

'Oh,' says the voice again after a while, 'it's you.'

'Who?' asks the man, bewildered.

'The Pipers,' says the voice. 'Of Peter Piper's Pickles and…'

'Ssshhh!' The couple seem nervous, having to shush an apparently invisible man.

'Changed your mind, then? About not wanting anything to do with us?'

'Have you seen the posters?' whispers the woman urgently. 'They're starting up public burnings again. Here!'

'Of course they are,' replies the disconcerting voice. 'You didn't really think they were just relocating Citadel witches, did you? That it didn't have to be your problem as long as you kept quiet?'

'It's not like that,' whispers the man. 'We kept ourselves to ourselves because... our powers... they'd scare people.' He lowers his voice even further, leaning close to the door. 'Rose, she... she can...'

'Freeze things in time, I know,' replies the voice, matter-of-factly. 'I know a fellow who can turn the ground to jelly. So what?'

'You know?' The man frowns. 'And you know about me? About the children?'

'Children?' comes the voice 'Thought you were the guy with the rats?'

'Rats *and* children,' whispers the woman. 'From birth to... what would you say, Pete? About eight years old? He hears them. Their thoughts.'

'You hear babies' thoughts?' exclaims the voice, much louder than the couple would like. 'Cool!'

'No,' replies the man in a whisper, 'very not cool. Most of the time they're just scared and hungry and angry. But... so many of them are magical. It's just... inside them. It's how people are born. It's how *lots* of people are born. About... a quarter? A third?'

'That many?'

'If people knew... I don't know what would happen. An uprising, maybe? Or a... genocide. So many babies.'

'The woman they're killing,' continues the woman, 'she was based at a bakery not far from our plant. She just fed the hungry. If they're willing to kill someone for that, here, in public, and make a... festival of it...'

'I hear you,' says the voice. 'In you come, then.'

172

The door stays shut.

'Are you going to open up for us?' asks the woman.

'Oh!' says the voice. 'Yeah, I was wondering why you hadn't already come in. It's unlocked and everything; just give it a shove. I'd do it myself, but no hands, you see.'

The couple finally spot a brown house spider next to the door jamb. The woman pushes the door open to the cobbler's shop. It is absolutely full of people.

The weak, early winter sun gets as high as it's going to manage for the day and starts sinking back down for the comfort of the horizon, like someone who's decided that directly after a heavy meal is the best time to attempt their first push-up in several months. Experimental steam-driven vehicles are not known for being particularly fast on any terrain, let alone a ruined dirt road, so it takes until darkness has fallen to get within a few miles of the Citadel. Once the walled city ahead is a complex pattern of lights, Gretel decides that even the dark won't be able to hide their approach for much further, and she pulls the land water-tank over to a stop.

'We should go on foot from here,' she says. 'Take a small advance party, get Buttercup, regroup with the others, save the big machines for the second wave.' She gets out, along with the others, and waits for Jack to grow some camouflage greenery over the land water-tank.

'Um,' says Jack.

Gretel turns.

The tank is gone. Not 'well covered by shrubbery' gone, but actually vanished. Jack hasn't even had a chance to grow anything yet.

'What?' asks Gretel.

Jack taps against thin air. The thin air, improbably, clanks. 'It's still there,' he says. 'It's gone invisible. I didn't know any of us could make things go invisible.'

Everyone turns and looks at Hansel, who shrugs.

'I don't *think* it's me,' he says, 'but maybe? I'm still not a thousand per cent on what all my powers are.'

'There's only a hundred in a per cent,' Gretel reminds Hansel gently.

'Still, though.'

'Well, whoever it is doing this, it's very useful,' says Gretel. 'Maybe they could see their way to doing it for all the machines? And maybe us…?'

Before she can finish her sentence, everybody has gone. She looks down at herself and sees that she too has disappeared.

'OK,' she says, 'thanks. Um… is there a magic word we use to break the spell, or does it just break at whatever moment would be the most dramatic?'

There is no reply from the invisible crowd. Someone invisible bumps into her. Somebody else invisible says, 'Ow, who's on my foot?'

Gretel decides to hope that whoever did just turn them invisible, whether by accident or not, is going to turn them back at some point, because the drawbacks to making a crowd of fifty people invisible are becoming very quickly apparent.

'Come on, then,' she says, and turns to the Citadel, bumping into one person and getting her heel trodden on by another. 'Try to stay together,' she adds as an elbow catches her ear and several disembodied voices behind her complain about nudged ribs and trampled toes. 'Maybe not *too* toge—' Her open mouth is suddenly full of feathers.

'Sorry,' says Hex.

The winter night asserts itself fully. It's clear, starry and cold. It is a pretty night all over the land, but in the Citadel it's stunning. The lights in the streets aren't quite enough to mask the stars. Instead, they complement them, bright pinpricks everywhere one looks in the darkness, all shining off the thin rime of frost that's settled on roofs, statues and trees. The Midwinter decorations look delightful, caught in the sparkling little lights of nighttime. Buttercup would enjoy it much more were she not being dragged to a scaffold in front of the castle where she's to be burnt to death.

Some of the decorations don't look all that Midwintery, on closer inspection. Buttercup suspects that they've been put up to celebrate her imminent painful public death, which isn't very nice. There's a crowd in the big square where the scaffold stands. It's a big crowd, and its atmosphere is… odd. Buttercup has never been magically attuned to the emotions of others, but she can still sense the strange tension here. There are celebratory areas of the crowd, cheering, jeering, banging drums, waving green ribbons and flags with Morning's face painted on. There are other areas with grim, angry expressions, casting dangerous looks at the huntsmen and their supporters. There are other groups, just… watching, with a worrying blankness that looks as if it could turn into something else at any moment. It isn't a crowd united in excitement at the imminent death of a witch. It's a crowd on the cusp of something worse than that. It's a silo full of flour and the stake is a lit taper. Buttercup breathes roughly with panic. Admittedly, she was expecting to be a bit panicky, what with the whole 'about to be burnt at the stake' thing, but there's something worse. Her eye catches another pretty, sparkling thing above the heads of the crowd. A spider's tethering web.

Oh no.

That's when she starts to cry.

25
Midnight

The crowd descends into an uncomfortable, pregnant silence when Buttercup is tied to the stake. There isn't even any applause when Morning steps to the front of the stage. As the Head Huntsman's voice rings out loud and clear into at least a thousand pairs of ears, the only other audible voice is that of the witch at the stake trying desperately to stop crying.

'Evening,' calls Morning.

There is no reply.

'Well, as you can see,' she continues cheerfully, 'we've reached a new phase in our good fight against unnatural wickedness. This one was found right here, in the Citadel, in our community.'

'Only because you set fire to her home,' comes a voice. It's not shouted, just spoken out loud. People turn and murmur with a hushed urgency, but nobody seems able to locate the source of the voice.

'Not very nice, is it?' Morning continues, pretending she hasn't heard the dissenting voice. 'Bit scary, knowing that they're right here.' She pauses. 'So, I'll tell you what. I'm willing to negotiate. I know that there are other witches in the Citadel with this one. Chances are, they're here tonight, maybe planning a little rescue? I know that there are humans here tonight who came into contact with this witch, or other witches. So let's end this silliness now. Come forward, stop living in the shadows, stop trying to keep it a secret, and you have my word right now, the huntsmen will be merciful, to all of you, including this poor wretch here.' She indicates to Buttercup. 'No more burning alive at the stake, no more torture. Just a quick crossbow bolt to the head. Swift, painless, dignified. What do you say? Otherwise I'm afraid it's a burning, and it'll be slow. For her, tonight, and for all of you when we find you. Because we will find you, I'm afraid. You, and the people hiding you. And any kids you might have, just in case.'

There is a movement in the crowd. A handful of people are approaching the scaffold. Morning peers into the darkness. There's a woman in a headscarf coming towards her, dragging an odd, faintly elvish-looking man, and an older couple in patched clothes. She sees the woman in the headscarf shudder and jerk backward a little, as if something very cold just pulled her back by the shoulders, but the older couple in patched rags push on.

'No,' moans the witch at the stake, 'no, no…'

'That's enough,' booms a different voice. Everyone stops, and looks in its direction. It is coming, somehow, from an unused megaphone that has been tied to the top of a statue of Patience Fieldmouse, not far from the scaffold.

'It's her again,' whispers one of the huntsmen on the scaffold, fearfully. 'That Ghost, from Nearby.'

'Nah,' mutters another huntsman. 'That's a bloke's voice.'

'Coo,' adds the male voice, impressed. 'Don't I sound loud. Echo! Echo! Echo! Anyway, where was I? Oh yeah. That's enough, I said! Why are you lot standing for this? And I'm not talking to the witches here tonight, and yes, there *are* witches here tonight, loads of them, actually, well done for working that one out I suppose, Your Huntsmanship, but that's beside the point. Witches, this isn't on you. It's not all on you to keep sacrificing and sacrificing in the hope of getting the people who want to hurt you to go a little bit easier on you for a while. I'm talking to the rest of you. You normal humans, standing around watching this and knowing deep down that it isn't right.'

Morning slowly, casually hops down from the scaffold and makes her way towards the statue.

'Look at what you're doing,' continues the voice, 'because you are doing it, even if you're not the ones who tie witches to the stake or set fire to the Darkwood; if you're letting it happen, if you're giving permission, then it's still you doing it. Why are you letting the huntsmen do this? You've got the power to change things – you changed them before, why not now? Because things are a little easier for you now, is that it? You're happy to swap innocent lives for that, are you? You think that's a fair society? You think that's a free society? People living in shame and fear and pain right under your noses? Your neighbours? Your families?'

Morning reaches the statue's plinth and hauls herself up onto it. Throughout the Citadel, bells begin to chime out midnight. She'd planned to set the bonfire alight to the sound of the bells. It would have been really dramatic. And now this distraction's sent her timing off. How annoying.

'Are you going to stand up for everyone,' continues the voice, 'or just yourselves? Is that the kind of person you are? Selfish and small? Or are you decent? Are you brave? Do you want a better world, not just for you, but f…'

Morning knows what she's looking for – a largeish house spider at the mouth end of the megaphone. She grabs the spider and holds it aloft for all, especially the witch at the stake, to see.

'Argh,' cries the spider, its little legs flailing helplessly against her finger. 'Help!'

Something has started up in the crowd. Raised voices and jostling at the back. People pushing forwards. She can't make out any individuals, just a general surge.

'The witch's familiar,' Morning shouts above the growing clamour and the tolling of the bells. 'A horrible great hairy spider spouting out her propaganda. Just another of their cheap tricks.

No more.' Morning squeezes the disgusting little body in her fingers until there's a crunch and the flailing legs go limp.

'Trevor! *No!*' The wail starts from the scaffold where Buttercup is tied, and quickly spreads through the crowd. Morning throws the little broken body onto the plinth and hurries back to the scaffold. The jostling and shouting are turning into something else – something bigger and angrier than what she was expecting.

The outraged howl continues to grow, drowning out the Citadel's bells raggedly counting to twelve. The square becomes an impossible, angry, grieving roar, from hundreds of mouths. Morning can't actually see many people screaming in the crowd, though. There's something very wrong with the crowd in the square. As many people as there are, it seems louder and more densely packed than it should be. Large parts of it are… muddled, somehow. She expects not to be able to see people very well in the half-light of the lanterns, but this is different. This crowd is not fully natural. It isn't right. The square churns with movement, a tide of bodies, seen and unseen and half-seen, rushing towards the scaffold, rushing towards her.

The bells stop. There is only the roar.

And suddenly, she sees people pushing through that she was sure weren't there before. People wearing the faded browns of country folk and farmhands. People who aren't even people. A Werewolf. A man with a raven's wing. The princess, unmistakable in grisly armour. All armed.

So, this is it. This is the uprising. They brought it to her after all. Morning turns to another huntsman.

'This is it,' she tells him. 'Tell Lieutenants Grey, Richard and Fennel to go ahead with Operation Home Turf.'

'Now?' asks the huntsman.

'Yes. Now.' She nods at the surging crowd. 'Kill them.'

'But, the civilians…'

Morning looks at the crowd. Something else is happening. A chant has started up amongst the roar of rage. 'Princess Snow,' it goes. 'Princess Snow, Princess Snow.' Fighting has started up, but it isn't the Citadel citizens fighting back against Snow and her invading army. Some of the citizens are fighting against the magical filth, but most of them seem to be fighting *with* the princess. Curse that spider.

There is a rumbling on the scaffold. Shards of rock pierce the wood, splintering the stake that Buttercup's tied to, setting the witch free, sending sharp fragments of wood and stone flying, causing many of the huntsmen to scatter. So, Hansel Mudd is here, too.

Morning can't stay here. There's one thing she knows she has to do, to keep this dangerous nonsense from spreading further, and then she has to retreat. The chant rings in her ears. 'Princess Snow! Princess Snow!'

Insurrection. The Citadel is likely lost. How disappointing. And she has to accept that this is, at least partially, her fault. She was too merciful. Too free and easy. Gave the people an inch, and they've taken a mile. Let them think it would be OK to try to instil more change, unacceptable change. She'll have to set up base somewhere even further from the forest now. Maybe a port town like Goldenharbour. And the abomination lists will have to come back, if this is where leniency and moderation gets her. Curse. That. Spider.

'Did I stutter?' she asks the huntsman, with a warm smile. 'I said, kill them.'

26
After Midnight

'Trevor!'

Buttercup is, at least, no longer tied to a stake, nor is she currently on fire. These are the only upsides to the situation that she can see, right now. All around her is chaos. Fighting. Screams. Blood.

Trevor. Oh no, Trevor.

Small hands grab her. A blade cuts through the rope. Buttercup looks around to see Gretel.

'Trevor,' manages Buttercup.

Gretel is crying. 'I know. Snow's trying to find him.' She nods out at the turmoil beneath what's left of the scaffold. Buttercup can just make out Snow, fighting towards the statue. 'I'm so sorry. We tried to get to him...'

'No. This is my fault. Snow said. She said!'

Buttercup clambers down, pushing her way towards Snow. Behind her, she hears Gretel shout, 'Oh no you *don't*,' and zap someone with her dynamo on a stick.

Buttercup screams for Snow, but her voice gets lost in the pandemonium. A baton flies at her head, followed by a chair leg wielded as a club. She blocks both with her hands, causing stale baguettes to crumble harmlessly in her hair.

She slips on something wet, and hopes it's just a spilled drink or something. She is caught by the impossibly warm, surprisingly strong arms of Old Nikolas. Something about seeing his usually merry face creased with concern threatens to break Buttercup even harder.

'Trevor, he point out Midwinter lights to me,' Nikolas tells her, setting her back on her feet. 'Ask if they make me more strong; I say no, is just pretty. He say, sometimes just pretty is all we need...' Nikolas effortlessly reaches out over Buttercup's head and yanks a morning star out of a huntsman's hands. 'No! No toys for you – naughty!' Nikolas turns his gaze back to Buttercup, pulling her steadily through the crowd towards Snow, like an ox with a plough. 'Is last thing he say to me. You find, for Old Nikolas, yes? Midwinter miracle?'

Buttercup's eyes widen with a spark of hope. 'Can you fix him?'

Old Nikolas shakes his head sadly. 'Is beyond my power. But maybe somewhere here... Is many witches, many powers. Maybe one can fix... I say, no!'

Old Nikolas turns suddenly towards a much bigger huntsman and grabs at the sword being swung at Buttercup.

'Go!' insists Old Nikolas. 'We hold off!'

Buttercup sees what he means by 'we' – Bellina leaps from the safety of Old Nikolas's collar onto the huntsman's head and starts stabbing his ear with the spikes of a holly leaf.

Buttercup ducks under the struggling arms and tries to push through the crowd between her and Snow. Hands push back. She can't make herself heard over the chanting. They're chanting for Snow. She recognises some of these people, mostly from the village, but a couple of them from the bakery in the Citadel. She remembers giving that lady a cake, and there's Carpenter Fred, and there's Homily Goggins, and...

As if by magic, Goggins turns and looks Buttercup dead in the eye. There's a moment of recognition in the old woman's face, then sorrow, then, oddly, gleeful excitement. She shakes Snow's shoulder and shouts something to her.

Snow looks, the visor of her helmet raised, and sees Buttercup.

Buttercup has seen Snow cry before, but not like this. The crowd of Snow's supporters part and allow the witches to run to one another.

'Buttercup,' wails Snow at the same time that Buttercup sobs, 'Snow, I'm sorry.'

Snow pulls her into a tight, pointy, utterly uncomfortable, utterly loving embrace. 'Sorry? For what?'

'You wanted me to stay safe, you told me. You worried over and over again that people would get hurt, and now... and now Trevor...'

'We'll find him.' Snow is using the voice she puts on when she wants people to think she definitely knows what she's doing. 'We'll find him and fix him, it'll be OK. It has to be.' She tries to kiss Buttercup's forehead, discovers, not for the first time, that she can't do that with her helmet on and quickly removes her head armour. 'I'm the one who's sorry. I shouldn't have sent you away,' she tells Buttercup. 'We're supposed to be a team.'

'And I just got myself in trouble,' Buttercup cries.

Snow chokes out an amazed little laugh. 'Is that all you think you did? Look at the people fighting with us – Citadel folk. Patience said what you did.'

Patience manifests next to Snow. 'Trevor isn't on the plinth,' she announces. 'He might have managed to crawl somewhere. I'll keep looking.'

'You think he's still alive...?' Buttercup asks, but the Ghost has vanished again.

Snow takes Buttercup's head in her hands. 'Buttercup, you doubled our army, by... being nice, doing the things that you do. We'll find Trevor, I promise, and then we're going to win this thing. Not because of my failed mission in Ashtrie, but because of you. And then... and then, when everything's OK, will you...?'

'Ooohhhhhh,' chorus a number of voices above the fray, to Buttercup's bewilderment.

'Will I what?'

'You know,' mutters Snow.

'No,' replies Buttercup, 'I honestly don't.'

'She's asking you to marry her,' shouts Homily Goggins, ducking out of the way of a halberd.

'What?' calls Buttercup.

Snow grabs the intruding halberd in her gauntlets and wrestles it out of the protesting hands of its unseen wielder. 'I'm asking you to marry me,' she tells Buttercup, seriously.

Buttercup doesn't know what to say. She wants to say yes, obviously, but there's the fight, and Trevor, and... and...

She puts her hands over Snow's. The halberd and one of Snow's gauntlets turn into flaky pastry.

'I...' she says.

But then one of the friendly-looking figures in the protective huddle around them is shoved aside and replaced with a new figure – still friendly-looking, but with something malicious behind those bright, amiable eyes. A wonky, toothy, silly smile and hair like a dandelion. The face of someone you instinctively want to trust. Laughter lines. Soft hands. A knife.

It all takes less than a second. Morning moves so fast. Buttercup raises her hands instinctively; Snow half-turns. Several of the group surrounding Snow notice what's happening but, like Buttercup, they're too slow to react.

The knife should just harmlessly glance off Snow's armour, but Snow has taken off her helmet. When Morning jabs around at Snow from behind the princess' back, the blade hits the vulnerable skin of Snow's throat, and sinks in.

And sinks in.

And sinks in.

The noise around Buttercup is deafening, and yet she's acutely aware of the sound of her own heart, her own breaths. She doesn't scream. She can't. She can't do anything.

Snow doesn't make a sound. She stares at Buttercup, surprised and sad. The pastry remains of her gauntlet flake away as she raises her fingers to the knife now jammed to the hilt in her throat. Blood runs down the white bone of the skulls adorning her armour, over her black hair.

For a moment, Buttercup is no longer aware of the battle around her. There is only the red of the blood, draining out the last of her happiness. Snow. Trevor. Morning is killing everyone she loves.

Somewhere, in a dark edge away from the fighting, Trevor is dying. It doesn't hurt too much – that's a mercy, he supposes – but his abdomen is crushed, his exoskeleton cracked. He wouldn't be able to survive for long like that under any circumstances, but in this case, his chances of survival have become even bleaker, since he is being carried away in the mouth of a frog. Frankly, he's surprised that he's made it this far still just about alive and uneaten. He is more surprised when the frog stops in a dingy alleyway and gently spits Trevor out onto the ground.

Since these things surprise him, when the frog then turns into a sad-looking woman, he ought to be completely flabbergasted, but actually under the circumstances it makes more sense than not.

'I heard what you said,' says the woman in an Ashtrian accent. 'You are a brave little thing.'

'Oh, you're from Ashtrie,' manages Trevor. 'I got some mates from out your way; you don't happen to know a fella called Hex, do you? Or a lady by the name of Odette?'

The woman smiles strangely. 'After a fashion,' she replies in a manner that's needlessly cryptic, considering how she's talking to a spider with surely only a few minutes left to live. 'I thought,' she adds with more frustrating mysteriousness, 'perhaps you might be one of mine, but you're not, are you?'

'Sorry, lady,' replies Trevor, 'I've never met you before in my life.'

'You really are just a spider,' mutters the woman. 'All of this, for a spider and a fat girl who makes cake.'

'Is Buttercup OK?' asks Trevor, choosing to let it slide that the woman likely intended her description of his friend to be an insult. There isn't much time for him to deal with the weird human distaste for bigness of body, what with him dying and all.

The woman gives him another strange, sad look. 'Yes. She will be.' She pauses. 'That genuinely makes a difference to you, doesn't it?'

Out in the square beyond, another outraged wail goes up. The ground rocks. There is the sound of masonry being grabbed and flung by unseen, impossibly strong hands.

'Hansel's here?' Trevor whispers.

The woman nods. 'I tried to get him to stay with me, but I couldn't, so I decided to disguise myself and go with him instead. See what it is that's so powerful it could push back against my will.' She pauses, regarding Trevor. 'He was right. Spiders are fantastic.'

'Thanks,' replies Trevor. 'I'm afraid we're a bit fragile, though. Don't have the longest lifespan at the best of times, not much cop in a battle.'

'Your skeleton's cracked,' notes the woman. 'I can't fix that.'

'It's OK,' Trevor tells her. 'I think my time is up.'

'A cracked skeleton isn't always fatal,' mutters the woman.

'For a spider, it is.'

'Hmm,' replies the woman. 'There's one thing I can do.'

Trevor can feel himself slipping away. 'You can't.'

As the dimness of death descends, Trevor sees this sad little woman shine with the last embers of a fatigued glamour. She takes on a cold, haughty air.

'I am the most powerful witch queen that ever there was, insect. I just turned a whole army invisible, for hours. You don't get to tell me what I can't do!'

Full darkness descends upon Trevor. 'Not an insect,' he sighs.

'Well, not any more, certainly,' says the woman's voice in the dark.

And then there is something. Not light, not yet, but something.

Pain. Yes, that's what it is. Trevor's body is suddenly filled with a terrible pain that he has never experienced before.

27
True Love's Kiss

'The princess!' Gretel hears the agonised cry spreading around the battle. She tries to stop people, ask them what has happened and where and how she can help, but everybody is too busy in their own fight. Slowly, painfully, she fights her way towards the epicentre of the rumbling earth that marks the presence of her brother. Somewhere in the skirmish, a foot hits the back of one of her legs, and knocks her to the ground. She tries to get up, but the fight continues around her, over her... somebody treads on her, accidentally. Gretel tries to get up, but a huntsman spots her and leans towards her, brandishing a dagger.

'You're all going to die, freaks.' The huntsman leers. 'Just like your feral princess.'

'What?' shouts Gretel, although her voice is drowned out by that of a man on the ground next to her, wailing over an expensive-looking coat that has been torn entirely in two. The huntsman draws back the dagger to slash at her, but is attacked by a bear, which for some reason is wearing a tutu. The huntsman scrambles and runs, pursued by tutu-wearing bear.

What was that about Snow?

She can hear more mentions of Snow amongst the battle above her, along with the words 'blood', 'stabbed' and 'dead'. She still can't get up; people are still helplessly treading on her as the battle fills the square. She feels small and helpless again, a little mouse, a little bird, Ella was right about her, and now Trevor is dead or dying, and something has happened to Snow, and this whole mess could have been avoided if she'd just given herself up to the huntsmen the first night they came for her. She is nothing special; she's small and ordinary and perhaps she'll die like this, trampled to death…

A small hedge erupts beneath her, shoving her back up onto her feet in a rather undignified and uncomfortable manner, but at least getting her out of the way of the trampling feet. Jack grabs her hand, and pulls her out of the brambles.

'Have you found Trevor?' he asks, in anxious tones. 'Have you seen Snow?'

Gretel shakes her head. 'But I heard…'

'Me too.'

The ground trembles again. Somewhere off in the throng of battle, thick tentacles of shadow thrash and smack against the tall buildings, tearing at some of the bricks like hands.

'It's definitely bad,' mutters Gretel. 'Hansel's really upset.'

'We'll get you to him.' Jack, with Hex's clothes tied around himself like numerous bulky belts, waves up at the giant raven pecking at huntsmen from above. Hex glides in to land, but as he does so, Gretel hears a new sound, coming from the distance.

She meets eyes with Jack. He recognises the sound, too. The huntsmen's flying machines.

'Not here,' says Jack, his voice one of pleading as much as disbelief. 'Not in their own territory.'

But it isn't the huntsmen's territory any more. Gretel has seen this all before, in the battle for Nearby. The Citadel is lost to the huntsmen now. There are just too many civilians fighting back against the huntsmen. Too many people who have sided with witches and magicals. The huntsman army will likely fall back now, but not before scorching the ground in their wake.

'Hex,' she shouts to the raven, 'you need to go. Tell Daisy it's time for the next wave.'

The raven gives her a glance of understanding, turns in the air and soars away.

Jack slaps an approaching huntsman out of the way with a vine as he watches his boyfriend go. 'There were supposed to be other birds with him,' Jack notes. 'Snow was going to...'

He trails off. Gretel realises that Jack is still holding her hand, from when he pulled her up. His hand is shaking.

Somewhere in the crowd, Mopsa and Dorcas stumble, unable to balance in the dangerous throng with their damaged feet. Dorcas is wailing.

'The frogs! I lost the frogs!'

Mopsa tries to pull her back up, but falls to her knees herself. 'Leave them.'

'Mopsa, they're people!'

A large figure stands over them. Two big hands haul them both up. A man regards them both.

'You're those two witches they brought back from Ashtrie,' he notes.

'Not witches,' Mopsa tells him. 'Her sisters.'

'Ugly sisters,' groans Dorcas. 'The frogs...'

'Makes no difference,' announces the man. 'Not now.' He props up a sister on each shoulder. 'You two can't fight; what are you even doing here?'

'We snuck,' says Mopsa.

'One of the frogs wanted to come,' adds Dorcas.

'Mad as a bag of weasels,' mutters the man. 'Let's get you somewhere safe.'

He tries to walk them away from the fighting. It isn't easy – there is a *lot* of fighting, so whenever he moves them away from one fight, they end up in the middle of a different one.

'Rescued by a handsome stranger,' says Mopsa.

'I'm married, miss.'

'What's the name of our handsome prince?' asks Dorcas, ignoring the whole 'married' nonsense.

'Freddery Clump,' replies the man gruffly, 'but everyone calls me Carpenter Fred, on account of how I'm a—'

And that's when the huntsman's sword swings from behind him, into his neck.

The crowd of supporters around Buttercup and Snow have formed a wall encircling them, shielding them from the battle. There are shouts beyond; after Morning stabbed Snow, she took opportunity of the shock and happily slipped back into the crowd. Some are trying to catch her, screaming curses at her.

It doesn't matter, now. Snow clangs to her knees, and then clatters onto her side.

'How could she?' comes one voice. 'In front of everybody!'

Morning did it in front of everybody because Snow, in spite of her best efforts not to be, had become a symbol. Morning did it in front of everybody so that everybody would know that that symbol was gone.

And it doesn't matter now.

The only things that matter now are the dagger, and the blood, and Snow's rasping, fading breaths. Buttercup can't remove or transform the dagger; it hurts Snow too much to even try to touch it, and it's too late now, surely. There's too much blood.

Buttercup takes Snow's hands in hers, and lies down next to Snow. Years ago, they lay like this on the moss, and looked up at the patterns that the branches of the Darkwood cast against the bright sky. Now, the sky is dark and twinkling with the cool light of the stars. The ground is hard, and wet with blood. Snow's hands are growing cold.

Buttercup hears the familiar rumble of the huntsmen's flying machines approaching. So, the huntsmen are going to run, and burn them as they go.

It doesn't matter.

'Yes,' she says.

Snow rasps a low, questioning sound.

'Yes,' repeats Buttercup. 'I'll marry you.'

Snow's rasping sigh becomes peaceful.

'I love you,' Buttercup tells her.

Snow no longer rasps.

Years ago, lying on the moss, Buttercup leaned over and kissed Snow. It was so warm, that day. Warm, dappled sun, warm lips, warm arms, the warm bark of Snow's happy laughter afterwards.

Snow is silent now, and still. Buttercup leans over, and kisses her cold lips.

Snow chokes. And coughs. And tries to sit up suddenly, accidentally headbutting Buttercup.

'Ah?' squeaks Buttercup in tear-stained surprise.

The hilt of Morning's dagger clatters to the ground. Snow grasps at her throat, wiping blood away from skin that no longer has a stab wound in it.

'The princess lives?' manages one of the crowd circling them, in the same state of puffy-eyed shock as Buttercup.

''Tis witchcraft,' says another. 'Y'know, since she's a witch and all.'

''Tis true love's kiss,' announces Homily Goggins, with an approving nod at Buttercup. 'Always does the trick, that.'

'Oh, no,' mutters Buttercup, 'that's not a thing. And even if it was, I don't... I can't... I really do just do cake.'

Snow is still choking and coughing. She reaches round and thumps herself on the back. Something in her throat dislodges with a wet, phlegmy sound, and she spits it onto the blood-soaked ground.

It is perfectly shaped like the blade of Morning's dagger.

A slice of apple pie.

28
Love and Sausages

Jack's hand continues to tremble as he pulls Gretel through the crowd, towards the epicentre of the churning ground and thrashing shadows. Unseasonal foliage springs up as they push through the battle, creating a leafy corridor. When they get to Hansel, he is conscious and focused, but crying. He doesn't seem to have even noticed the Werewolf, ferociously protecting him from attempted huntsman attacks.

Scarlett pauses, her form a combination of human and wolf, as Jack and Gretel approach. Her faintly pointed ears prick at the sound of a great howl in the streets beyond the square.

'Your pack's here,' says Jack. 'They'll need you. We can take it from here.'

Gretel reaches beyond the magic shadows pouring out of Hansel, and lightly touches his shoulder.

'Thank you for helping him,' she tells Scarlett.

'Good to be needed,' growls Scarlett through a wolfish muzzle, before bounding away to join the pack.

Hansel meets eyes with Gretel, briefly. Gretel is relieved to see that he recognises her. She's never seen him able to remain in control so well while expelling so much magic before. Neither has she seen him so exhausted.

'You OK?'

Hansel shakes his head. Fair enough, that was a bit of a silly question. None of them is OK. Above, the prow of one of the huntsmen's flying machines comes into view from beyond the high buildings surrounding the square. Hansel glowers at it, and long, dark tentacles climb up to pull it down onto the rooftops.

'That's only the first,' he gasps. 'They must have a dozen more. I can't ground them all, and we don't have time to clear the square.' He gazes at Gretel again, horrified. 'There's civilians here. Huntsmen, too! They wouldn't... Morning wouldn't, would she?'

Down several side streets, away from the fighting, Morning Quarry is displaying a newfound urgency. She runs down alleyways, searching dark corners, peering inside outhouses and behind bins. Her robe and hands are dark with the princess's dried blood. She is carrying a bag of dog treats.

'Sausages?' she cries. 'Sausages! Come on, girl, this is no time to play, we have to go!'

'Morning!' shouts a voice familiar to her. The huntsman lieutenant Fennel runs up to her.

'Have you seen Sausages?' Morning asks.

'Is now really the time?' Fennel asks her.

'You question me?' Morning snaps. She stops herself and softens her tone, at her old friend's expression. 'You know I love that dog, Fennel. And we have to leave, now. The cleansing is imminent.'

'All weapons are mobilised,' Fennel tells her, 'but we still have a few hours. We still need to extract our people, before...'

'No.'

Fennel's expression darkens more. 'Beg pardon?'

'We must allow as few as possible of those witches and witch lovers to escape. Just enough to get the word to the rest of the land that their princess is dead, and the Citadel destroyed. The cleansing needs to start within minutes.' She looks around herself again. 'Just as soon as I find Sausages. Sausages!'

'Our people are still in there,' argues Fennel. 'Grey and Richard are still in there, overseeing the land assault. Morning, they're our friends! They've been on your side from the start…'

'And their sacrifice will be honoured,' Morning tells her. 'Sausages! Come *here*!'

'It isn't a sacrifice if they haven't agreed to be killed,' shouts Fennel. 'It isn't a sacrifice if they don't even know about it! It's just you killing them!'

'We are huntsmen, Fennel. We are prepared to give up everything for the good fight. Even our lives. Like Patience Fieldmouse,' she adds brightly. 'Be more Patience, and so on. Now, help me find my dog.'

But Fennel has stormed off. Morning rattles the dog treats again. 'Sausages!!'

Her heart leaps at a familiar bark. Her dog appears at the end of the alleyway, panting happily, tail thrashing.

'Sausages! Silly girl, where have you been?'

The dog barks at her merrily, but makes no attempt to approach Morning.

Morning takes a few steps towards the dog, still shaking the treats. 'Come along, girl, we have to go now. Walkies! Big, big walkies!'

The dog still stands there, wagging her tail, barking.

'Shush,' says Morning, but Sausages doesn't shush. In fact, Sausages is not the only dog barking nearby. Other dogs join Sausages at the end of the alley. Big dogs. Little dogs. Feral dogs. Wolves.

'Oh,' says Morning, realising.

'Oh,' she says again, hurt. 'You, too?'

The other dogs run off, followed by a huge pack of pet dogs and wolves, running together in a great stream of canine joy. Sausages gives her another happy bark and turns to join the pack.

'Sausages?' manages Morning, in a small voice, but Sausages is gone. Part of the pack now. Doubtless led by that disgusting

Werewolf. Morning throws the bag of treats against a wall. The bag splits and treats cascade out.

Morning leaves the alley and heads straight for the nearest gate out of the Citadel, alone.

The first of the huntsmen's flying machines is already in the process of collapsing slowly against the rooftops of the Citadel, its crew slipping and scurrying over the roof tiles, as four more large flying machines sail into view.

Hansel magically rips a chunk of masonry off the side of a building and hurls it at one of them, but there is an explosion from beyond the square, and a screaming sound that Hansel and Gretel haven't heard since the invasion of Nearby. The huntsmen are using the explosive catapults, too. A fiery missile knocks the magically propelled masonry off its course and towards some of the people trapped in the square. Both Hansel and Jack raise their hands to protect the people in the path of both the missile and the masonry, but stop when both projectiles suddenly freeze, hanging in mid-air. Even the flames licking the missile are completely still.

'Who's doing that?' mumbles Jack.

'Must be a witch who can do timelock spells or something,' Gretel replies, marvelling at the motionless flames.

Hansel's attention is back on to the new flying machines already. Gretel squeezes his shoulder again.

'It's OK,' she tells him. 'It isn't all on you, this time. We've got this.'

There is the sound of more flying machines, coming from the east. They quickly appear overhead. The new flying machines aren't sleek and scary-looking like the huntsmen's crafts. These ones look hastily cobbled together out of odds and ends, tin baths, flour sacks, farming equipment.

'The witch-lovers made their own flying machines?' shouts one voice from the battling crowd, surprised.

There is a pause, and then a chorus of mocking laughter.

At the prow of the front makeshift flying machine, an elderly, green scaly figure clambers out and clings on, flapping its own weathered wings to stabilise itself. Mavis the Wyvern. She lowers her head, lifts her wings, and showers one of the huntsmen's flying machines with a jet of fire.

The mocking laughter on the ground comes to an abrupt stop. A second of the huntsmen's flying machines is crashing now, in flames, its crew leaping out and deploying their large sheets of fabric to slow their fall to the ground – not to safety as such, but at least to a terrain that isn't crashing or on fire.

More missiles fly. A firefight between the flying machines fills the air. The square remains a loud confusion of clashing weapons, magic and magical creatures, while all around rings out with the barks and howls of hundreds of dogs and wolves. Buttercup and Snow run through the battle, hand in hand, calling for Trevor and fending off attempted blows with axes and pastry power.

'All this time,' gasps Buttercup. 'I had magical healing kisses all this time and we never knew!'

'Does explain why my scars always heal so fast,' manages Snow, punching a huntsman to the ground. 'Always assumed it was just good breeding.'

'I just hope we find Trevor in time.'

'Can't believe my future wife is planning on kissing a spider.'

'To save our friend's life!'

Patience manifests in front of them suddenly. Buttercup and Snow don't quite stop in time to avoid stumbling inside the Ghost's form a little, which is an unpleasant experience for everybody involved.

'Sorry,' says Buttercup.

'Um,' says Patience.

'What?' asks Snow.

'I think I found Trevor,' says Patience.

'But...?' prompts Buttercup, worriedly, noting the Ghost's expression.

'Something's happened,' replies Patience, before leading them towards an alley instead of just telling them, which might have been easier, but that's Ghosts for you.

In the streets beyond the embattled square, a huntsman lieutenant named Richard is manning the catapults, or at least attempting to. His battalion keeps getting chased by dogs. And then there were the little stinky hairy Dwarves that floated down from a rickety enemy flying machine, waving axes and screaming, 'Yummy!' They used the same fabric sheets idea as the huntsmen, which was frankly cheating. To add injury to insult, they managed to carry Richard's best catapult operative off, screaming. Another of his catapults was crushed by a sort of sideways water tank, on wheels. And now... now, there's a bear the size of a shed crashing about, with a tiny old woman on its back screaming, 'See what you did? Yer woke Baby!'

Frankly, Richard has had enough. It's pretty obvious that the Citadel has been lost. He just needs to hold out a little bit longer for Morning to send orders to stand down and then he and the other huntsmen can move on, and establish a new base somewhere less indulgent of witches. Maybe there he will finally be able to get that cushy desk job Morning was promising him before he helped her become Head Huntsman.

'Richard!' It's Fennel, hurrying towards him. 'Time to stand down.'

Richard really does want to stand down, but at the same time, Fennel is the same rank as him and he'll be trousered if she gets to be the one to tell him to stand down.

'Is that Morning's order?' he asks tartly.

'Richard, it's over.' Fennel looks up. Richard follows his gaze. There are only two huntsman airships still flying and functional. Both have turned, and started flying back to where Richard's catapults are stationed. 'We have to go.'

As Richard watches the flying machines and resists Fennel tugging at his sleeve, Grey, the third huntsman lieutenant, comes sprinting out of an alleyway towards him, screaming and pulling rats off his robe with one hand while his other arm hangs at an odd angle. He stops briefly in front of the other two lieutenants, panting.

'Got to go. Now.'

'What, because of a few rats? And whatever it was that happened to your arm?'

'Swan broke it,' puffs Grey. He looks across at Fennel. 'I couldn't get word to the flying machine pilots.'

'They have their orders already,' argues Richard. 'From Morning…'

'I know.' Fennel pulls the last of the rats off Grey. 'Let's go.'

As Richard watches, one of the huntsmen's flying machines launches a fireball down at the rebels… no. No. Not at the rebels. Towards the catapults. He turns and runs. Fennel and Grey are already running.

'She mistimed!' Richard shouts as the fireball explodes behind him, the flames licking at his heels as he runs.

Behind them, the huntsman flying machine is hit by a blast of a Wyvern's fire from a pursuing enemy craft, and Richard is surprised by how relieved the sound of his own side's weaponry slowly crashing makes him.

'How did she mistime? That could have killed us!'

'Yes,' shouts Fennel back at him as they run. 'It could.'

Everything about Trevor hurts. It's a pain the likes of which he's never felt before. Everything is too much, much too much. There's too much of him, and yet somehow not enough. The world is too loud and too bright and yet too small. All the colours are wrong. He feels as if he's been turned inside out. The woman with the Ashtrian accent is gone, but he can hear others approaching the secluded corner where he's been left.

'Oh, fruit.'

Trevor gazes up to see Snow and Buttercup standing over him, with Patience wafting nervously overhead. Trevor is as relieved to see them as he is concerned by their expressions.

'Did...' mutters Buttercup, 'did he land on Trevor?'

'That *is* Trevor,' Patience replies. 'I feel it in my ectoplasm.'

'Don't be ridiculous,' snaps Snow.

'Guys?' wheezes Trevor, which in a deep, aching recess of his mind troubles him – he doesn't usually wheeze. 'I really hurt. Can we go home yet? I left a half-eaten bluebottle in the kitchen that I'd really like to get back to...' He trails off, struck by two terrible realisations. Firstly, the kitchen, and any flies therein, got blown up by the huntsmen days ago, and secondly, he isn't hungry for bluebottles. The very thought of sucking the goo out of one makes him feel physically sick. He *must* be in a bad way.

Above him, Buttercup clutches at Snow's arm. 'It *is* him!'

'Told you so,' says Patience.

'But that's...' says Buttercup.

'I know,' says Snow. 'But how?'

'I'm as surprised as you are that I'm still alive,' Trevor tells them, 'but there was this frog. And then she was this woman with a sad face and a foreign accent, and now I don't feel so deathy any more, but I really, really hurt.'

'Ella,' breathes Snow. 'Ella must have found a way to follow us. We have to get to Hansel Mudd!'

'Who's Ella?' Trevor asks Buttercup. 'I feel like I've missed loads here; how did you escape and why are you two covered in blood?'

Buttercup reaches down to help him up carefully. 'Long story. I have magic healing kisses.'

'Oh.' There's something wrong with the way he's being helped up, but Trevor can't quite put his finger on it. Funny. He's never wanted to refer to 'putting his finger on' something before. After all, he doesn't have fingers.

'Snow was dead for a bit but I brought her back. I was on my way to do the same for you, but looks like this "Ella" person beat me to it.'

'That's lucky.' How are his feet still on the ground while he's being picked up?

'Yes,' says Patience curtly. 'Isn't it fortunate that you lot have discovered two different ways to bring recently dead people back tonight, instead of, say, a few months ago, when other people could have made use of them?'

Trevor is aware of feeling cold now, as well as a very sharp pain in his abdomen. He still feels like there's far too much Trevor going on for him to cope with.

Snow turns to help Buttercup carry him, and since when did it take two people to carry him? As she turns, he sees his reflection in her silver breastplate.

Oh. So that's why he feels so weird.

Staring back at him, in the place of a very handsome largeish spider, is a very handsome largeish man.

The huntsman catapults have stopped, and the last huntsman flying machine is slowly sinking onto a bell tower, with one wing still on fire. There are a few buildings on fire, as well. Hansel is just thinking about the best way to put them out when the air fills with soft, fat white flakes of snow, smothering out the flames. It seems impossible, when only minutes ago the sky was crisp, clear and starlit. It seems more impossible that the vast majority of the snow is falling straight onto the small fires.

'Ho ho,' calls a voice from the square, 'merry happy!'

The last few huntsmen are running.

Have... have they won?? Hansel allows the magical exhaustion to take him, at last. He sinks to his knees. Gretel puts her arms around him.

'You did it!'

'*We* did it,' he mumbles. 'We all did.' He looks around the square. Some people are running, others are milling about, with lost expressions. Many are crouched in groups, tending to the injured. Oh, there are a *lot* of injured, and more besides, just lying there, completely still, with nobody going to help them. The people for whom it's too late.

'Who did we lose?' he asks.

'We don't know yet,' Gretel replies.

He looks into his sister's eyes. 'Trevor,' he says. 'And there were no birds. Snow…'

Gretel and Jack cast their gazes down.

'What's that about us?' calls a distinctive, arrogant voice.

'Snow!' cries Gretel, relieved. 'Buttercup! Patience!'

'Another naked hot guy,' exclaims Jack. 'Why do those keep happening to me?'

'Wait, I'm naked?' asks the large naked man, propped up between Buttercup and Snow. The naked man speaks using Trevor's voice. He glances down at himself before adding in Trevory tones, 'So that's why I'm cold.'

Hansel, Gretel and Jack respond in the way one would expect when a naked man starts talking at you using the voice of a spider. They scream.

29
Cinders

The battle is over. Her time approaches. Her time to rise through the rubble and fill up the delicious power vacuum. She's still diminished – turning that whole army invisible so soon after her initial fight with the Mudd Witch drained her a lot, and she really shouldn't have stopped to help that dying spider... she's still not entirely sure why she did that. Perhaps it was simply because she could. Drained as her magic is, the Mudd Witch is even more exhausted, magically and physically. She will use the last of her power, and he won't be able to stop her. These useful idiots just won the crown of Myrsina for her. Queen Ella will sit proud and cold and beautiful on a throne of pain and fear once again.

The sky is clear again. Everything twinkles with stars and little lights and frost and a few flurries of snow here and there. Perfect. She picks her way through the wreckage, weaving herself a dress that shimmers like dewdrops on a spider's web... for pity's sake, that spider really did get to her, didn't he?

She opens her arms wide to the Citadel as she approaches. 'This land needs a queen,' she announces. 'One has arrived.'

That filthy Princess Snow steps forwards, her hand resting warily on an axe. 'Oh no you don't.'

'Pretending to defend your crown, Princess?' She gathers more reserves of magical power. 'You don't even want it.'

'This isn't about wanting some shiny hat. This is about defending lives from people like them…' She nods at the departing huntsmen. 'And people like you.'

'People like me?' Ella keeps her tone light. 'You fight side by side with someone just like me.' She gestures to the exhausted Mudd Witch.

Now the Mudd Witch's scrappy, ordinary sister steps forward. 'He's nothing like you. He's better than you.'

Ella laughs, and her laugh is like tinkling crystal. 'We'll see about that,' she says. 'We'll see about that… to death!'

'That doesn't make any sense,' says Jack Trott.

Ella pulls together as much magic as she possibly can, and hits the Mudd Witch with a wave of it. The Mudd Witch is too exhausted even to defend himself. His sister throws herself backward, against the Mudd Witch, attempting to shield him with her distinctly unmagical body. The boy she turned into a raven – whatsisname, Septa's brother – lands in front of the twins and transforms. Well… mostly transforms; he still has a wing. With his one human hand he grabs Jack Trott, who joins him in front of the twins. Trott gestures, and plants begin to grow – vines with big pumpkin fruits blocking her way. She has to spare some of her magic to try to get rid of them, make them think they're something else. And now Princess Snow stands in her path, hand in hand with the rubbish Cake Witch. Pigeons fill the air and fly at her. Ella has to divide her magic some more to make the pigeons think they don't have wings. A Ghost manifests in front of her, telekinetically flinging small pieces of rubble at her. She has to use yet more magic to deflect them. At one side of her, that pack of dogs and wolves again, led by the great red Werewolf, and at the other side, the Bear Witch of the north approaches, on the back of a giant bear, flanked by Dwarves. One of the Dwarves is dragging a big sheet behind it. More besides are closing in. Witches from the Citadel. Witches from the villages and towns. A swan… she recognises that swan. Her focus and her magic are too divided… oh no.

Something hits her in the face. It's soft and wet. It doesn't hurt, but it's a shock. She wipes it off her face. A cream pie.

'Come on, now,' says a voice near her feet. That spider she turned into a man, weirdly splayed on all fours. He can't stand up yet in this new body, but he gazes up at her with... with understanding. Almost with sympathy. 'It's over,' says the man-spider. 'You're not going to have the crown here. But you can have something better.' He smiles the smile of somebody who still isn't used to having lips. 'You can have friends.'

Suddenly, Ella feels so very tired. She's divided her magic too much. Whenever she tries to attack one, they all turn up, and they do it not out of fear but out of love, and it's just too much. The glamour fades, like a candle sputtering out. She sinks to her knees, just a sad, tired woman in rags.

'That's better,' says the man-spider, still with that weird smile. 'You look more like yourself now. People should just be themselves.'

'If that's your way of asking me to change you back, it doesn't work like that,' she sighs.

'No, it's OK,' replies the man-spider. 'But I was wondering if you could maybe see your way to giving me one or four more limbs...?'

The defensive group around Hansel relaxes as it becomes obvious that Ella really has exhausted all of her power, and all of her will to keep fighting, for now.

'What about me?' Hex asks. 'Could you turn me back, if you wanted?'

Ella shakes her head. 'Not me. Spell's too old. You can try True Love's Kiss; that sometimes...'

Jack is kissing Hex before Ella can finish.

'We've already done that lots,' Hex mumbles through Jack's kiss. 'I still have the wing.'

'Then you'll just always have a wing.' Ella shrugs. 'You probably don't need the nettle shirt any more, though.' She nods her head at Jack, who is really, really trying to make this particular True

Love's Kiss work. 'Looks like he's volunteered to be your nettle shirt for you.'

She turns to the swan. She's definitely seen that swan before. She's done something terrible to that swan. 'Same should go for you,' she tells it. 'True Love's Kiss.'

The swan casts its gaze down.

'He's alive,' Ella tells it. 'He's here. I travelled here as a frog in a pocket. I wasn't alone.' She closes her eyes and holds out a hand. From her expression, it's not so much that she's concentrating on a spell, more as if she's letting go of something.

Another naked man stands up amongst some of the witches from the Citadel.

'Uurp,' he says, momentarily bewildered. He looks across at the swan. 'Uurp?' he asks.

'It's OK,' Ella tells him. 'It doesn't matter any more.'

'Uurp,' replies the man. He goes to the shocked-looking swan, takes its small, white head in his hands and presses a light kiss between the creature's eyes.

The swan sheds its feathers like leaves in an autumn storm. It unfolds and rises, and becomes a woman, tall and elegant and just as naked as the man. The romantic moment is rather marred not just by the fact that they're both shivering and naked, but also because this is the moment when Snow notices the Dwarves and runs towards them with a delighted shout of 'LADS!'

'Odette?' gasps the man, who seems to have found something in his vocabulary besides 'uurp'.

'Siegfried?' cries the woman.

'So many naked people now,' exclaims Jack, who has finally stopped kissing the similarly naked Hex.

'I know,' says Trevor, still folded up on the floor, 'and trousers, but it's *freezing*.'

With a still wobbly Trevor propped up on his shoulder, Jack sweet-talks some of the Citadel residents to help him get all of the naked people over to a neighbouring inn to get warm and dressed.

Gretel helps her brother up. 'You OK? You need rest.'

'I'll be all right.' Hansel looks about, troubled. 'Where's Daisy?'

'Who do you think was in charge of all those airships? She'll be with us once she's landed.'

'And Stepmother and Stepfather?'

Gretel looks out across the square full of groaning, injured bodies. For all the medics, their stepparents included, the fight has only just begun.

'Lads,' cries Snow into the matted fur of one of the Dwarves as they scramble around her like tatty kittens, 'you were supposed to stay in the village; what are you doing here? Especially you, Oi, you were on your last legs.'

'Yummy,' says a Dwarf that Gretel's pretty sure is Oi.

'OK, well, as long as you stayed on the outskirts of the fight and were careful...' One of the Dwarves licks her. She licks it back. 'All right, all right.' She laughs with a mouthful of hair. 'I love you too.'

'Snow?' calls Buttercup in a trembling voice.

The group follows her to a cluster of people among the groaning injured of the square. Mopsa and Dorcas clutch at one another, in shock. Homily Goggins is on her knees, following Nearby Village's tradition of putting leaves over a dead body's eyes. There are no medics here for Carpenter Fred.

'It were too late by the time I found him,' says Mother Goggins before anybody can get a word in. 'Chances are, it were too late half a second after the sword swung, that's a good, quick, clean slice to the neck, that. He shan't have felt a thing, and besides, I like to think he'd have appreciated skilful chopping like that, bein' a carpenter.'

Buttercup kneels down by him. 'I have healing kisses...'

'Come off it, lass, his head's nearly off, and he's been dead a good half hour. You ain't healing that, and I'm not sure his widow would appreciate you snogging what's left of him, at this difficult time.'

'He used to hate witches,' breathes Hansel. 'He didn't need to fight for us…'

'He wanted to,' Goggins assures him.

'He saved us,' mutters Mopsa.

'Aye,' replies Goggins. 'He was a good 'un, our Freddery. If you don't count all of the times he was a pain in the trousers.'

'He was *our* pain in the trousers,' says Gretel quietly.

The group bow their heads solemnly around the fallen carpenter. Ella sinks to her knees next to Mopsa and Dorcas, her mind a muddle, full of stories about change, and forgiveness, and sacrifice, and love.

'I humbled you,' she says to her sisters.

They nod.

'I need you to teach humility to me,' she tells them.

'Really?' gasps Mopsa.

Ella takes her sister's hands. 'Really. No more hurting each other. Let's go home.'

'We don't have a home any more,' Dorcas reminds her.

'Then let's find a home, and go there.'

'But how?' asks Mopsa. 'We can barely walk.'

Ella looks at Jack Trott's giant pumpkins, left over from the stand-off.

'I have an idea.'

30
Ever After

The castle is cold and empty. The walls have been stripped of the tapestries that Snow remembers from her childhood, and the departing huntsmen have haphazardly taken everything they could carry with them as they left. Chairs are upturned, shelves have been left half-stripped. The whole place looks horribly sad.

'The throne is still intact,' Charles the Magnificent tells Snow as he clops through the stone hallway alongside her, the loud echoes of the castle highlighting how the Unicorn still walks with a slight limp. 'We'll have to get you a new crown done, but that shouldn't be a problem; just get your Dwarves to find some gold and hey presto.'

'Why are you giving me the tour of my own childhood home, again?' asks Snow.

'Because I am a majestic Unicorn,' replies the Unicorn.

'You hid in here instead of fighting,' says Snow, 'didn't you?'

Charles the Magnificent sniffs. 'I was securing the area.'

Snow reaches the throne room. She cautiously approaches her mother's throne.

'Have a little sit in it,' says Charles. 'Try it on for size.'

Snow looks at the throne. She doesn't want to sit here. She wants to sit in a little wooden chair in a cakey kitchen and get told off for putting her feet on the table.

'I can't.'

'Well, that's a lie,' Charles the Magnificent tells her. 'You just don't want to. But it's not about what you want, right now, is it? It's about what the country needs. And what it needs, right now, is anything but a power vacuum, for the regrouped huntsmen, or a rival witch queen or something even worse to fall into.'

Snow thinks about Ella's attempt to snatch power, and about all the escaped huntsmen. She drums her fingers on the armrest of the throne.

'How come you know so much about power vacuums and political machinations?'

'Majestic Unicorn,' replies Charles the Magnificent, matter-of-factly, and it's clear that that's the only answer Snow is going to get.

A night and a day's journey west of the Citadel, Morning stops, exhausted. With the country on high alert, she hasn't been able to hire or flag down a single carriage on the Citadel road. The couple of carriages she has seen actively sped up once the drivers saw her huntsman robes. She has ditched the robes since, but has still had no joy. If she continues on foot, there's still another three days' travel ahead of her to get to Goldenharbour. She needs food and sleep, so she stops at a small town with an inn.

She's not sure how, but rumour has managed to make it to the inn before she has. She quietly picks her way through a very leek-heavy pie as the inn's landlady chats breezily with her regulars about the end of the huntsmen's reign and the return of the princess.

'Well,' says a man whose complexion suggests he is a very regular customer at the bar, 'queen now, not princess.'

'I saw her once,' adds another man, 'back in the good old days, when she was just a little dot. Very regal, she was. Poor thing, what they did to her.'

'I never had any truck with those huntsmen,' announces the landlady.

'Yes you did,' mutters the ruddy-faced regular. 'You shopped Myrtle the pot-washer to 'em last year for knowing the seven times table.'

'Ooh, I never!'

Morning tunes out of the conversation. So. That's which way the wind's blowing, now. She'll have quite the uphill struggle when she gets to Goldenharbour.

She finishes her bad pie, and goes up to her room – the last one available, right up at the top of the inn, since she arrived so late. She'll get up early, maybe take one of those horses in the stables. She enters, sits on the bed and removes her boots. The door to her attic room opens again.

'We thought you'd stop here.'

Morning looks up and beams at the trio in the doorway. 'Fennel! Richard! Grey! How lovely! You managed to get ahead of me!'

'We got hold of some horses,' Fennel tells her, in a dangerously polite tone, 'after you left.'

Morning continues to smile, warmly, watching the three huntsmen as they enter the room. 'I knew I could count on my best guys to prevail.'

'Mm,' replies Fennel.

Morning gets up and opens her arms wide. 'Since you're all here, let's go downstairs and let me buy you a drink. We can ride out together at dawn; we'll be planning our bright future in Goldenharbour by tomorrow night. Start again from fresh.'

'And you're not worried about any sort of miscalculation in your timings there, Morning?' asks Grey. 'Such as the "mistiming" that had the flying machine fire on our own catapults?'

'Grey.' Morning smiles. 'What happened to your arm?'

Grey, his arm in a sling, glowers at her.

'Swan broke it,' says Richard quietly.

'Answer me,' demands Grey, over him.

Morning's smile doesn't falter. 'Better to destroy the weapons than let the enemy take them.'

'You almost got me,' Richard exclaims.

'Exactly what did "start again from fresh" mean to you, Morning?' asks Fennel.

'I'm not sure I get your drift,' lies Morning. She eyes the doorway. It's completely blocked by Fennel and Grey. Richard is against the window. She can't get out that way, either.

'You left us to be killed, Morning,' says Fennel.

'And the other huntsmen,' adds Grey, 'and all of the civilians still loyal to us.'

'Yeah,' adds Richard, 'but mostly, us.'

'Yeah,' says Grey. 'Leaving *us* to be killed… that's beyond the pale, Morning. We were supposed to be your friends.'

'You are!' Morning still has a knife in her tunic pocket. Very subtly, she tries to reach for it.

Fennel notices her hand move. Nobody says anything.

There's nothing left to be said.

Quietly, Fennel shuts and locks the door.

The next day, at dawn, three figures ride west, their huntsman cloaks abandoned on top of the body in the very top room of the inn. By the time the landlady finds it, they'll be miles away. They won't go to Goldenharbour. Perhaps they'll go to Tide, and catch a ship from there. They'll settle somewhere, eventually. They'll start again, from fresh.

31
Happy

Days pass.

The dead are buried.

Weeks pass.

The injured heal.

Midwinter comes and goes. People get nuts in their slippers, and feast together, and enjoy the warmth of good company, and have a merry jolly time.

A month passes. And another. And another.

Day, very gradually, starts winning ground back from night. Old Nikolas, the ancient witch of Midwinter, settles down for another nice long sleep until the time of dark and frost returns and his specific magic is required once more.

Odette and her fiancé, Siegfried, magical creatures no more, wave their friends goodbye on a coach bound for Odette's childhood home in Ashtrie.

Rumpelstiltskin the part-elf and his friend Salad settle their shop in one place. It is renowned as the finest cobbler and wigmaker in the land. Also, if you need anything turning into gold, just ask for Rumpel, although it will cost you.

A man, who was until very recently not a man, slowly and cautiously learns to walk on what he keeps referring to as his 'hind legs'. He collects stylish hats, and almost always has one on. Often it's the only thing he actually does wear, since he still finds trousers, shirts and boots impossibly tricky.

In the Darkwood, green shoots begin to appear amongst the charred husks of the burnt-out forest fires. Wildlife returns to it – birds, Jackalopes, Fairies, dormice, magical and non-magical living together as they always have. A Thumbling named Bellina decides to go on holiday there, meets a pack of fellow Thumblings, and thinks she might stay a while longer after all.

The refugee camp in Nearby empties. Not all of the creatures go back to the Darkwood. Some go off into wider Myrsina, to build shelters under bridges, or to swim free through the open rivers. Some choose to stay in Nearby Village. A Centaur sets up a new carpenter shop there. Gregor Smithy is finally able to retire as village watchman. There's nothing for him to watch for any more.

In the Citadel, the damaged buildings are rebuilt. Little flags start to go up, bearing the colours of the old royal family of Myrsina. Matching bunting begins to line the streets. The inns and boarding houses fill up.

And then, comes the day. The big day. The streets aren't just full of little flags; they're full of people, waving the little flags. The air throngs with petals, music and cheers. The crowds part noisily. Through them walks a queen. She is barely recognisable as the fabled White Knight of the Darkwood. For starters, she's had a wash and is wearing a pretty frock. Her 'ladies in waiting' are rather odd, though. True, they've all been shampooed and combed, but they're still terribly hairy and have little to say except 'Yummy', and, when they see gold, 'Hi ho'.

The queen strides up the steps of the castle, to a platform that has been erected in the newly named Battle Square. There, she stops, and turns to her people. A very small circlet of gold is placed on her head. The crowd goes wild. The 'ladies in waiting' are pretty pleased as well, although that seems to mostly be about the gold.

The queen turns to another woman on the scaffold, in a dress so interwoven with flowers it's hard to see where fabric ends and flowers begin. The crowd finally shuts its collective trap.

The vows are short but personal. They make several people cry. The queen's bride cries custard, but everybody's too caught up in the emotion of it all to mention it. Rings are exchanged and now instead of one queen, there are two. The two queens lift one another's veils, and kiss. And kiss. And kiss a bit too much for a big public wedding, to be honest. The crowd erupts again.

Queen Snow turns from her wife to her people.

'Happy now?' she shouts to the crowd.

The crowd cheer.

'You've had your fancy coronation and your emotional royal wedding; you've all got your commemorative tankards and whatnot?' adds Queen Snow.

The crowd cheer again.

'Good,' replies Queen Snow. She takes off the circlet. 'Then, I quit.'

'It's not quitting, dear,' murmurs her wife. 'It's called abdication.'

'Then, I abdi-what-have-you.' Snow passes her circlet to Buttercup, who accidentally turns it into a large doughnut. 'Good luck with the whole election thingie tomorrow, and the… what did you call it again, New Girl?'

Gretel Mudd steps forward on the platform. 'Representative democracy,' she says, and not for the first time. 'Remember, guys, you're voting for your local representative in the new parliament; you're not voting on a single leader at this stage. Once we see which political alliance has the most seats, then…'

'Shouldn't you be providing the seats?' calls one voice from the crowd.

'Yeah,' shouts another, 'what if a chairmaker gets voted in? They'd have an unfair advantage!'

'That's not what I…' Gretel pinches the bridge of her nose. 'It's all in the pamphlet, OK? Did everyone get a pamphlet?'

'Yes,' chorus the crowd grumpily.

'I'm illiterate, though,' complains another voice.

'There were diagrams,' shouts Gretel irritably.

'Yes, yes,' calls Snow, 'as I say, good luck with the whole new political system, which has been hurriedly devised by three children and a dead woman.' She waves her hands dismissively at Gretel, Daisy, Hansel and Patience.

Hansel raises a finger. 'I didn't really do much; mostly I just held up the chalkboard.'

'*Two* children and a dead woman,' Snow corrects herself. 'Anyway, it's your problem now.' Here, she gestures happily to the whole crowd. 'Humans, witches and magicals alike. Enjoy. I'm off to eat cake with the missus. Laters, taters.'

She makes a valiant attempt to sweep Buttercup up into her arms and carry her off, but she quickly finds getting off the platform while carrying a full-grown and slightly overweight woman rather tricky, and a very nervous Buttercup asks to be put down anyway, so in the end they just walk to the smaller, private wedding reception together. And they do have cake. And Snow and Buttercup do indeed very happily never become royalty ever again, for there is no longer a 'royalty' for them to be.

And that's how the restoration of the Myrsinan crown, from coronation to royal wedding to dissolution, lasted for all of twenty-seven minutes.

The next day, a parliament is elected, with representatives from all over Myrsina and all walks of life. Since a quick census has discovered that indeed around a third of Myrsina's population is magical, that proportion is echoed in the candidates available for people to vote for. The resulting parliament is actually around two-fifths magical. Gretel, Daisy and Patience's final headache as overseers of the transition is to find out how they're supposed to seat three Unicorns and a Centaur in the castle's grand hall, especially since two of the Unicorns hate one another. It's not perfect and it's very early days, but it does seem preferable to both huntsman rule and the aloof monarchy that paved the way for the huntsmen to take over. None of the Mudd family stands for election. Neither do any of their friends from Nearby or the Darkwood, unless you count Charles the Magnificent. All of them are glad to let somebody else change the world for a while – except, as was just mentioned, Charles the Magnificent.

Spring explodes with petals and pollen. The days lengthen, the wind blows warmer. Bees hum in bright flowers. Bears lumber from hibernation. In the foothills of Bear Mountain, Gilde Locke's friends fulfil an old promise to rebuild her broken cottage. Gilde is surprised by just how many people turn up. The cottage is as good as new within a few days, which is good because she's running out of porridge to feed everyone. The cottage still has three chairs and three beds, but she knows her former housemates aren't going to stay, this time. Scarlett wants to move back down south, near to where she grew up, and Hex has a whole new life now, with his sweetie. It's all right. She'll keep the extra chairs and beds, for anyone going up into the mountains who needs a place to stay – or in case any more of those mountain Zombies manage to dig their way out of the collapsed mine shaft upriver, poor things. She'll be fine. She feels connected to the world beyond the bears and the forest for the first time in all her long years. She doesn't even mind that Hex slips away with his sweetie before her housewarming party, or that Scarlett spends most of that night talking to Trevor. She doesn't need to cage them. She doesn't need to cage nobody. She spends the next day sitting outside the little cottage with Baby, and the spring sun isn't too hot or too cold. It's just right.

In the Citadel, blossom tumbles onto the cobbled streets like pale confetti.

A Ghost haunts the castle. Patience has promised to stop throwing cutlery and leaving messages in frost on the walls, in return for the new government changing the statue of her in the square outside. Now, it no longer shows her in a huntsman mask and robe, and the plaque underneath simply bears her name, the years she was alive and an advert for her new self-help book for the recently dead. The Ghost gets on well with the other residents of the castle, especially the new prime minister, a Citadel resident named Lucy Toads. The Ghost occasionally gets lifts with travellers and merchants back to the Darkwood and Nearby, to see her old friends. Prime Minister Toads always asks to give her regards to Hansel and Daisy in particular. 'Tell them the lace merchant's wife says hello,' she says. 'They'll know what you mean.'

In the unpopulated highlands to the west of Bear Mountain, a couple stop hiking, and rest.

'There,' says Hex, pointing with his wing to a distant mountain crag. 'Do you see it?'

Jack peers in the direction his boyfriend is pointing. He sees nothing but clouds and rock for a moment, and then a slow movement. It's hard to make out – grey bodies moving against the grey mountainside. Also, Jack has started to cry, which is blurring his vision.

'It's a family of them,' Hex tells him. 'Dad, mom, a juvenile and I think I see the dad carrying an infant. Spotted them going out to hunt when I was stretching my wings after Gilde's thing. Thought it would do you good to see them.'

They watch the family of Giants plod their gentle way across the mountain. It would look a bit more serene if one of the adults didn't have two yak slung over their shoulder, but everyone needs to eat.

'Do you think they've decided it's safe to start coming back?' asks Jack. 'Or have they been hidden up here in the mountains all this time?'

'Does it matter?' asks Hex.

'I suppose not,' says Jack. 'Thank you for showing me.'

They watch the family until they have lumbered off into the mist.

'Want me to fly you home?' asks Hex.

'Could do,' Jack replies. 'Or you could show me Ashtrie. Or we could keep going north; there's a whole continent beyond these mountains.'

Hex regards the mountains speculatively. 'What do you want to do most of all?'

'Well.' Jack gets out the same ring he's been offering Hex since coronation-and-abdication day. Hex just rolls his eyes.

Jack grins. 'I'm not hearing a "no"!'

In Ashtrie, birds sing in the forest again. For the first time in decades, the trees and shrubs are allowed to grow as wild as they please. Three sisters live together in a humble but comfortable cottage near the woods. Nobody who visits ever sees the face of the deposed queen when they look at the youngest sister. It's still Ella's face – drawn, thin, rather ordinary, but peaceful. They just don't recognise it. It's one of the few things Ella uses her magic for, these days. Sometimes, she checks up on her many husbands. They all seem to be doing fine. They're getting used to being men again. Two have already remarried, feckless things. Siegfried and Odette are expecting. Ella hopes that Odette doesn't accidentally lay an egg. She's sure it will be fine. Sometimes she does use her magic to turn pumpkins and other large squash into carriages, and she and her sisters go riding, the wind in their hair, the air whipping away their laughter. She forgives, and is forgiven in turn. She learns to find delight in kindness rather than revenge, and in love rather than fear. She is always, always good to spiders.

In a different cottage on the other side of the forest, close to Nearby, a Werewolf, who after thirty-five years still isn't quite used to how many legs she should be using at any given moment, lives with a man who definitely isn't used to his current number of legs. Even after almost half a year in human form, Trevor still falls over sometimes, and forgets that he can't walk up walls any more. Once, during a thunderstorm, Scarlett finds him trying to hide in a crack under a skirting board. They end up spending that night under a bed. Scarlett hates thunderstorms, too. Besides that, it's not so bad being human-shaped, he finds. He likes carbohydrates, and no longer being terrified of cats. He is informed by several women and a couple of men that his human shape is a very attractive one, and he does like having his handsomeness recognised at last, by potential partners who are less likely to eat him. He's even able to sign up for the new government's Intelligence & National Security Initiative, although nobody's got back to him, yet.

In Nearby Village is a new bakery and cake shop run by a witch and her grumpy wife. It needs fixing quite often, as sometimes bits of it get turned into shortbread. The grumpy wife swears at the villagers a lot, especially when they accidentally call her 'Majesty', but on the whole, she's getting used to living amongst humans again, as much as she loudly complains about it. Sometimes she leans out of the window to talk to the birds, and woe betide anyone besides Buttercup who dares to call it adorable.

'Jack's coming back,' says Snow. 'Little birdie tells me he and Hex started heading south again yesterday.'

'That's nice!'

'I know why they're coming back,' announces the Mirror hanging on the wall. 'If you ask me in rhyme, I can—'

'Bet they're getting married,' says Snow at the same time that Buttercup asks 'are they getting married?'

'Who told you?' the Mirror huffs.

'Oh, Jack's been flashing an engagement ring around for months,' says Snow. 'He's not exactly subtle.'

'And besides, a wedding's something you'd come back home for,' adds Buttercup, 'isn't it?'

'This isn't "home" for them though, is it?' replies Snow, sitting at the table. 'They're unlikely to stay. It's not going to be like how it was.'

'I know that.' Buttercup pushes Snow's feet off the table. 'I know things have changed. Everyone's off doing their own thing. Jack and Hex. Patience. Gretel…'

'The lads,' sighs Snow wistfully. The bakery is markedly free of Dwarf hairs.

'Trevor and Scarlett,' adds Buttercup. 'Didn't see that one coming.' She pauses, thinking. 'It's nice that they come and visit so often, though.' She pauses again. 'I do wish they'd remember to wear clothes, though. Or at least something other than a cloak and a hat. People in this village are terrible gossips.'

'They'll get the hang of it eventually,' Snow tells her wife.

'We're all "getting the hang of it", I suppose,' sighs Buttercup. 'Whole new world, now. My little family's flying the nest.'

'But you do still like the nest, right?'

Buttercup smiles. 'I love the nest. And I love that you're in it with me.'

Three days later, there is a scrabbling at the door from a single Dwarf. After long years, Oi's six Dwarflings have finally reached maturity and gone off by themselves. Snow doesn't even have to ask Buttercup to let Oi stay. She opens up her doors to people who are lost and alone. It's just what Buttercup does. Although she still gets Snow to sweep the Dwarf hair up from her nice clean floors twice a day.

Spring turns into another hot, hazy summer in Nearby. On the outskirts of the village, a farmhouse stands. The kitchen is bright and warm, and used. There are five chairs around the table, and five breakfast bowls soaking in the sink. Everybody is outside, by the pig shed.

Three teenagers sit together with slates while Mr and Mrs Mudd busy themselves feeding the pigs.

'What do you think of this?' asks Daisy Wicker, handing her slate over to Gretel Mudd.

Gretel nods. 'Yep. Could work. Maybe if we incorporate the measurements of my design...'

'What are you two inventing this time?' Gretel's stepmother asks cheerfully. 'More of those whatchamacallits for monthlies? They're ever so good; I shan't be going back to that old belt loop thingy again.'

Daisy proudly turns her slate to show Mrs Mudd. 'We're making a sign!'

Hansel Mudd, the most powerful witch known to Myrsina, frowns at the sign for a moment and then slowly reads aloud in the hesitant voice of one for whom reading comes less naturally than tap dancing comes to fish. 'Wicker. And. Mudd,' he manages, 'In...'

Everyone waits patiently.

'In... ven... tors.'

'Well done.' Gretel grins. Daisy kisses him on the cheek.

Behind them, in the pig shed, Mr Mudd shivers and piglets squeal in panic.

'Oh,' says Hansel. He blows a plume of vapour out into hot summer air.

A Ghost manifests in front of them.

'*Leave this plaaaaaaaace,*' it howls.

'Stop it, Patience. You're scaring the livestock. What are you doing back h—' Gretel stops short. She stares at Hansel and Daisy in horror. 'Oh no.'

'It's Saturday, geniuses,' Patience tells them. 'You're not even dressed for the wedding yet; come on, you need to get washed and changed. Even Gilde managed to find a nice frock to turn up in.' Patience frowns. 'I'm a little bit worried she might have stolen it off a corpse. Come on! Chop chop! If you hurry to Buttercup's you might still make it in time to see Trevor trying to get into a pair of trousers; he's been at it for nearly half an hour already.'

And with that, she disappears.

And so, Hansel, Gretel and Daisy walk down the hill to the bakery to see their friends.

And all of them live happily ever after. Except for Monday evenings, because Bin Night is still absolutely terrible.

THE END

Acknowledgements

Thanks to Dom Lord & Abbie Headon for all their support and help. Thanks to Pete and Fanny at Duckworth. Thanks to everyone who bought and recommended Darkwood and Such Big Teeth, especially Jess, Paul and Lucy. Thank you to my mum, whose name is Rory (it's a long story) and special thanks to The Lovely Nathan, and my kids Violet and Alex, particularly since the last quarter of this book was written during lockdown. Absolutely no thanks to my cat Spooky, who didn't help one tiny bit.

I stand by the message of these books, that most people are fundamentally good, and brave, and willing to stand up for others. If you are one of those people who stand up for the powerless, thank you for inspiring all of us.

About the Author

Gabby Hutchinson Crouch (*Horrible Histories, Newzoids, The News Quiz, The Now Show*) has a background in satire, and with the global political climate as it is, believes that now is an important time to explore themes of authoritarianism and intolerance in comedy and fiction. Born in Pontypool in Wales, and raised in Ilkeston, Derbyshire, Gabby moved to Canterbury at 18 to study at the University of Kent and ended up staying and having a family there.

Also available

Magic is forbidden in Myrsina, along with various other abominations, such as girls doing maths.

This is bad news for Gretel Mudd, who doesn't perform magic, but does know a lot of maths. When the sinister masked Huntsmen accuse Gretel of witchcraft, she is forced to flee into the neighbouring Darkwood, where witches and monsters dwell.

There, she happens upon Buttercup, a witch who can't help turning things into gingerbread, Jack Trott, who can make plants grow at will, the White Knight with her band of dwarves and a talking spider called Trevor. These aren't the terrifying villains she's been warned about all her life. They're actually quite nice. Well… most of them.

With the Huntsmen on the warpath, Gretel must act fast to save both the Darkwood and her home village, while unravelling the rhetoric and lies that have demonised magical beings for far too long.

Take a journey into the Darkwood in this modern fairy tale that will bewitch adults and younger readers alike.

OUT NOW!

Also available

If you go down to the woods today, be sure of a big surprise.

The Battle of Nearby Village is over, and deep in the Darkwood, Gretel and her friends journey into the hostile mountains of the north, seeking new allies in their fight against the huntsmen. There they find Gilde the Bear Witch, along with a Werewolf named Scarlett and a winged man named Hex. Meanwhile, Hansel and Daisy set off on a dangerous trip of their own to the Citadel, where they end up in the middle of a political battle for the future of the whole country.

Can Gretel and her friends persuade Gilde to join forces, or at least stop fighting them at every step? Can Hansel find a way to heal the land's divisions and make the huntsmen change their ways before disaster strikes them all? And how did Trevor the spider get hold of a wig? Discover the answers to all these questions and more in *Such Big Teeth*.

OUT NOW!

Note from the Publisher

To receive updates on new releases in the Darkwood series – plus special offers and news of other humorous fiction series to make you smile – sign up now to the Farrago mailing list at farragobooks.com/sign-up.